To Beki.
Thanks!
Geoff

THE SEARCH

A STORY ABOUT A JOURNEY

BY
GEOFF PRICE

THE SEARCH

Print Edition
ISBN: 978-1-3999-6913-0

FOR MY DAUGHTERS

KATIE AND JO

CHAPTER 1

Kenton, North London, February 1990

'HELLO JACK,' SAID the young woman standing on his doorstep. He stared blankly at her, never having seen her before.

He had been jolted awake from his afternoon doze by the ring of the doorbell; it had an extravagant melodic chime, something that Margaret had liked. Now that he was on his own, it didn't ring very often, not unless it was the Jehovah's Witnesses or some smart alec trying to sell him something he didn't want or need. Perhaps the Kleeneze Brush man or an Avon lady. It had taken him a few moments to gather his thoughts. He was at home alone, in his armchair, on a weekday, and it must be nearly tea-time. Getting to his feet took a little longer than it used to do. From the floor, where it had fallen, he had picked up the *Daily Mail*, full of stories about Nelson Mandela's release from prison. He folded it neatly and put it aside on his table.

The bell had rung again, a much longer ring. He hadn't been expecting anyone and experienced a sense of minor panic in case they went away before he had made it out into the hall to answer the door. What if he had won the Pools? He hadn't checked his coupon this week? What if someone had seen a prowler?

When he looked through the frosted glass panel in the front door he could make out the image of a woman, not one he recognised. He opened the door to reveal her; probably mid-thirties he thought, not what he would call very fashionable, but a professional type. It was raining but he couldn't see that she had an umbrella.

Looking back later on this moment, his word for his feeling was 'flabbergasted'. How did she know his name? Perhaps a canvasser for the elections, but she had no clipboard or leaflets, so he ruled that out. She was well-spoken, with a hint of a Midlands accent that Jack remembered.

'Hello,' said Jack, 'Can I help you?'

She didn't answer, just gazed back at him.

'Go on then,' he said with a forced smile, 'Give me a clue.'

'Do you ever think about Nottingham?' she said, still with no hint of a smile of her own.

'Blimey, it's a long time since I was in Nottingham.'

'Yes, about thirty-five years I would think.'

'That's right, nineteen fifty-five it was, a very long time ago. Are you from there?'

'Yes, not far away,' she replied, again giving nothing away but intense.

At first, Jack couldn't work out who this woman was, why she should be standing on his doorstep. Yet, at the back of his mind, a thought stirred, and it wouldn't lie down again. Could there be a connection? Is she bringing a message? He shifted uneasily from one foot to the other, unable to meet her eye.

'Have you come from there today?'

She nodded.

'Have you driven?' He glanced towards the road but couldn't see a car.

'No, I came to London by train and then out on the Tube to here.'

'What, just to see me?'

"That's right, just to see you. But it has been a long

journey just to find you.'

Jack saw Mrs. Hodges from number 42 walking past, staring at him with an inquiring look. It would not be long now before everybody in the street would know he had had a visitor, and a young woman at that. He didn't know yet who she was, and perhaps he should have sent her packing. However, as the rain was now quite heavy, he said, 'I think you'd better come in out of the rain.'

He stood back and ushered her into the front room.

'Thank you,' she said.

'Please sit yourself down,' he said, gesturing towards the cream settee. 'Can I get you a cup of tea?'

'No, thank you,' she said pleasantly, 'but a glass of water would be nice.'

Jack went out to the kitchen and brought her a glass of water, but didn't stop to make himself a tea, struggling to put his thoughts into some sort of order. He sat again in his favourite chair, the rocker with a big cushion behind him, opposite her.

He had seen her looking round the room; the tall cottage-style dresser, with Willow-pattern plates carefully stacked vertically on every shelf, the few family photos, nothing ostentatious, clean, tidy and dust-free, gas fire on low. Not much had been changed since Margaret died. He was dressed in his usual fashion; wool cardigan, corduroy trousers, twill shirt and tie, even though he wasn't expecting any visitors. He felt fortunate that he was still quite lean and fit for his age.

She seemed confident in the way she was looking at him. He hadn't offered to take her navy anorak, so she kept it on, even though it was quite soaked. She wore jeans, sensible flat black shoes, a multi-coloured scarf loosely tied round her neck. No make-up, hair a little windblown, rucksack on her back, which she had now set aside. She wore a plain ring on her right hand, but nothing on her left.

She then put him further on edge by not starting a conversation, just looking him in the eye, firmly, expectantly. Jack ran his fingers through his wiry, grey hair while he looked her over again. She was not glamorous or pretty, but he thought she had a pleasant face. Did she remind him of anyone? Medium height and build, nothing to take your attention in a crowd. He had always had an eye for the ladies, not in any crude or lustful way, but he enjoyed their company and would appraise their appearance. He liked to see that they had made the best of themselves. This one was plainly dressed, but neat, not scruffy. There was something about her firm gaze which he found intimidating.

That thought at the back of Jack's mind hadn't gone away; on the contrary, it was assuming greater prominence, and it was making him curious. Did she have a message for him? He had an idea about what the reason for the visit might be and took the initiative.

'I was sent up to Nottingham for six months, to open a new depot for us, up and down every couple of weeks.'

'So I believe.'

More silence, this time she gave way.

'Am I right to think you're on your own here?'

Jack sighed.

'Yes, I am. Since my wife died, two years back.'

'I see, I am sorry to hear that.' She paused again, briefly. 'Do you know who I am yet, then?'

'Not for certain, no, but perhaps I can guess.'

'Go on then.'

He took a deep breath.

'Are you related to Pamela?'

'That's right, I'm her daughter.'

His curiosity grew stronger.

'Right, I see. What's your name then?'

'Samantha.'

Jack paused to take this in.

'I've always liked that name.'

'Thank you.'

Hesitantly, 'and how is Pamela?'

Samantha gathered herself before replying. 'She died three months ago, at the beginning of December.'

'Oh, no!' Jack drew in a deep breath and looked out of the window, away from her for a few moments, his anticipation crushed. 'I'm so very sorry to hear that.' There was a catch in his voice. He shuffled uneasily in his chair and again ran his fingers through his hair.

'She hadn't forgotten you, you know.'

Jack stared at her for a moment, eyebrows raised. It was quiet again, as he composed himself. That year had been a big one in his life for several reasons; new baby, away from home with his job, certain tensions. Memories and images from that year tumbled through his mind. He began to feel uneasy about the direction of the conversation.

'Did she tell you anything about me?'

'She said that you were a nice man who lodged with her after Norman had left home.'

'And she was a very fine lady, a real lady. But I must have been there before you were born. Norman wasn't your father, was he?'

'No, I came along well after he'd gone.'

'And are you in touch with Norman?'

'No, I've never met him. He means nothing to me; he did the dirty on my mum, that's all I need to know about him.' She finished the sentence on a firm note, implying there was nothing else to say on that subject.

'So why have you come looking for me now?'

'I wanted to meet you, to see you for myself.'

Jack relaxed a little and chuckled. 'Hmm, not much of interest to see, is there?'

'Oh, I wouldn't say that,' said Samantha with a chuckle of her own. Jack felt himself blushing, and that hadn't happened for a long time. He took a cloth from the spectacle case on the small table by him and cleaned his glasses. They were not smudged, but he needed to buy a little more time to think.

After thirty-five years can I trust my memory? Did what I think might have happened, really happen? Or not?

He now had a clear idea of where this conversation was going, so he sent it off in another direction.

'Do you have any brothers or sisters?'

'My mum remarried, and I have two younger half-sisters.'

'You have a stepfather, then?'

'I did, but he died of cancer a few years ago.'

Jack waited for a moment.

'And was your mother's death a peaceful one?'

'It was for her as she had Alzheimer's and was quite at ease. But she then had other health problems, and it was quick after that.'

Another pause, but Jack felt less tense now.

'So why have you come looking for me? And how did you know how to find me?'

'I have my reasons. Mum always kept her address books, and I found you in one of them. I have a friend down here who checked the local phone directory and saw that you still lived here. I decided to take a chance to come to see you.'

Jack squirmed in his chair.

'So, who's your father?'

'That's what I want to know.'

A pause.

'Ah, I see, you think it might be me?'

Samantha looked him firmly in the eye now.

'I think that it is possible that you are. Well, tell me, could you be?'

Jack took his glasses off again.

'What a question to come out of the blue like this. It is important for you to know, I expect?' he said, gently.

'It is, I have good cause for wanting to know more about my biological father. Having met you now, I was hoping that it would be you. I can see why Mum thought you were a very nice man.'

"Thank you. Didn't Pamela tell you who it was?'

'She always refused point-blank to tell me anything, who or how. She could be very stubborn at times. I felt there was a story there that she didn't want me to know.'

Yet another silence, before Jack spoke again.

'It was a very long time ago, a lot of water under Trent Bridge since then.'

He took another deep breath. 'This is quite a surprise and I'm so sorry to hear that she's no longer with us. I definitely need a cup of tea, are you sure that you don't want one?'

'Please get yourself one, I'll have a top-up of water if I may? Could I use your loo, please?'

'Of course, top of the stairs straight ahead.'

The February afternoon was drawing on now, the rain still battered the windows. He brought in his tea, settled back in his chair and switched on a table lamp. Samantha had sat again on the settee but had taken off her damp anorak and her scarf, which now lay beside her. She wore a smart, purple, V-necked sweater with a thin silver necklace. If she had hoped for a quick look round while she was upstairs, she was out of luck for all the bedroom doors were kept closed. All she could see was a clean and tidy bathroom, quite spartan in decoration, with a strong smell of disinfectant.

Jack felt the need to explain.

'My firm found me digs with your mum in Sneinton. That was ideal for me, the house was always spick and span, meals were ready when I wanted, packed lunches provided. Not far to the Colwick bus stop, I thought that I'd struck lucky. She'd been saddled with a big house and not much income, so she felt obliged to take lodgers to survive. It was not how she had wanted her life to be, and I was very sorry for her. Did she still live in that same house?'

'Yes, that's where I was brought up. Did you know Nottingham before then?'

'No, I didn't, so I had to find my way around.'

Samantha leant back, relaxing now, clasping her left knee with both hands. 'I guess things were a bit different in those days.'

'They were. I tried to ring my wife every night from the call-box down the road, but I'm not sure that helped very much, she was always stressed, on her own with the children.'

'Were there other lodgers at our house as well?' asked Samantha.

'Most of the time, they tended to come and go a bit, there was nobody else there for the whole six months that I was. Some blokes, commercial travellers and the like, might only stay a night or two. A few stayed for a couple of weeks. She had three rooms she could let out. I never socialised with any of the others. To tell the truth I was shattered by the end of the working day. And of course, I wasn't there some weekends, when I caught the Friday evening train back here.'

'Which room did you have?'

'The nice room at the back on the first floor, very peaceful it was. I was comfortable there.'

'And you must have got to know Mum quite well in that time?'

'Well, yes, I did,' said Jack, hesitating. 'I was angry about the way she'd been treated, even though it wasn't my business. She was a bright, intelligent lady, I'm not at all surprised to hear that she re-married. We walked out to go for a drink once or twice, up Sneinton Dale, she didn't want to be seen with me at the pub on the corner. There weren't any coffee shops or wine bars to go to in those days, you know, not like today. I bought the drinks, I insisted on that.'

'Was it your idea to go out together?' asked Samantha, a question which made Jack feel uncomfortable, as he shifted in his chair again.

'Ooh, I don't know really. It was summer, a Thursday evening I think, we'd both had a hard day and one of us must have said "I feel like a drink," and we took it from there. She drank a Babycham, they used to be very popular, always served with a cherry in it. She was good company, chatty without being trivial, if you understand my meaning, she knew what was going on in the world, had some quite definite opinions.'

'She would have been quite choosy about who she was seen out with,' said Samantha, very firmly.

'I think so.'

'So, tell me, could you be my father?'

And they looked again at each other, trying to anticipate the next move.

CHAPTER 2

Kenton, North London, February 1990

JACK DID NOT think of himself as unhappy. He felt that he'd had a good life and a sound marriage, and he was proud of his family. He accepted what life had brought him now, but he was lonely, missing Margaret much more than he would have anticipated.

He had never lived on his own before and had never imagined that she would die first, the women seemed to him to always outlive their men. She had been a good wife, attentive, loyal and diligent, even if she was a little cautious about change or anything new. They had lived in the same house since they were married forty years before, and he remembered his children growing up there and he still expected to see Margaret when he went into the kitchen.

An organised man, his many years in a building supplies warehouse had taught him the benefits of "a place for everything and everything in its place." His workshop at the bottom of his garden was a paragon of orderliness, with shadow boards for his tools and neatly labelled containers for the screws and nails.

He sometimes went to the Parish Church, had occasional nights at the pub where he would banter with a few acquaintances. He followed the football and cricket with interest. He would chat to the neighbours when he went to the shops. And he had his memories.

It was now two years since Margaret had died, a

slow, sad decline, leaving him on his own. His children and grandchildren were sometimes in touch but didn't live nearby. His sister, younger than him, still lived in their old family home up in Lancashire, but she only rang to tell Jack her troubles, and never asked about his. On the table in the hall, by the telephone, was his son David's business card, something grand in finance in the City of London. He always told his father to contact him whenever he needed to, but Jack never knew which country he was in. The need to call did not seem to arise very often, as Jack did not have much to tell him.

JACK LOOKED BACK at Samantha but couldn't quite meet her gaze.

'I'm sorry if this isn't the answer you want, but no, from what I can remember, I don't think I could be.'

Samantha sighed, shrugged her shoulders and folded her arms. Then she leant forward.

'You say "you don't think", are you really sure about that?'

'Yes, I am.'

For a moment Jack thought she was going to cry but she fought it off, looking down at her hands. Jack waited.

'Are you going back to Nottingham tonight?'

'No, I've a friend in Watford, who I have arranged to stay with for a couple of days, I have an open ticket back. She says she's going to show me the sights of Watford,' replied Samantha, managing a grin.

'Good Lord,' said Jack, 'I wouldn't get too excited about that. I only go there when I really have to.'

Samantha chose to ignore this remark.

'When exactly were you in Nottingham?' she asked.

'Nineteen fifty-five. From around April until September-October time.'

'And I was born in June fifty-six, so you were definitely around when I was conceived.'

'Ah, right.' Jack checked the arithmetic. 'Our Elizabeth was born in June fifty-five.'

'And where is she now?'

'She and her husband moved to New Zealand after they were married, over ten years ago now. He's a doctor. They have two girls, born out there.'

'Have you been out to see them?'

'No, I'd love to go, they are in Christchurch, which looks great, but Margaret had never flown, hated the idea of it and of being in a strange country. We always took our holidays in Devon or Cornwall. They've been back here a couple of times. The last time was Margaret's funeral, so I'm hoping that they will make it again this year.'

'Do you have any other children?'

'Yes, just one, a son,' said Jack, in all innocence.

'And where is he?'

'David is in Surrey, wife and two kids, a boy and a girl, he's two years older than Elizabeth. He has a top job in international finance, done very well for himself, nice house, but don't ask me to explain what he does, because I haven't a clue.'

To Jack it felt like he and Samantha were a pair of old boxers, circling round each other in the first round, sizing up the opposition, looking for potential weaknesses and openings for a quick jab. If there is not enough action after a minute or two, the crowd start to become restless, urging them on to try something. The more experienced fighters know that is a mistake, the savvy one will wait for the other to be careless, because that will be their opportunity. He used to enjoy the boxing, he had been at Wembley Stadium in 1963 for the famous fight when Henry Cooper came close to beating Cassius Clay, later known as Muhammad Ali.

Jack gazed out of the window, the rain was still heavy. It was he who gave way first, she was staring down at the carpet.

'Where do we go from here then, Samantha?' The name was unfamiliar to him and did not yet roll easily from his tongue. He still hadn't recovered from the shock of this stranger's arrival, the news she brought and the questions she was asking that he did not yet feel totally ready to answer.

'You tell me. I hadn't thought this through beyond meeting you. I do have my motives for wanting to know, can you understand that?'

'I can. My own childhood wasn't straightforward, I was sent by my parents in Lancashire to come to live down here with an aunt and uncle. My mother wasn't at all well, and Dad thought it would be for the best for me. It was during the Depression, and he thought there would be more opportunities for me down here. I was only twelve and it was a bit of an eye-opener coming to the big city.'

Jack realised as he finished that he had talked about himself and had not addressed her question. Samantha folded her arms again and showed that she had also noticed that.

'I definitely have my reasons,' she continued, 'I have been thinking about this for a long time and feel that it's stopping me from moving on with my life until I've sorted it.'

A glimmer of an idea was now starting to form for Jack. Perhaps, just perhaps, there was a way to deal with this. Vague memories of days and events long gone were coming back to him now. He did not want to commit himself immediately, he might say something that he would later regret. He recognised that she needed help, even if he hadn't given her a completely definitive answer to her questions. And yet, just possibly....

'Look, this has come as a bit of a shock. Can I think about it a bit longer?'

'What's there to think about?' she asked abruptly.

'I need to think this through,' said Jack with a smile. 'I do understand your predicament and I would like to help you if I can. Could you ring me tomorrow please?'

'OK,' sighed Samantha looking at him with a raised eyebrow and a smile of her own. 'It will be in the evening as I am going shopping with Jenny tomorrow. She's a nurse, and it's her day off.'

Jack took a page from the notebook that lay next to the phone and wrote down his number.

'That will be fine, I'm not going anywhere in the evening. Here's my number.'

'Thank you.'

The conversation had been stilted and the parting wasn't easy either, he shouldn't kiss her, a hug felt wrong, shaking hands would have been just silly. He just put his hand on her shoulder and said, 'We will get there,' not knowing what he meant by that.

'Thank you,' she said, also not knowing. 'See you again,'

'Yes,' said Jack, 'See you again.'

WHEN SHE HAD gone, he realised that he hadn't asked her much about herself. Husband, children, job? How could he be sure that she was Pamela's daughter? She said that she had her mother's address book certainly, but she could be a niece or even a neighbour. Because he lived in London, might she have thought that he was rich and there was money to be had, or demanded? At least she should now realise that there was no fortune to be made here. What might he be letting himself in for? He realised that she could be disturbing his calm, peaceful life. Well, a little excitement would not go amiss. After all, he took up the challenge to go to Nottingham in the first place, didn't he? That was a gamble.

HE TOOK HIS meals at the kitchen table, for that evening it was steak and kidney pie, carrots and potatoes, followed by tinned rice pudding. Afterwards Jack was restless and could not settle. He fiddled about for a while in his workshop where he did carpentry work, but he did not achieve anything useful. He looked at the television briefly, just daft quiz shows, not his taste at all. After that he confirmed to himself that he had read all that he could possibly want to know from the *Daily Mail*. His mind turned back to Samantha, and he tried to put himself in her shoes.

He knew several people locally who were uncertain about their origins. One lad, Clyde, had worked for him for a long time. Big strong fellow, dark-skinned, black curly hair, born in nineteen-forty-four, good footballer, he and his mother lived alone. She was from Harrow and the word was that his father had been an American serviceman. The War had been a big upheaval for many families, with their children evacuated, fathers called up and mothers going out to work for the first time in their lives. In London in particular, many hours were spent underground, taking cover from the bombs in Shelters and Tube stations. He knew that many had had a reckless attitude of, "Who cares, we might not be here tomorrow." After the War, times were still tough. Back when he had been up in Nottingham, it had only been a year since food rationing had ended.

So Samantha would not be the only one with a mysterious background, although those conceived in wartime were older than she was. Certainly, the nineteen fifties were still a time when to be illegitimate was a real stigma, both for the mother and the child. Many a youngster would come home from school with the cry 'Bastard!' ringing in their ears, embarrassing their mother by asking her what the word meant.

He could appreciate Samantha's wish to know more. One day she could have children who wanted to hear about their grandfathers. If it had been him in her place, he would probably have just shrugged his shoulders and got on with life, but not everyone was like him.

Jack did not know how much he could trust his memory. He had recently been to the funeral of an old colleague, Mike, where he talked to the family. He was surprised to find that events he had recalled did not happen in the way Jack thought they had. He had believed that this man had come to work with him straight from school, only to be told by his brother that Mike had worked for the local council for three years before that. Or, at least, that is what the brother remembered.

How reliable is my memory? Have I invented things that perhaps I wished had happened? Or tried to forget things that did happen? Who knows?

Of concern to him was the reaction of his own children if they heard about this, especially if he became involved in Samantha's quest. To Jack's eyes, David saw things too much in black and white, and he was likely to be suspicious of Samantha's motives and telling Jack in forthright terms to keep clear. Elizabeth had become more distant from Jack since she and her husband had emigrated. To him there was a lot of her mother in her, and he hoped she would be more sympathetic, although she had always been careful not to fall out with her brother. *Yes, suddenly, there's a lot for me to think about here.*

CHAPTER 3

Kenton, North London, February 1990

JACK WAS A decent man, who usually liked to help others if he could, and he realised that he was probably the only person now who could help Samantha in her search. As he was around at the time in question, it was possible that he had met some of the likely suspects. He spent all of the evening and then some of the night in bed, chewing it over in his mind. He eventually awoke with a start, an hour past his usual time of 7.30am, having slept through the alarm, and that put him in a poor mood to start the morning.

He had a project in his workshop down at the end of the garden, beyond the carefully cultivated vegetable plot. It was to make some wooden toys on his lathe, something he had been putting off for a while. After lunch, he made himself start on that, little wooden trains that he had made before, nothing very challenging, but he found it satisfying to hold in his hand a solid product that was all his own work. They would be sold at to raise funds at the Church fete in the summer. He liked being part of the Church, not that he had any strong religious feelings, or ever gave much thought to it. He felt that we must be on this Earth for some reason, it could not be all just a big accident of nature.

He sometimes contemplated his own death, hoping it would be quick and pain-free. How long before it came, he would wonder and then go on to think about how to spend the intervening months and years. He was thinking that he should be doing something useful in that time, while he could.

Samantha's visit had made him realise that he was bored and drifting, living from day to day. He now glimpsed that there could be an opportunity here to occupy himself more usefully. Besides, he had also taken a shine to Samantha. She wasn't glamorous or fashion-conscious, but she had a determined air that he appreciated, and he wanted now to know more about her story. And, after all these years, somehow his link to Pamela was now renewed. Even though he now had to accept that she was gone, that connection was important to him.

For his meal that evening, Jack kept it simple, one of those Vesta curries: he had never been to an Indian or Chinese restaurant, but he had tried these meals since living on his own and quite liked them, they were easy to prepare. Margaret had always done all the cooking; his job had been the washing up.

Then he sat down and waited, picked up the paper and put it down again. His phone very rarely rang these days; sometimes David quickly catching up, always in a rush ('Got to go Dad, it's Round Table tonight'). Occasionally it would be Elizabeth, by prior arrangement from New Zealand and, very rarely, his sister Brenda from Lancashire. He had been braced for the call all day, but it still made him jump when the phone gave its shrill sound just after 8.30pm. In his usual style he recited his number and waited, literally holding his breath.

'Hello Jack,' said a female voice.

'Hello, is that Samantha?' he asked, even though he knew that it was. Still he found that her name did not come easily to his lips and a part of his brain was wondering why, even as the rest of it was listening intently for her reply.

'Yes it is,' said Samantha, at first sounding slightly flustered and impatient, then taking a deep breath. 'Have you had a good day, what have you been up to?' This was in a calmer tone. Jack wondered if she was on her own or if her friend was listening in.

'Oh, this and that. I did some shopping this morning and I have been in my workshop this afternoon.' He went on to tell her about the model trains he had been making.

'They sound lovely, I would like to see those sometime.'

'Why, do you like trains? asked Jack.

'No, I know someone who does.'

Jack didn't quite know what to make of that, so he moved on.

'And how have you got on, what did you think to Watford, then?'

'I could see what you meant,' she said with a laugh, 'It's not special is it? But Jenny knows a nice new Italian restaurant and we had a good lunch there with a glass of wine and later we did some clothes shopping. She's got a better eye for fashion and colour than I have.'

'The restaurant sounds posh. Who is Jenny, how do you know her?'

'She's from Nottingham, an old schoolfriend, found herself a good job at the General Hospital here, she needed to put some distance between herself and her family.'

'Well, she's a bit different from you then, you're trying to get closer to yours,' Jack couldn't help saying, and immediately thought that he might have overstepped the mark, but fortunately Samantha laughed again.

'Very true.'

Jack paused, relieved that she had taken it that way. He had spent much of his working life on the phone with suppliers, customers and customers' customers. Personal calls he had never found to be as easy.

'What do you think then, Jack?' The sixty-four-thousand-dollar question.

'For the moment, if we assume that your father was someone who lodged with your mother that summer, although it might not have been, it is probable that I met them. Right?'

'Right.'

'And there is nobody else around from that time to help you. Right?'

'Right again.'

'I know it's a long shot, but we just might be able to track down the culprit, needle in a haystack job as it is. Right?'

'How can we do that?'

Jack answered one question with another.

'When are you going back to Nottingham?'

'I'm not sure yet, probably the day after tomorrow, Saturday.'

'Have you the time to come over again, so we can talk about it?'

'Yes, I could come tomorrow afternoon,' Samantha replied quickly.

'Let's do that then, I'll see you then.'

'OK, tomorrow, about three o'clock?'

'See you then. Bye.'

WHEN SAMANTHA RETURNED the next day, Jack had slept a little better, but the morning had dragged slowly again. Just a few minutes after three, the doorbell rang again. It was another blustery February afternoon.

'Hello, do come in.'

Samantha took off her anorak this time and Jack hung it in the hall. She sat again in the same place on the settee, Jack settled again in his rocker. Once more they looked each other in the eye. He had already made himself a cup of tea and she refused any drink.

'Let's get this out of the way now, before we go any further. Pardon me for asking, but how do I know that you are Pamela's daughter, or even if Pamela had a daughter?'

'That's a fair question,' said Samantha, delving into her rucksack. She came up with a piece of paper, printed in red, with handwritten content in black ink and passed it to Jack. It was a birth certificate, dated 13 June 1956, for Samantha Jane Charlton. Born in hospital in Nottingham; Mother Pamela Hilda Charlton, nee Briggs; Occupation Housewife. Father's details were left blank.

'And that's still your surname, or did you take your stepfather's name?'

'I took his name, and I became known as Samantha Townsend.'

'And is that still your name?'

'No, I'm Mrs. Samantha Jenkins now, although I am separated from my husband.'

'But it still doesn't prove that this is you, anyone could have got hold of this.'

'What sort of proof do you want, haven't you seen enough yet to convince you?'

He was getting that stern look and sharp tone from her again and felt on the defensive, being mean in doubting her. However, he persisted.

'I agree that you have plenty of evidence, but you might have been caring for her or a niece or something similar.'

'Well, I promise you I am Pamela's daughter, the

person on the certificate and you will have to bloody well believe it, or we will get nowhere. Just as I have to believe you are the real Jack Rodgers, not just someone living in his house. We've got to trust each other, haven't we, if we are going to achieve anything together?'

Jack leant back and put his hands up, palms outwards.

'You're right. Perhaps you've got a photo of you both together which you could show me some time?'

'Oh, I am a fool. I have, I will show you one next time I'm down here.'

'Look, you have taken me completely by surprise, I'm still in shock to hear that Pamela has gone. I'd never heard from her in over thirty years. It wouldn't have occurred to me that she might have died. When you first arrived I dared to think that you might have a message for me from her.'

It was Samantha's turn to look surprised, eyebrows raised. Once more, he stalled by cleaning his spectacles.

'I would like to see if I could help you find out who your father is, for your sake and for your mum's sake. You were born on June thirteenth, nineteen fifty-six, do you know if you were premature or late at all?'

'Mum used to say that it was no wonder that I'm such a stickler for punctuality, as I was born exactly on my due date.'

Jack smiled and gave her an approving look.

'Oh, you are my sort of girl.' Jack realised that he had put his foot in it again, but this time it took some of the tension out of the room as they both laughed.

'So that would take us back to September thirteenth, nineteen fifty-five, approximately, give or take a week or two? Those estimates for birth dates were never very systematic, were they?'

'No, but somewhere around then.'

'Well, I can check, but I am pretty sure that it was October time before I finished up there. So, I don't have an alibi to prove I was somewhere else, as they say on *The Bill*.'

'No, you don't, do you?' said Samantha, very firmly. 'Jack, I have to say that it feels as if you are sending on a fool's errand to divert me away from the truth. Were you my mother's lover or not?'

CHAPTER 4

Harrow, April 1955

I ALWAYS WORRIED when I heard the words, 'The Boss wants to see you, now, in his office.' This time my heart fluttered; the optimist in me starting to think about a pay rise, yet the pessimist was remembering all of my little mistakes, wondering if they added up to enough to merit the sack.

It was Fred, our foreman, who brought the message. I had always got on well with Fred. He was close to retirement then, and had some old-fashioned ways and views, but I thought he was a good bloke who had helped me a lot with the odd quiet word when I needed it. When he passed the message on, I thought I saw the slightest hint of a smile. I remember when Tony got the push, Fred couldn't look him in the eye.

Gladwin's was still a family business, Builders' Merchants, supplying everything the building trade required from bricks and sand to hammers and nails. Mr. Ernest started it near Harrow-on-the-Hill station with his brother Horace when they came back from World War I in 1919. Mr. Horace had been badly gassed in the trenches and died soon after. Mr. Ernest was still around but was rather frail now and his only son Brian had just taken over the business. I wasn't too sure about Brian; he was a bit loud for my taste. He liked flash cars and, while he was married with two kids, as the blokes in the yard put it, 'he is having it off with Elaine in the office,' and he didn't seem to care who knew. What Brian did in World war II is a mystery, something to do with him having bad feet.

I gave him credit for seeming to be ambitious for the business, which I liked. He had brought in a lot of new customers who were building all the new houses that were going up in Harrow and further out along the Metropolitan Line, towards Northwood. We had been really busy in the last couple of years. Fred reckoned there were a few backhanders being given, bottles of scotch, tickets for The Arsenal and Test Matches and so on.

I joined Gladwin's when I left school at fifteen in 1938 and worked for them until being called up in 1941. I 'did my bit' in the Army in North Africa and came back in 1946. They kept my job open for me and I went straight back, never thought about going anywhere else.

I had only been in the Boss's wood-panelled office a few times, mainly to see Mr. Ernest at Christmas, when the annual rises were given out. It was always full of smoke from his pipe, and he would lean back in his big revolving chair and say, 'How are you, lad?' He gave me a bigger rise when Margaret and I were married and used his contacts in the trade to help us to get our house. Mr. Ernest would quiz me about my cricket and football, asking if they were still playing me at centre-half, when he didn't think I was tall enough to play in that position, and that would be about it.

It was rather different this time. I had to wait outside the office while Elaine made a big thing of phoning him ('Brian, Jack Rodgers is here to see you') and then asking me to sit down and wait. She was big, brassy, and blonde, but not a real blonde, I could tell. She made sure that we all noticed when she tottered across the yard in her tight skirt and high heels. After about five minutes, her phone rang. She answered it and gave Brian a little giggle before saying that I should go into his office.

The old pictures of Harrow in 1914, had now been replaced by colour photos of racing cars. I noticed one of Fangio winning the German Grand Prix. The old faded Persian carpet had gone, with a brightly coloured replacement, golds, reds, and purples, in its place. Senior Service fumes now, where there had been pipe smoke before. I had never been a smoker myself, not even in the War, when nearly all the others did, and the air didn't now seem as pleasant. Brian was studying a letter intently and just waved me to take a seat to the side of his desk. After another couple of minutes, he put the letter down, swivelled his chair and looked straight at me, displaying his yellow socks and suede shoes.

'Hello, Jack, how are you, mate?'

'Very well, Mr. Brian, thank you.'

'You don't have to bother with the Mister bit, we are in the nineteen fifties now, you know.'

'Oh, right.'

'How long have you been at Gladwin's now, Jack?'

'It's about thirteen years now, I think, either side of the War. I came back in February forty-six.'

'And you've always worked in the warehouse and on the counter.'

'Mainly, but I have been out on deliveries a lot'

'Fred says that you know all the stock well and you are good with customers.'

This was a surprise, nobody had ever said that to me before, and I blushed.

'Don't hide your light under a bushel, mate, you've got to look confident in business today, it's a tough world.'

I nodded.

'What are your ambitions, then?'

I took a deep breath and, taking note of what had just been said, I went for it.

'Well, I know that Fred will be coming up for retirement before long, so I would like to think I would be in with a chance of his job. After that, perhaps there could be something on the Sales side, finding new customers.'

'Well said, mate. Gladwin's are going places, and we will need all of our best blokes. I have big plans.'

He stopped and looked straight at me again, then lit another cigarette. He stroked his moustache approvingly.

'How well do you know Nottingham?'

That threw me.

'Nottingham? Well, I went up there for the Test Match a couple of years ago. Saw Denis Compton make a century.'

He laughed. Brian often laughed, but it never seemed to be with much humour.

'We have taken a lease on a building on a new industrial estate up there. It will be ready in about three months' time, and it will be Gladwin's second branch, but not the last, there will be more to come. We want you to go up there and set it up for us. I want it run in the Gladwin way and think you are the chap to make sure of that. When it is shipshape after another three months, we will take on someone local who knows the area and you will come back here. You're on eight pound a week now, aren't you?'

'Seven pounds eighteen shillings, actually.'

Brian laughed that laugh again.

'We will pay you twelve quid a week while you are there. We will pay your fares and for your digs. You can come home once a fortnight. What do you reckon?'

Nobody at Gladwin's had ever been made an offer like that before. Nor had anything like that happened to any of my pals in their jobs with the Post Office and the Co-op.

Gosh, what will Margaret say? Shame that my old Dad's gone; he would have been proud of me for that. 'Work hard and be helpful to people and you will get on,' he would say. Although that didn't do him a lot of good once he got his lung disease from the asbestos.

'Don't answer me now, you'll want to talk it over with the Missus, I expect. You've got a mortgage and a nipper and another one due soon, I hear. The money will come in handy.'

'Thank you.' I managed to reply. 'When do you need an answer?'

'By Monday if you will, please.'

It was Thursday. When I got back into the warehouse it was busy, Fred was occupied dealing with one of our regulars, Wally from Ruislip. Wally needed a lot of watching, inclined to help himself to stuff in the warehouse if he thought nobody would notice. Sometimes he would complain that he had been short-delivered when Fred and I knew very well that he had not.

I wandered around the yard outside for a while, dazed, staring at the heaps of sand and stacks of bricks. Afterwards, Fred took me on one side.

'What do you think then, son?'

'I don't know what to say really, it's so unexpected. I've never thought about working anywhere else, especially away from London. I don't think Margaret will be happy about me not being home every night.'

'Well, she's got her mum and her sister just round the corner, so she should be all right. When's the baby due?'

'Nine weeks to go, and she had a hard time with our David. I just know this will worry her, and I don't like to see her upset.'

LOOKING BACK LATER, I could only marvel at the risk that Gladwin's took. I had no experience in management at all and finished up being responsible for all sorts of things that I had never done before, dealing with the site builders, recruiting staff, advertising and so on. Really, I was the low-cost option, just a few extra pounds a week for a few months. Fortunately, I was excited; I should have been terrified.

AS I CYCLED home to Kenton, I was wondering how to broach the subject. When I arrived, Margaret was very flustered; David was crying, she was boiling nappies with the awful stink that they made, and tea wasn't ready. I decided to leave it until later in the evening.

It was about nine o'clock before David had finally gone off to sleep and we had eaten. Margaret was already yawning and had switched off the radio. I felt like a pint, not that we were able to get out for a drink very often then.

'I need to talk to you, I was called in to see Mr. Brian today.'

She gasped and put her hand to her mouth. She would always fear the worst, rather than hoping for the best.

'It's all right, it isn't bad news, but it is something that will take some thinking about. Gladwin's are opening a new branch in Nottingham, and they want me to go there and set it up. I would be away for six months, home every fortnight, but they are paying all of the expenses and there would be a big pay rise while I'm doing it.'

She looked at me and I thought she was going to cry, but I ploughed on.

'It's great that they are asking me, it's a real vote of confidence. I have told Brian that I'm looking for promotion and would like to move into Sales later.'

I waited; Margaret was holding back the tears.

'What would it mean, when would you go, when would you get back? What would happen when the baby is born? What about if I have a hard time again?'

I reeled under the avalanche of questions.

'I don't know, we haven't got down to that sort of detail yet.'

'It might be detail to you, but it isn't detail to me. Have you already said yes?'

'No, I haven't, but they want an answer by Monday. They want to open there in three months.'

'How much more money?'

'Twelve pounds a week, it's more than a fifty percent increase, it would really help with the mortgage, you know how tight things are for us at the moment. You've got your mum and Barbara here to help you.'

'Huh! Barbara can't help much with three kids of her own and you know what a worrier my mother is.'

There was a long silence and she yawned again.

'Let's talk about it over the weekend,' I said.

THE SUBJECT WAS not mentioned at all on Friday evening, but I could feel the tension in the air, with odd remarks about me needing to do certain things in the house, 'if you're around, that is.' Pregnancy didn't suit Margaret; some girls seemed to blossom, but her legs were painful, and she tired quickly. She insisted on keeping the house in apple-pie order, which I was usually very happy with, but then it felt excessive. She didn't get to see her old friends from the typing pool, like she used to, and I was sure she missed them.

By Saturday evening, I couldn't stand it any longer and said to her that we had to talk.

'You want to do it, don't you?' she said.

'I am flattered to be asked.'

'If you don't do it, who else will they ask?'

This was a good question, which I hadn't thought about.

'Don't know really. Fred's too old and wouldn't go. Cyril in Sales would think he could do it, but he's all mouth and doesn't know how to run a warehouse. Besides, he's only been with us for six months and is always telling everyone how he is going after other jobs. None of the other blokes know half as much as me and most of them aren't as ambitious or care as much I do about the job. You're right, he doesn't have many other choices.'

'I just like having you here. Mum would come round, but she gets on my nerves when she starts wittering on about stuff or telling me what that Mrs. Roberts has done. Barbara's got her hands full, and her Richard is no help at all, just sits in front of their telly all the time. It's hard enough coping with David, I can't imagine what it will be like with another baby as well.'

There wasn't much I could say to that, I knew it was all very true, and that was the end of the discussion. By the time I got to bed, she had already turned her back on me. I lay awake for ages. I wanted to go, it really seemed like a big opportunity, make or break you might say. The day-to-day routine at work was comfortable enough, but it did get boring at times. I also knew this would be a big boost financially. I did all our accounts, paid the bills, and Margaret had no idea how tight things were sometimes, keeping in the black while still paying up the mortgage.

ON MONDAY MORNING, I went up to the office and told Elaine that I would like to see Brian again. Fred had given me a firm stare but had not asked about my decision; I reckoned he knew what I was going to say. Brian kept me waiting; I couldn't concentrate, and it was an hour or more before I had the call to go to the office. As before he made me sit and wait while he read a long letter.

'Jack, you wouldn't know what bastards some of our customers are. Reg Davis complaining about the quality of our sand.'

I wasn't surprised at that one. We had changed to a cheaper supplier and the new stuff was too damp and was often contaminated with soil.

He swivelled his chair again, red socks today. 'Right mate, what do you reckon then?'

'I would like to accept your offer, thank you.'

'Missus OK with it?'

'I wouldn't go that far,' I said, and Brian laughed that mirthless laugh. 'I would like to be back for a few days when the baby arrives, due in nine weeks.'

'We'll sort something out on that, don't worry,' he said with a dismissive wave of his left arm, flicking fag ash far and wide.

'Right, it's a deal. We would like you up there from next Monday. Go and see Angus, he's got all the details.'

Angus MacDiarmid was the Finance Director, a real tight-arsed Scot who had never been seen to smile. He had worked for Gladwin's for ten years then, but by the next Christmas he was gone. Elaine said there he had had some big arguments with Brian. Fred's view was that he was going to be somebody else's little ray of sunshine.

I didn't manage to see Angus until the Wednesday and then it was all a frantic rush to sort everything before the weekend. He was actually quite helpful and methodical, taking me through everything about the Nottingham site, plans, drawings, and such. Angus told me the arrangements for expenses, but still hadn't said anything about where I was going to stay. He seemed a bit surprised when I asked.

'Oh, Elaine is sorting that out, go and see her.'

Elaine greeted me with a big beaming smile and a wink when I went to see her.

'I think I've found you some really nice digs in Nottingham with a Mrs. Charlton. Here's the address and phone number, it's not far from the station and just a bus ride from our new site. She sounds very nice and quite young, I would say, I think you'll be all right there.' She was still wearing the smile and I was treated to another wink.

'Bed, breakfast and evening dinner, she'll do you a packed lunch if you want one. You pay her cash each week and then claim it back from us with your travel fares. There will be a float of £25 here for you on Friday to collect before you go.'

AND THAT WAS it, really. Not much useful guidance on anything, it was going to be seat of the pants stuff. The Army in North Africa had been like that for me, with quick changes of plans. The RSM would tell me one thing and half-an-hour later the Major would order me to do the opposite, so I had learnt to be flexible. I could never forget the dash west after El Alamein, hair-raising and chaotic it was. That was when we lost my best pal Ted Kenworthy from Yorkshire, I saw him being run over by one of our own trucks.

CHAPTER 5

Kenton, February 1990

SAMANTHA'S USE OF the word 'lover' made Jack wince and he waited a while, once more shuffling in his seat, before he could bring himself to answer.

'Even if I were, that still wouldn't be definite proof that I was your father, would it now?'

'No, but please don't start that again, suggesting that she was the sort of woman to sleep around, because I know she was not.'

Jack again put his hands up, a signal of submission.

'I agree, she wasn't, she was fun, but she was a proper lady.'

'But you still haven't properly answered my question, have you? First of all you said that you weren't.'

'No, I haven't, and I can't right now, not being put on the spot like this. It was a very long time ago. Memory is such a funny thing, what you wanted to happen and what actually happened can merge into one another. After thirty-five years, you can't rely on it to be accurate. I can't take responsibility for anything at this stage. I had a lot on my mind at the time. The job there was a big task for me, as much as I could cope with, if not more, and without much help. Also, I knew that back at home Margaret wasn't at all happy with me being away. My memories of that time are very confused. I'm not used to talking about things like this with anybody, it makes me feel very embarrassed and uncomfortable.'

Samantha gave an exasperated sigh.

Jack kept going but moved in a more positive direction.

'You found me in her address book. Were there many other names in there?'

'The usual family and friends, in an alphabetical index, but also there was a plain notebook section at the back. There was a long list of men's names and addresses, from all over the country, not alphabetical, just listed. I presume that was in the order that you all came in.'

'How long did she take lodgers for, do you know?'

'She stopped in the spring before I was born, and afterwards she didn't seem to want to do it again. "That's behind me now" was all she would say about it.'

'From what she told me, she'd been taking lodgers for three or four years before, soon after Norman had buggered off.'

'I think so, your name was quite a way down the list,' she confirmed.

'We would have some clues to identify your father from the other names around me on the list, as they are the ones who would have been there at the same time?'

'Yes, we would.'

'The other thing is, it's coming back to me now, I paid her cash and needed to have a receipt from her to take back to the office so I could claim the money with the rest of my expenses. She had one of those little books, tear-out receipts with carbon copies, you haven't got any of those, I suppose?'

'Ooh, I hadn't thought of that. There are some in her bureau, but I haven't looked at them, that's a really good idea,' said Samantha, sounding for once as if she was warming to the task. Jack was happier now with the direction that their conversation was taking; finding out facts, discovering some clues about where their search could go.

'I can remember one or two of the men who stayed. There was Barry from South Wales, who liked to joke that he travelled in ladies' underwear. Pamela was very embarrassed when he started waving some of his samples about one night. And a strange man, Cedric, from the West Country, wouldn't make conversation with anybody, he was there for a few weeks. No idea what business he was in. As I say, many I never met. I tried to be away by seven in the morning and some of them hadn't shown their faces by then. But with only three of us there at a time, you were sometimes forced into conversation round the dinner table.'

'I'm trying to picture it, did Mum eat with you?'

'Oh no, she always had her meal in the kitchen on her own. Anyway, she had usually eaten by the time I got back. The buses from Colwick weren't the most reliable. I never understood how she did it, I didn't go in the kitchen very much, but there was always a meal ready for you, hot or a salad in summer, whenever you arrived.'

'That sounds like her.'

'You felt that the kitchen was her territory, she wouldn't take help with washing up or anything like that, said we were paying guests. She was a very capable lady. Did she go out to work again later?'

'Yes, when we had all gone to school, at first it was mornings only, then full-time. She found a job as a receptionist with a hosiery company in the Lace Market.'

'And what do you do for a living?'

'Oh, nothing very special, just a clerical job in Local Government, working for my local council. It is handy and convenient.'

Jack stopped there, he did not want to push too far at this stage with personal questions, even though there was plenty more he would like to know. If she lived on her own, had any children, relations with her half-sisters, her education, those sorts of issues. He waited a minute to see if Samantha was going to take up the running again, but she was just gazing back at him.

'Are you still going home tomorrow?'

'Yes, I'm going for a mid-morning train, I'll be home soon after lunch-time. I did enough shopping in Watford to last me a while, so I won't stop to look round the Nottingham city shops.'

Jack was feeling cramp in his right calf and stood up to stretch it. Samantha seemed to take this a signal that the conversation was at an end and started to gather up her things.

'Hold on a minute,' he said, waving her down, 'I suffer with cramp, it's my age, I just need to stretch my legs.'

Nevertheless, he remained standing while he spoke, stretching his leg, which meant he was looking down at her and she was forced to crane her neck to see him.

'You're on a mission, aren't you? You're not going to be satisfied until you have a result here, are you?'

'No, I'm not. I really feel the urge to find out who is my real father.'

'But you'll struggle to do it on your own, and I am probably the only person who has the time, any knowledge and some inclination to help you, is that right?'

Samantha sighed. 'It's very frustrating for me, you do understand that don't you?'

'OK, please don't push me on the detail just yet, but I would like to help you, for your sake and to honour Pamela. We'd have to be clear about what we want to achieve, if we found a guilty party, what we'd do about it, what their reaction is likely to be, if they thought you were after money from them or something like that? Do you get my meaning?'

She looked him directly in the eyes, as if she still thought that perhaps Jack might be her Dad. Jack was willing to help her, and she had few other options.

'Are you really sure that you want to do that? It could take up a lot of your time?'

'That's OK, I've plenty of that. None of us know how long we've got left, and I'm near the end of my three-score years and ten. But I am still healthy at the moment, touch wood, so it would be good to do something useful while I can. There's no big rush on your part, is there, but it's something that you want to sort and then be able to move on, is that right?'

'That's right.'

'Go back home, think about it. Give me your number but call me when you have got some thoughts and we will make a plan. I like to have a plan when I start something.'

Samantha smiled at him. 'So I see. I think you're quite looking forward to this, aren't you?'

He smiled back. 'You could say that.'

The parting was easier this time. He put his arm round her shoulders and gave them a little squeeze.

'What are you and your friend up to tonight then, a disco in Watford?'

'I think I'm past that now. Anyway, Jenny's on nights, so it's an early takeaway before she goes, settle down with my book and say goodbye to her in the morning.'

'She knows what you are doing here, then?'

'Oh, yes, she knew mum very well and she understands how I feel.'

'Keep in touch.'

'I will.'

HE HAD ENCOUNTERED some resentment back in 1955, as a 'Southerner', being sent to tell Nottingham people what to do. The local accent and dialect to him were, in many cases, impenetrable, and he constantly had to ask people to speak more slowly and clearly, which didn't please them.

The extra money had been very welcome for Margaret and himself, with a mortgage and a young family. He didn't have much time on his hands on those weekends when he was in Nottingham. He would sometimes go into the City Centre, and he managed to watch Forest twice, but he didn't feel that he belonged in the area, it felt like a foreign country.

The other issue that had weighed on his mind during those months was Margaret. He would ring her every night, from a call-box down the street (it would not have been right or discreet to use Pamela's house phone). Sometimes he would have to wait outside the box for ages while some old dear chatted away to someone. The calls weren't easy, Margaret had invariably had a hard day. At the start she was pregnant and had a toddler to cope with, and then later she had the new baby as well. There wasn't much of interest for her in his day, only the problems he had experienced. Jack never told her about taking Pamela for a drink, he knew she would be suspicious, whether there was any reason to be, or not.

AFTER SAMANTHA HAD gone, Jack made himself another cup of tea, sitting down in his chair again and starting to think again about Pamela. They had parted on good terms; at the time Jack thought there was a chance he would need to be going back up to Nottingham again for a while, but it never happened.

He had not forgotten her. To him, she was very

attractive, not just in a physical way, but he had really liked her personality. She was humorous, interested in the world around her and not afraid to air her opinions, but only if asked. Pamela could not stand people who she considered to be stuck up and pretentious. She was honest and straightforward, organised and tidy. Perhaps, thought Jack, we were too much alike to be a good couple, and he smiled at the idea.

He realised he had seen many of Pamela's characteristics in Samantha. There was a slight physical resemblance, nothing very striking, but he could detect in her a very similar personality, direct almost to the point of bluntness. Jack had always thought of it as being a Northern thing. To him, Nottingham was 'The North'.

No, it was not as if Pamela was always on his mind, she had never been an obsession. If he saw Nottingham on TV, Trent Bridge cricket or the City Ground, then his time there would re-surface in his memory. And then he would remember Pamela, wonder how she was, and hope she had found some happiness, because he thought she deserved some. It wasn't as if he had imagined himself living there. With her. Not often, anyway.

CHAPTER 6

Kenton, Late February 1990

'HELLO JACK, IT'S Samantha.'

'Hello,' said Jack, 'I was hoping you would ring, how are you?'

Samantha sighed. 'Up and down, had a few issues to deal with, but I'm OK now.'

'Hope it was nothing too serious,' said Jack, hoping this might bring more illumination on her life and circumstances.

'Nothing for you to worry about, anyway. I've had time to do some research and I have been looking through Mum's receipt books, that was a good idea of yours. They're not all here, there are some gaps, I don't know why, she was usually very meticulous about keeping stuff and storing it.'

'Do you still have her house, or has it been sold?'

'No, it hasn't been sold, that has been one of my problems. Let's just say that my two step-sisters and I have different views about what should happen next. Nothing has changed yet since she went into a home more than a year ago. I go in regularly and check it all out, but everything is as she left it.' Samantha continued, 'Now, you're still keen to help me to trace my real father then, are you?'

'I am, yes.'

'Why are you so keen?'

'To know the truth, for your sake and Pamela's. I

feel there is a mystery here to be solved and I can do my bit to help. It gives me a project, something to work on, the days get a bit empty sometimes.'

Samantha absorbed this for a few moments.

'Let's press on then. I've had another look round Mum's house. Perhaps there are other receipt books somewhere, but I haven't found them yet. Over a period of four-and-a-half years I think there are two or three books missing.'

'That's odd, isn't it, you can't think why she would have done that, can you?'

'No, you can't.'

'Am I in there, then?' asked Jack.

'You certainly are,' replied Samantha with emphasis. 'Unfortunately, one of the books that's missing covers part of the time that you must've been there. There were a hundred receipts in each book, and she usually used seven or eight each week, so there's a period of three months not covered, after you had first arrived.'

'So, what have you learned?'

'Hmm, well, there are a few names that I can match up in her address book, but not all, especially those who only came once for a single night. I've started by making a list of all of them.'

'OK.'

'What have you been up to, Jack?'

'It's hard to know where to start, where you can find information, so I've been to our local library. I went first here in Kenton, then the bigger central one in Harrow. I felt a bit conspicuous, especially in Kenton Library, I recognised one member of staff who lives on this road. I didn't want her questioning me on this, not at this stage, people could get the wrong impression.'

'Did you learn anything?'

'I spoke to a nice Asian guy in the Harrow, he was

quite helpful, although I am not sure that he really got my meaning. He directed me to the reference section, where they had some phone directories but only for round here, I thought they might have had more than that. He said they have a lot of stuff on what he calls microfilm, but I didn't like to say that I wasn't clear what that was.'

A disappointed tone became evident in Samantha's voice. 'Oh, I see. Not much further forward then.'

'No,' acknowledged Jack. 'How many names have you got for when I was there?'

'Quite a few, although the missing receipt books don't help. What I do know is that you arrived for the first time on Monday April eighteenth, nineteen fifty-five, which was the week after Easter that year. You stayed for two weeks, until Friday twenty-ninth. You came back on the Monday, May second and stayed for the rest of the month, not going home until Friday twenty-seventh, which was a Bank Holiday weekend. I have the names of the men who stayed with her in that time, but not address details for all of them. After that, the books are missing, no more information until mid-September.'

'One date I can remember is that our Elizabeth was born on June twenty-second, and that was in mid-week. She was overdue, so Margaret had to be induced, and I know I stayed home all that week, went back the next Monday, while she was still in hospital. Was I there in September?'

'On September twenty-third you paid for two weeks, presumably from Monday the twelfth. You were back on the twenty-sixth for three weeks until Friday October fourteenth. No record for you after that.'

'I think quite early on I dashed back home to Kenton, just for a day, Saturday afternoon to Sunday afternoon, out of my own pocket, just to keep Margaret happy. I think I also once found an excuse to come back on a Thursday night, perhaps the August Bank Holiday weekend. August Bank Holidays were at the beginning of the month in those days. I think they changed them in the seventies sometime.'

'Oh, I didn't know that. I can see that it must have been tough for you and your wife, being away from home for so long, all that travelling up down. With a new baby as well.' Samantha was sounding quite sympathetic for a moment.

'What about the names you found, are there many?' Jack tried again.

'In the six weeks at the start, there were about twenty names, and I have addresses for about half of them. At the end, that's five weeks and about fifteen names, addresses for a few more then. On some of the receipt copies, she has written what I assume are the names of the companies who had booked them in, so we might have some information on their employers. Do you want me to send you what I have; names, addresses, the odd bits of information that Mum wrote on her receipt copy?'

'Yes, please, especially the odd bits,' replied Jack. 'Most of the men I met worked for a company, but one or two were freelance, like Sales Agents for several different firms. I can put my thinking cap on and see who I can remember, that would be a good start. In the meantime, I will see what else I can find out about how we track people down. It's hard not knowing where to start and I don't want to have say too much about why I'm looking.'

'Yes, please,' said Samantha, 'Like you, I'm a bit nervous about saying too much to people in our library.'

'Thank you, I'm glad you understand my position on that, but I realise I'll have to put myself out a bit more, if I am going to be of any use to you.'

'All right, then,' said Samantha, 'I will crack on and copy this stuff out and send it to you.'

'Very good, speak soon.'

'Yes, speak soon, let me know what thoughts you have when you have seen the list.'

'I certainly will.' Jack was warming to the task.

A FEW DAYS later, a large buff envelope carrying the name 'Amber Valley Borough Council' landed on Jack's doormat. He was perplexed at first, as he had never heard of Amber Valley, and it sounded quite a glamorous name to him. However, it appeared to be a local council in Derbyshire, and the package was from Samantha. Inside was a hand-written note from her, together with some photocopies. A brief note, showing her home address, was attached.

> *'Dear Jack,*
>
> *This is what I have found so far, please see what you can make of it. I'm sorry if I sounded ungrateful when we spoke last week. I do appreciate what you are doing to help me, and I realise that you could have shut the door on me and sent me away. You still might do that, I wouldn't blame you. I've started a journey and have no idea where it is going to take me. As you are now aware, I do have other things to deal with at the moment, so please forgive me if I am distracted at times.*
>
> *Hope to hear from you again soon,*
> *Best wishes, Samantha'*

Jack looked through the bundle. She had photocopied the relevant pages of her mother's address book, from Jack's name onwards to include those who would have stayed in the six months that he was there. It gave Jack quite a start to see Pamela's handwriting again. She would sometimes leave him little notes to tell him that there had been a call for him, or to say she was out and would not be back until later – 'Dinner in the oven'.

Samantha had also written out in her own neat hand the names from the receipt books from April onwards. There had been two D. Smiths, Dennis and Donald, and there was some confusion about which was which. Looking first at the addresses, he could see that many parts of the country were represented, from Exeter to Aberdeen, Blackpool to Tunbridge Wells, and also Belfast. No post codes back then. There were phone numbers for a few of them. He saw names of the two men he had told Samantha that he remembered, Barry Watkins, the knicker-waver from Cardiff, and strange Cedric Luscombe from Newton Abbot. He had a vague recollection of one or two of the others.

The list she had made from the receipt books gave him a few more clues, as they were in date order. He could recall very little from his first couple of weeks, as his mind was so confused, adjusting to Nottingham, trying to understand how to carry out the job he had been given and thinking about Margaret and how life was at home. He recalled that he had been pleasantly surprised at how much he had missed his wife, it was the first time they had been apart since they had been married in 1950.

He pulled down the front of his bureau to form a desk and set about making his own record on an A4 pad. He put the names into alphabetical order, by surname, the dates they stayed at Pamela's, then their addresses and the names of their firms where that was on the receipt copy. Samantha had mentioned some comments that her mother had made, not in the address book, but on her copy of the receipts. Samantha had added these to her own list, and Jack was relieved to see there was nothing against his name, one way or the other. Barry Watkins had earned the comment 'Good riddance!' One had paid her £2 short, and another chap was noted as having paid in dirty £1 notes. She wouldn't have liked that, thought Jack, making a mental note that none of these should rank very high on a list of potential suspects.

It was so frustrating for him that the information was incomplete. However, it did seem likely that the names on which they would concentrate their attention would be in the address book; he marked them with an asterisk on his list. It then occurred to him that some who stayed when he did, were regulars who had been coming for a while and therefore would have been in the address book from an earlier date. There were several of these, some would book again for the same week in the following month. It was starting to feel complicated, he would have to discuss that with Samantha.

He looked at his list of asterisks, seventeen names. For a moment, he let his mind drift. *Where are they all now? I bet they would be surprised to think that someone is looking at their name thirty-five years later. Some seemed even then to be getting on a bit, definitely in their fifties, if not their sixties, probably dead and gone now. What sort of life was that anyway, commercial travelling, they called it? We used to get them at Gladwin's all the time, coming into our yard in Harrow. Some you knew and were all right, just finding out what you needed from them, telling you about new products and special offers, write down the orders and then they'd go, see you next month, no problem. Others were a real pain in the backside, managing to come at your busiest times in the morning, parking their flash cars in the way of our customers and our lorries. They wouldn't take 'No' for an answer, downright abusive some of them. Brian wouldn't see them, not unless they were one of his favoured few, in which case all the dealing would be done in Brian's office, and we would be later presented with a list of what he had bought, whether we needed it or not. In his day, Fred would look at the list and ask, 'What the bloody hell has he bought those for, daft bugger, we'll never sell them in a thousand years.' And he was right. Yes, a funny job, being a traveller like that, not my scene at all.*

Seventeen names. Even their Christian names dated them; Keith, Ron, Brian, Barry, Cedric, Malcolm, Graham, Geoffrey; nobody was giving names like that to their kids any more, more likely now to be Damien, Darren, or Lee. At least Jack was making a bit of a comeback, although he himself had been christened John, but had always been called Jack, the same as his grandfather.

Then one name jumped out at him, taking his breath away for a moment. 'Oh yes, I remember you now,' he said out loud, 'very well indeed. I should have realised we would come up against you sooner or later. Very interesting, but I am not going to say anything to Samantha, not yet, let's see how things go first.'

CHAPTER 7

Nottingham, April 1988

'HELLO VERA, HOW'S Mum today?' asked Samantha.

The Care Assistant was usually bright and cheerful, a West Indian woman in her fifties, but today she frowned and puffed out her cheeks in a show of exasperation.

'Mrs. Townsend?' Samantha's mother bristled if the staff called her 'Pamela,' she liked to be called by her second married name. 'You might say we've had better days.'

Samantha gasped as the wall of warmth hit her as she stepped inside the home.

'Oh, it's like that today, is it?'

''Fraid so, bit aggressive, and then sometimes just miserable.'

'Has she been down in the Day Room with the others yet?'

'Yes, but she just sits there and glowers at them. She tells me that they're all crazy.'

Vera gave a deep chuckle as she stood to one side to allow Samantha through.

'OK, I'll see what I can do to cheer her up. She's back in her room now, then?' asked Samantha, feeling nervous about her mission for the day. Preferring not to use the lift, with its intense odour of disinfectant, she climbed the two flights of stairs to her mother's room, which was one of the smaller ones on the top floor.

PAMELA HAD BEEN at Oak Tree House now for three months, ever since the Alzheimer's had taken a firm grip. She had been found wandering around the local streets a couple of times, confused as to her whereabouts, standing outside the corner shop, gazing vacantly in the window. Phone calls from Mary Barthorpe, the next-door neighbour, had asked Samantha to rescue her mother. Some days Pamela hadn't been recognisable as the careful, tidy person that her daughter had always known. Not that she had changed physically very much, but her whole demeanour and appearance were so different now, often with a vacant look in her eyes.

The home was a fifteen-mile drive from Samantha's house into Nottingham, often in rush-hour traffic. She always dreaded what she might find when she arrived. The staff were caring but harassed, and she sometimes wondered what went on there when she wasn't present.

Oak Tree House was a residential home, but if Pamela continued to deteriorate, then it might be necessary for her to move on to a place with a higher level of care. The big house had been built in Victorian times as a family home for one of the many successful Nottingham merchants. Many original features had been retained, such as the lovely fireplace in Pamela's room, now with a gas fire fitted. The building had a forbidding look on the outside, with a heavy red-brick gloom. The modern concrete ramps and metal rails to circumvent the front steps could only ever look like afterthoughts. However, Pamela's room was bright and airy, with some inoffensive pictures of rural scenes on the walls, and a view through the sash window over the well-tended rose garden and vegetable patch, where a gardener was working. Samantha feared the eventual move to one of the modern nursing homes out in the suburbs.

‘Hello Mum.’

Sitting in her usual chair, by her bed, gazing out of the window, Pamela looked up and gave a watery smile. At least she still thinks that she knows me, thought Samantha, even if she is not sure who I am. She was dressed in clothes that Samantha did not recognise; a red skirt clashing with an orange blouse, which Pamela would never normally have tolerated. There was a tea stain on the blouse.

‘How are you?’

‘I’m waiting for my tea.’

‘Well, it’s only just gone two o’clock, so I don’t think it’ll come for a little while,’ said Samantha. It was a Saturday, so Samantha was earlier than usual, making her mother feel that it ought to be tea-time. Taking Pamela’s hand, she sat by her in the single guest chair. They exchanged smiles. From these meetings Samantha had learned that it was best to wait a while before embarking on a conversation, blending into the background, as it were. Vera knocked on the door and looked in with raised eyebrows. Samantha gave her the thumbs up, and the door closed again.

‘Mum, I’ve brought you some photographs that I thought you might like to see.’

There was no comment from Pamela, but she looked expectantly towards her daughter as she took an envelope from her handbag. The first one she was shown was of a family outing.

‘Who are this lot, then?’

Pamela stared hard and, giving a genuine smile, looked immediately more like her old self, pointing at the faces.

‘That’s me and Ken, and you, Emma and Rachel, that’s a nice one.’

‘I wonder who took it, perhaps Mary from next door came on the train with us. Yes, it’s taken on a day trip to Skeggy, isn't it? Ken liked Skeggy, he'd been going there all his life, hadn't he?'

A day trip to Skegness had never been top of Samantha's list of great days out, but they had had some good times there, especially if the sea was far enough in to be seen. She produced another photo, this time of her holding the hands of her half-sisters, Emma and Rachel, who were respectively eight and six years younger than her.

'Why are you asking me this? That's you and Em and Rach of course.'

This was unusual, Pamela had always resisted shortening any of their Christian names. 'If I wanted you to be called Sam, I would have had you christened just that,' she used to say. She herself hated being called 'Pam' and would always fix Ken with a stony stare when he forgot, which he was inclined to do. Nevertheless, Ken was never 'Kenneth.'

With a sense of trepidation, another photo was offered, this time of three men, not known to Samantha, in sports jackets, collars and ties. Pamela stared hard for a long time and then produced another beaming smile, pointing to the man on the right of the rather self-conscious group.

'That's Jack,' she said firmly. 'Now he was a nice man, one of my regulars. Very pleasant and reliable.'

This was unexpected and Samantha caught her breath and tried not to look surprised, not wanting to lose the moment.

'Who are the others?' asked Samantha.

'No idea,' said Pamela, just as crisply as before.

'They're some of your lodgers, aren't they? It's taken outside our house.'

Pamela peered in again, adjusting her smudged glasses.

'I suppose it is, but I've never seen them before.

When's my tea coming?'

'It will be here soon. What did you have for lunch?'

'Lunch? Not sure really.'

There were two more photos of uncomfortable men herded into groups outside her house, but Pamela claimed not to know any of them. Samantha paused for a moment before producing one more, of a relaxed, smiling man, who she guessed to be in his early thirties, with a nearly full pint of bitter in front of him, sitting in a pub garden.

'I've told you before, weren't you listening, that's Jack Rodgers again?'

'And there's another drink on the table, with a cherry in it.'

'Well, that would be mine of course, I always drank a Babycham in those days. Just the one, mind you.'

'Tell me about Jack, then.' Samantha feared that she might now be pushing too hard, but Pamela quickly replied.

'Oh, he was a very nice man, came from London for quite a long time one summer.'

'Did you take the photo, Mum?'

'Couldn't tell you. I had a lovely little camera, a Brownie 127 they were called. I don't know what happened to it. You haven't got it have you?'

'No Mum, I haven't. It's taken at the pub, the one up the dale, isn't it? Did you go for a drink together?'

Pamela shifted uneasily in her chair and glared at her daughter.

'Might have done, I don't know.'

'Just the two of you, was it?'

'Well, it was a very nice evening.'

'Did you like him, then?'

Pamela pulled a face again but then smiled.

'He was a very nice man, a gentleman, not like some of the others.'

Then, right on cue, tea arrived, cheese sandwiches and a slice of Battenburg, and the conversation was at an end.

DRIVING HOME, SAMANTHA mentally kicked herself as she sat in a queue of traffic, at the roundabout, waiting to pass under the M1 at Junction 26. She had found the photos in her mother's dressing table drawer, kept near at hand, which might indicate something. When Ken was alive it hadn't seemed right to ask too many questions and now was probably too late. She realised she should have shown them to her before. It seemed more urgent now. Pamela was going downhill fast, and she was not going to get proper answers from her any more. But there had been enough of a signal that one bloke stood out for her from all the others.

'Jack Rodgers', she thought, *'that's the name to remember. He looked pleasant enough. And she did seem to remember that one particular evening.'*

She shouted out, 'Where are you now, Jack, I wonder. Will I ever find you?'

The man in the big Mercedes alongside pretended that he hadn't heard her.

HER MOTHER'S CHOICE of Ken was difficult to understand, he just didn't seem her type, although he made it easy for her to keep complete control of the household. Not the sharpest blade in the box by any means, but not unpleasant, and he had always been respectful to Samantha. Turned down by the Army in wartime, obviously not considered suitable for combat, he had then drifted through various low-grade jobs. He worked in shops and factories, not often out of work, but never in a job for long either. He was definitely not a grafter by nature, and he didn't do much around the house. Pamela was over forty when she had Emma and Rachel, quite an advanced age for the early 1960s. It was as if she were determined to have more children and took the best option she could find to do that.

Ken was a near neighbour and a bachelor, younger than Pamela. From what Samantha had gleaned, he did not appear to have had a lot of relevant experience in personal relationships, still living with his widowed mother until they married. Gladys was particularly surprised, although not unhappy, at how events had turned out for her spoilt only child. She once whispered to Samantha while watching Emma and Rachel play, 'I didn't think he had it in him'. Samantha smiled at the memory; she had always speculated about what it was that Gladys thought Ken might not have.

SAMANTHA STOPPED ON the way home to pick up her six-year-old son from a friend's house and then drove the short distance to their home. Adam had been quite happy playing football in the garden with his friend and showed some disappointment to be going home.

'We need to be back soon,' she said, 'Your Dad is coming for you at five o'clock, you're staying with him tonight, remember?'

'Oh, yes.' Adam thought for a minute and then asked, 'Will Jessica be there this time?'

'I really don't know, that's your Dad's decision, nothing to do with me. Why, do you like her?'

Adam, in the front seat next to her, fiddled with the zip on his track-suit top.

'She's quite nice, but a bit funny.'

'How do you mean?'

He looked out of the window as they overtook a tractor on the dual carriageway.

'Don't know really, she goes all giggly, like she doesn't know what to say to me.'

'Well, she's quite young, isn't she, perhaps not very used to children of your age? And maybe she isn't as interested in football as you are?'

'No, perhaps she isn't. She's definitely not a Forest supporter anyway.'

By now they were home, and Samantha parked outside their house. Adam jumped out of the car and ran up the path and waited for Samantha to unlock their front door.

'Come on now, get your overnight stuff together. And don't forget Teddy this time.'

CHAPTER 8

Harrow and Reigate, March 1990

'DAVID, IT'S DAD, I'm in hospital, Northwick Park.'

'Oh God, Dad what have you done, have you had a fall?'

'No, nothing like that, I had this awful stomach ache and had to call an ambulance. They say it is an epigastric hernia, it's not unusual, but they have to operate quickly, so it is planned for tomorrow morning.'

'It's not like you, Dad, you usually seem so fit and healthy. Do you want me to come over?'

'No, there is no point in that, but they are already asking if there is anyone to look after me when I come out after a few days, so I might need to come to you.'

'Well, of course you can Dad. I'm in Geneva next week but I am sure that Louise and the children will be able to cope.'

'OK, I will let you know how things go here.'

'Oh dear,' thought Jack, 'Louise and the children. Margaret never got on well with Louise, thought she was too posh and stuck up. Very nice and very smart but living in a world that we didn't know or understand. It's a good job I picked up David's card on my way out the door, but I didn't think to pick up my address book. How could I contact Samantha now? I don't even have her phone number with me, it was all such a rush, the ambulance came very quickly. I hadn't even told her that I had received her package.'

JACK WASN'T EXACTLY a model patient. Sure, he was polite and friendly to all of the staff, but he was frustrated at not being in control and a little humiliated when they had to do personal things for him. He found some of the other patients on his ward annoying; the old boy on one side was rude to some of the darker-skinned staff, while on the other side was a fiftyish business-type who constantly complained about his treatment. It was a relief when he was told he could go out.

WHEN HE WAS ready to be discharged, David arrived almost on time to collect his father. He wore a navy, pin-striped suit, a white shirt and a bright purple tie. He soon became restless, checking his watch, prowling up and down and looking out along the corridor, because they were delayed waiting for Jack's medications to be ready.

'They're keeping you waiting, Dad.'

'Well I'm in no hurry, but I expect you are.'

'No, no, it's all right. What is an epigastric hernia anyway?'

'Big lump suddenly came up on my stomach, size of a cricket ball. Here's my scar,' he said, lifting his shirt and vest, 'what would you say, five or six inches long?'

'Yes Dad, at least that.'

A nurse had told them firmly that Jack must go to David's GP if there were any problems. More than an hour passed after David arrived before they could leave. Jack didn't drive any more, having sold his car soon after Margaret had died, reasoning that there was good public transport where he lived, and he wasn't expecting to do many long journeys any more. David's chosen route to Surrey was round the M25 from Heathrow to Reigate. Jack had never felt comfortable on motorways. The traffic was heavy, as it always seemed to be on that stretch, even though it was now after seven o'clock on a Friday evening. David was impatient, cursing other drivers under his breath and making generous use of his horn. When a clear space did open up in front of him, he put his foot down hard in the BMW, and Jack could see that his speed was over ninety miles per hour. He must have drifted off eventually, but he was suddenly aware that the car was stationary, and he could hear another voice.

'You do realise what speed you were going at, don't you, sir?'

'I'm sorry,' replied David.

Jack realised that they were on the hard shoulder and the voice belonged to a policeman who was leaning in the driver's window.

'I followed you at ninety-seven, the limit is seventy, so I'm going to have to give you a ticket, sir.'

'OK,' said David.

After the man had gone, David ruefully looked at his father.

'Not a word to Louise, if you don't mind, Dad. It's not the first and she's always on at me about speeding. Stupid, if you ask me, to have a car like this and not be able to go faster.'

Jack did not reply.

The next thing he knew David was pulling on to his drive, parking alongside Louise's pale blue sports car. David made a big play of carrying in Jack's bag and ushering him carefully to the front door.

Louise opened the door to greet them. She was wearing a smart white blouse and a tailored navy skirt and Jack guessed that was her work outfit.

'Jack, it's good to see you, how are you? You know we've been worried about you, don't you?'

Without waiting for an answer she enveloped him in an all-embracing hug; not that he found it an unpleasant experience, but hugging was a new habit which was foreign to Jack's generation, and anyway his scar was still rather tender. The children, Simon and Lucy, hung back, embarrassed and uncertain how they should greet their grandfather. Jack shook them both by the hand.

'Are you hungry, Jack?' asked Louise, 'what was the hospital food like?'

'Not too bad, but they served lunch at twelve, so I think I could manage a small portion of something now.'

'What about a drink, Dad?' inquired David, 'are you allowed anything alcoholic?'

'I don't think I should, but my mouth is dry. A glass of water, perhaps?'

'How about an orange juice?' offered Louise. They hadn't yet moved on from the large entrance hall.

'Yes, that would be nice, thank you.'

The house was a modern, spacious, five-bedroom detached in a Surrey suburb, elegantly furnished, into which they had moved when it was built, five years before. David took Jack's bag upstairs and wasn't seen for a little while after that. Louise sat Jack down in their conservatory and diligently asked him about the operation, and patiently listened to the answers. Jack carefully described the procedure but spared her sight of the scar.

Whenever he had stayed at David's house (to Jack and Margaret it had always been David's house, never Louise and David's), he had always felt uncomfortable, not knowing what to do or where to sit. Their lifestyle and tastes were a long way removed from Margaret and Jack's ways, which were more frugal from years of rationing and tight budgets. Margaret was always critical of their expenditure which she thought was extravagant. That criticism was always aimed at Louise, rather than David, as if he would not have had an input. His son was often away all week, and Jack's relationship with his daughter-in-law had been uneasy because of Margaret's attitude to her. He did not really know his grandchildren well enough to bond properly with them. The food was good, but often consisted of stuff that Jack didn't recognise. They lived too far out for him to walk to the village, so he felt marooned.

'OK,' said Louise, 'just give me a couple of minutes to dish up our supper.'

'How are you two, then?' asked Jack. Simon and Lucy studied their thumbs and mumbled answers. Jack couldn't remember how long it had been since he had last seen them.

'Simon, are you fourteen now and Lucy, you're twelve aren't you?'

'That's right,' replied Simon, 'although I will be fifteen next month.' Jack made a mental note to check the calendar when he was back home.

'And how's school?'

Simon answered again. 'Oh, it's OK, we have the GCSEs coming up soon to think about.'

'Don't you do O-Levels any more, then?'

'No, that's all changed now.'

'Are you at the same school as Simon, Lucy?'

The girl spoke for the first time; Jack was surprised to see how grown up she had become.

'Yes, I am now, this is my second year.'

'And do you like it?'

'I like it more now, it was a bit strange at first.'

'So you go on the same bus as Simon?'

'I try to go on the earlier one instead, there's too many horrible boys on his bus,' said Lucy, giving her brother an evil glance.

Jack wasn't sure what to say to that and a silence fell, broken only by the sound of David's heavy steps upstairs.

Louise called from the kitchen, 'Not long now.'

WHEN DAVID EVENTUALLY re-appeared, they sat down to eat in the dining-room. Carefully set out, good cutlery, linen napkins. A big bunch of daffodils filled a vase in the middle of the table. Jack's orange juice was waiting for him, and he drank it thirstily. The first course was half an avocado each, or that is what Jack assumed it to be. He waited to see which item of cutlery the others used. It wasn't a unanimous decision; David and Louise took up small spoons, Simon a larger one and Lucy a small fork. This was followed by white fish in a tomato kind of sauce, with a side salad. Chosen to be suitable for an elderly convalescent, thought Jack, but he found it very enjoyable.

'Is there anything else we can get you?' asked Louise. 'Ice cream, perhaps?'

'No, thank you, that was ideal, very nice indeed.'

His hostess graciously acknowledged the compliment, while starting to gather up the dishes.

'Can I help at all?' asked Jack, as he had always done the washing up after Margaret had prepared a meal.

'Certainly not,' came the crisp reply, 'you are recovering from a serious operation, and we are supposed to ensure that you are taking it easy while you are here. You go and rest yourself in the conservatory. It's all going in the dishwasher anyway.'

Jack and Margaret had never had a dishwasher or

even thought of buying one. He shuffled off obediently and gazed out on the garden. It looked good, with plenty of fancy pots, but he knew that David paid a man quite a lot of money to tend to it. The lawn edges were not trimmed well enough by Jack's standards, and he could see a rose bush that had been poorly pruned.

'How do you think the garden looks, Dad?' David, now in a pink polo shirt and jeans, had come in silently behind him and Jack was suddenly startled to remember that he for the moment he was not living on his own.

'It looks very good, David. How often does the gardener come?'

'Every two weeks, every second Tuesday he's here for a day. He mows the lawns for me in summer. I just don't have the time and I know how Louise loves to see it looking tidy.'

'That's all you can really do with a garden in winter, is to keep it tidy.'

JACK JOINED THE family while they all watched TV, a soap opera and a detective programme, but towards ten o'clock Jack was starting to feel drowsy. He excused himself and made his way up to the guest room. Tomorrow was Saturday and for a few minutes he wondered what the weekend would bring, but he was soon fast asleep.

THE NEXT MORNING, when Jack awoke, after nine o'clock, Louise and Lucy had already disappeared to go shopping. Simon was in his room, where David believed he was doing his homework. Cereals, fruit and toast had been left for Jack's breakfast. For a while, David busied himself moving a few things around in the garden, which amused Jack, as he was well aware that was not his natural habitat. After a while he came in and offered to make Jack a coffee, which he brought to the conservatory with his own. He put a plate of Kit-Kat fingers between them.

'We've got a big Round Table do on tonight, Dad, a dinner dance in Dorking, so we will be going out about six thirty, but don't worry, you will be fed. Is that all right with you?'

'Definitely, I want you to carry on as normal.'

'And how is life in Kenton, business as usual?'

'Not exactly,' said Jack, which was not the answer for which David was prepared.

'Oh, really, how come?'

'I had a young woman come and knock on my door, I didn't know her, but she knew who I was.' David's frowned and stared at Jack. 'She is trying to track down her real father and she thinks I can help.'

'What on earth do you mean, Dad?'

'Do you remember that I worked up in Nottingham for six months, about the time Elizabeth was born?'

David frowned, 'I think I remember you telling me about that. Was it to set up a new depot for Gladwin's?'

'That's right. I was in digs with this girl's mother.'

'For Christ's sake Dad, what are you telling me?'

'I'm just telling you what's going on in Kenton, like you asked me.'

'I mean, are you, no I mean, well… how can you help her?'

'With some information she has, we might be able to identify who is her father.'

'And you're going to help her?'

'I am, yes.'

'No Dad, leave it alone, bloody hell, that must be more than thirty years ago, all water under the bridge, what is there for you in that?' Jack wondered if David thought that he might have a half-sister who could be a competitor for a share of his father's estate.

'It would be something out of my routine and have the benefit of helping someone in need.'

'Dad, I think it's a big mistake, you don't know where it is going to take you, leave it alone.'

David frowned again.

'Well, don't say I didn't tell you about it,' said Jack as David retreated to the kitchen. Nothing more was said on the subject during Jack's stay.

CHAPTER 9

Reigate, Surrey, March 1990

THAT EVENING, AS they were going out to their dinner dance, Jack could not help thinking what a handsome and impressive couple Louise and David were. He, in evening dress, over six feet tall, with his mother's fair colouring, although his hair was starting to recede, more than Jack's wiry mop had, and his frame was filling out a little. She was nearly as tall, slim and elegant, jet-black hair, wearing a bright, peacock blue evening dress with plenty of jewellery. Smart and confident, he felt really proud of both of them, he could imagine the impact they would make, walking into any room.

Louise had prepared a chicken salad supper for Jack and the children; Simon and Lucy loaded up their plates and then moved from the dining room to the lounge to watch TV. This appeared to be their normal routine when their parents went out.

'You can come and join us if you like, Granddad,' called Lucy.

'I'm OK here, thank you,' replied Jack, who had never felt comfortable eating from his lap. After he had finished his meal, he took his *Daily Mail* off to the conservatory, where he felt most at home. Later, he did go into the lounge to watch the football highlights with Simon, after Lucy had gone to bed. Simon revealed himself to be a Chelsea supporter, although he had never seen them play a live match; he was thrilled that they were now back in the First Division. Jack mentioned his home town team, but it was not clear if Simon had ever heard of Preston North End.

ON SUNDAY MORNING Louise brought her coffee to sit with Jack in the conservatory. David had shot off to see someone on Round Table business and the children had not yet emerged from their bedrooms.

'How are you feeling now?' she asked.

'Not bad, still a bit weary, thank you. I don't think I would have been allowed out of hospital if I hadn't been able to come here. I really don't like those places, although they do their best for you, of course. Northwick Park was where Margaret died, if you remember.'

'Oh, yes, I can picture seeing her there, near the end, she was in a bad way wasn't she?'

'She was, you couldn't recognise her as the same person, especially when I think of the bright young thing I first met. She wasn't the prettiest girl I ever knew, but there was always something about her, a bright light in her eyes, that I fell for.'

'I wish I'd got to know her better, I really do,' said Louise. 'I don't think I ever broke through with her somehow, couldn't find the right words to say. I know a lot of my friends find their mother-in-law relationships to be difficult.'

'Times have changed,' said Jack. 'The world's a different place now from when we were setting up home. Things were tough, coping with rationing and all that.'

'Yes, we do tend to forget how it was.'

Jack guessed that times had never been too hard in Louise's parents' household.

'She was very pleased for David to have found you.

She felt that you were good for him.'

Louise laughed. 'I think that's a bit of a back-handed compliment Jack, if you don't mind me saying so. Like you're saying he deserves me!'

It was Jack's turn to laugh now.

'Fair enough. She felt you came from a different world from us. Your work, the way you dress, your parents' background and your education were all a long way removed from ours. I was thinking to myself last night when you went out what a handsome couple you are. And you looked great, if I may say so.'

Now she blushed. 'Feel free to say so, you could remind David of that from time to time, if you like.'

'We knew very well that he could be headstrong, and he didn't need someone who'd be a pushover for him.'

'We've never talked like this before, have we? I'm really glad you came. I wish Simon and Lucy were a bit more forthcoming with you. Simon has already gone for the grumpy teenager role and Lucy can be a proper little madam at times.'

'I think they're fine, very bright, a credit to you both. I am sure that they will do well for themselves, and I hope I'm around to see what they make of the world, even if their Granny can't.'

'I hope so too,' said Louise,' I think you're a good influence for them. You're making the best of your situation and haven't let yourself go to pieces since Margaret died. You know what is going on in the world and have your own views on that, I think that's a good example for them. They might not say much to you, but they are actually enjoying having you here.'

'At least there will be someone here to say hello when they get home.'

'Yes, I know it is not ideal,' she sighed, 'especially in winter.'

And with that she picked up their coffee cups and went back to the kitchen.

IN THE LATE afternoon, a taxi arrived to take David to Gatwick to fly to Geneva for the week, leaving Jack to share a quiet evening with Louise and the children. If David had said anything to her about Jack's revelation, it was not apparent. After that it was a quiet week for Jack, the children went early to school and did not arrive home until five o'clock. Louise would leave to go to her Financial Advisory company in Guildford by eight thirty, immaculately dressed and coiffured, and sometimes it was six o'clock before she arrived home. Once she had served up their meal, she looked tired and was not apparently in the mood for conversation.

Quiet days were something he was used to, but not in these surroundings. It was a forty-minute walk into the village, which Jack did not yet feel ready for, and, if he did go, there was only a little village shop and a grubby pub. On the Tuesday the gardener came but, apart from giving the lawn an early trim, did not seem to Jack to have done much that was useful.

Louise would remember every day to bring him the *Daily Mail*, so he always had the previous day's paper and its crossword, and they had the *Daily Telegraph* delivered. He wished he had a book to read; he had looked over David and Louise's bookshelves, but couldn't see anything there of interest to him, the novels were more Louise's choices than David's, he thought.

David arrived home late on Friday evening, very weary and sounding very frustrated with his week. From the kitchen, Jack could hear comments about 'the bloody obstinate Swiss, keep moving the goalposts'. He had poured himself a large glass of red wine and sat sullenly in his armchair for the whole of the evening, barely responding to any attempts by Louise or Jack to strike up a conversation.

On Saturday morning David drove Jack back home, after a fond goodbye from Louise, and more tepid ones from Simon and Lucy. The weather was fine, the roads were clear, and they travelled in silence for most of the way, until they were nearly in Kenton.

'Do you feel OK now Dad?'

'Not bad, I'm feeling stronger every day, thank you.'

'You're going to drop this crazy Hunt the Father idea, aren't you?'

'You think it's crazy do you?'

'You know it is. What do you think Elizabeth will say?'

'Well, I'd hope your sister would be more understanding,' said Jack, and David fell silent for a while.

'I'm going to say this Dad, although I know you won't like it.'

'What?'

'You could be opening a can of worms here, you don't know what you're getting into. She might be some sort of con artist, leading you into trouble. I am telling you to back off out of it with her.'

'And if I don't?'

'Don't expect me to bail you out, because I won't.'

'OK, you've said it now and I've heard you out.'

They were close to Jack's house by now.

'I thought what a grand couple you and Louise looked when you went out last Saturday night.'

'Oh, thank you.'

'Yes, and don't forget to tell her how good she looks from time to time.'

David grunted but made no further comment before they arrived. It was the best part of two weeks since

Jack had been there, and he felt so relieved to be back again. He had not been away for so long in many years and it all appeared to him as if through fresh eyes. 'It doesn't look too bad,' he thought.

DAVID MANAGED TO fit in a quick tour of the house to see if there was anything out of place.

'You keep everything very tidy and ship-shape, Dad.'

'Of course, that's how your mum liked it. Cup of tea?' asked Jack, although he knew what the answer would be.

'Better get back, Dad, if you don't mind. We're out again tonight at a fortieth birthday party, I've got some work to catch up with and Simon wants some help with his Maths homework.'

'Well, thank you for chauffeuring me and do please thank Louise again for looking after me. I couldn't have managed without all of you.'

'No problem, that's what we are here for. Do keep in touch, won't you?' He shook his father very firmly by the hand, staring hard at him. Jack understood the message and averted his eyes. Away went David, accelerating rapidly down the road.

AS SOON AS he had gone, Jack did what he had been desperately waiting to do and went straight to check his answerphone for messages. Nothing.

CHAPTER 10

Harrow, Late March 1990

JACK FELT MENTALLY drained after his week with the family, although he was becoming physically stronger. It had now been more than a fortnight since he and Samantha had spoken, and he knew that she could again be thinking that he had lost interest in her project. He wanted to look again at the information she had sent him to refresh his memory before he contacted her again.

He made a mental note that he must call her on the next day, Sunday. His hopes were raised when the phone rang, but he was to be disappointed.

'Oh you are there, I thought you had done a disappearing act.' It was his sister Brenda, calling from their old family home.

'No, I'm here all right.'

'Well, I rang this time last Saturday and there was no answer, so I rang again on the Sunday morning and no reply then either. Where were you?'

'I was at David's,' he started to say, but before he could explain further, the interrogation continued.

'David's! What were you doing there? You don't go there very often if you can help it, do you?'

'Not very often, I know, but I've been ill, you see.'

'Ill, you didn't say anything about that to me, what was it?'

'It was very sudden, an epigastric hernia.'

'Hernias aren't very serious, Gordon had a couple, just overnight jobs.'

Do older sisters always put a bloke on the back foot? Whatever you told Brenda about, she always knew someone who had had something similar, usually bigger and better than yours, or, in this case, less serious.

'Not one of those, these are in your stomach. A great big bulge came up with awful stomach ache, I was bent double in agony. It was all I could do to call an ambulance. They said it could have been really serious if I hadn't got to them quickly. The surgeon said it could have been life-threatening as it could have become strangulated.'

The doctor had not said that exactly, but Jack felt inclined to lay it on a bit thick in retaliation against his interrogator. Brenda reluctantly accepted his explanation.

'Oh, really? How long were you in for?'

'I think it was five nights in all. I had to wait until David could come for me. They wouldn't discharge me until there was someone to keep an eye on me. Of course, I could've come to stay with you,' Jack said, knowing that would alarm her.

'Good Lord, no, I couldn't cope with you here like that, not with my arthritis.'

This led, as calls from Brenda usually did, into a lengthy description of her various health issues, real and perceived, which Jack eventually interrupted.

'Look, it's good of you to call and I am sorry that there wasn't time to let you know what was happening, I didn't think to take my address book with me. I hope you haven't been too worried. If you don't mind, I've not been back home very long, I have things to sort out and I do feel rather weary. Shall I give you a ring in the week?'

The truth was that Brenda had never crossed his mind in the time he was away from home. However, it was if she hadn't heard him.

'So did you have an operation, then?'

'Yes, I did and I've a bright red scar right across my stomach to prove it.'

'And did it go OK?'

'The operation went well, but it knocks you back a bit. It seems to take longer these days to get over things.'

Still the probing continued.

'How did you get on at David's then, were you there on your own all day?'

'I was well looked after. Louise left me a salad lunch every day. It was quiet, but it suited me, I'm used to that.'

'How old are his kids now?'

'Simon's fourteen and Lucy is twelve, they're growing up quickly.' The pause gave him time to sign off. 'Look I will have to go, I'll call you in the week. OK?'

'OK, talk next week.'

Jack sat down with a great sigh, feeling even more exhausted. 'My lovely sister, she doesn't listen to a damn word you say.'

THEY HAD NEVER been very close. Brenda was born in 1920, Jack three years later. Brenda would say that she was never told that another child was coming, although to Jack that was proof that, even at such an early age, she didn't listen to what was being said to her. Their father was a labourer in a heavy engineering factory, while their mother stayed home, as was normal in those days. She was quite frail and suffered from anxiety and depression, which became more severe with time. Their father was made redundant at the start of the Great

Depression in 1930, which hit the North of England particularly hard, and they had to rely on the Dole and any casual work he could find to survive.

When Jack was twelve, his father sat him down one summer's day. Normally taciturn, by his standards it was a lengthy speech.

'Look son, you know times are real hard here just now, and I can't see that they'll pick up any time soon. Your Mam ain't well, and I don't think she's ever going to really get better either. I want the best for you, I think you're a good lad, sensible and hard-working and you can do well for yourself, but there ain't much here in Preston for you. There will be more chances for you in London, so you are going to live there with Edna and Tom. Brenda will stay here and help me with the house and your mother.'

'How long will I be going for?' asked Jack.

'I'm not sure, we'll have to see how things go, but you'll stay with them for the time being.'

'Why do they live in London, Dad?'

'Tom's from down there and they met during the War when he was sent up here with the Army in nineteen sixteen. You know that they are good, kind folk, they want to have you and look after you. They've never been able to have children of their own and they've both got steady jobs.'

'But what about all my friends here, Joe and Freddie? Where will I go to school?'

'Don't worry about that, Edna has it all arranged. You'll start when the schools go back in September. I'm sure you'll soon make plenty of new friends down there. I shall miss you lad, I'll tell you that.'

AND THAT WAS it, his father had arranged everything in letters with his sister Edna, who Jack had only met a few times. Until then he had never been any further from home than a single trip to Manchester. Edna was just a year younger than his father. She worked as a sales assistant at Marks and Spencer while her husband, Tom, was a postman. In the end, it had worked out well for Jack. It took time, but he did make friends even though they made fun of his Northern accent. Tom helped him to get the job at Gladwin's; they were on his postman's round, and he saw a notice saying that they had a vacancy for a willing lad.

Soon after Jack went to London his mother was admitted to a mental hospital, which she never left, dying three years later. When Jack's sister Brenda married Gordon, they moved in with her father and then took over the tenancy of their council house when he died. Their marriage was childless. Now Gordon had died, she was still a council tenant. She had said that they were too poor to take up Mrs. Thatcher's Right to Buy, even with the discounts offered, unlike many of their neighbours.

AT LAST, ON Sunday morning Jack was able to sit down at the dining table to look again through Samantha's package: the photocopies of the address book, and the list she had made from the receipt books. He compared them again with his own alphabetical list, and the names he had marked with asterisks, trying picture who they were. He then went to the phone.

'Hello, is that Samantha?'

'Jack, is that you?'

'Yes, it is, really sorry I haven't rung before, but I've been ill.'

'Oh, I am sorry, are you OK now?'

'Yes, I'm getting better, but I was in hospital for about five days after emergency surgery, and then had to stay at my son's for a week. I only came home last night.'

'That does sound serious.' Jack was immediately struck by the extra degree of sympathy he was receiving now compared to his sister's reaction. He gave her brief details of his illness.

'Did you think I'd done a runner?' he asked. Samantha laughed.

'Well, I rang a couple of times and did wonder if everything was OK with you. I was starting to wonder how I would make progress on my own. You received my parcel all right?'

'I did, thank you, I've had a good look through and made some notes. One thought I have had,' said Jack, 'is that you've copied the names in the address book from when I arrived onwards. But some of the blokes were regulars, who had been coming for a while, so they would be earlier in the list of names, if you get my meaning, and we are missing them. Some may be in the lost receipt books, but, of course, we've got a gap there.'

'Good point, I hadn't thought of that.'

'If you go back through the older receipt books, you'll probably see the same names recurring.'

'Yes, that's a good idea, I'll do that.'

'Anyway, are you OK? I haven't asked you how you are, too busy telling you about me. Have you got your mother's house sorted yet?'

'No, it's a real pain. My half-sisters want to keep it, or a part of it, so they have a base when they come back to Nottingham. As you know, it's a big house and they are thinking to turn it into flats and keep one; it's been left to the three of us jointly, but I want to sell it, and they can't or won't buy me out. The money would really come in handy, and a flat in Nottingham is no use to me. Either way, there's plenty of work to be done to sort out stuff first. Junk to be dumped, her clothes, her documents and so on, and my sisters seem to find it difficult to make the time to do that. I'm paying a local chap myself to hack the gardens into some sort of shape. Otherwise, life goes on, I'm OK, thank you.'

Jack still found it difficult to imagine what Samantha's life was like.

'Did anything strike you in all the names I sent you?' she asked.

'Yes, I recognised some, ones I had already mentioned to you. Some seem vaguely familiar, but after all this time, it is hard to put faces to the names. I have made a shortish list of my own, there are seventeen names on there. I am concentrating on those in the address book.'

'That's good.' She paused for a moment, 'You are still on, aren't you, to see what and who we can find?'

'Yes I am, definitely.' Jack winced and thought it was a good job that David could not hear him.

'You are sure about that?'

'I am sure.'

'Sure you're sure?'

'I'm sure I'm sure.'

'Fair enough, I won't ask again, you'll have to tell me if you want out. Look, I'm coming to stay with Jenny again in a couple of weeks, can we meet up then?'

'Of course we can.'

'Can you make it to Watford, we could go to the library there, take our lists with us and see if we can find out anything in their telephone directories, perhaps on the Friday afternoon?'

'No problem, I can take the Tube from Kenton to Harrow and Wealdstone and then the train through to Watford Junction, I don't think it's far from there.'

'OK, I'll call you next week and let you know my arrangements.'

AS JACK PUT down the receiver, a throb of excitement ran through him. He had found a new friend, who cared about him, and he had a project to occupy his mind. What if he had fathered Samantha, would that be such a bad thing? He would be quite proud for her to call him Dad. Margaret wouldn't know now. But then there was David to think about, he really didn't want to fall out with him any further. And then there was also Elizabeth, did she know about this yet? In his mind, he could hear David's voice on the phone to her, 'Do you know what the silly old fool is doing now? There's someone after a share of his estate, we can't allow that to happen.'

CHAPTER 11

Watford, April 1990

AFTER THEIR VISIT to Watford Library, Samantha and Jack found a nearby café, very basic, Formica and plastic, but clean. They had a coffee and a sandwich, for which Jack insisted on paying; roast beef for him, tuna salad for her. Their visit had not been very productive; they had found telephone directories, but only those for the local area around Watford. A brusque staff member had told them that something she called the 'Hundred-Year Rule' prevented them from seeing census returns until 2090. ('Can't wait that long,' Jack had said unhelpfully). She also said that the Library only held the Electoral Rolls, which they had thought might be another source of information, for Watford and the local area.

Nothing was said at first. Jack looked at Samantha, in her usual navy parka, who had seemed upset as they left the Library but now seemed to have regained some composure.

'We need a plan,' he said.

'Agreed, but saying that is the easy part,' she shot back. Jack withdrew, leaning back in his chair and waited for her to continue.

'I think the phone directories are the first part,' Samantha continued, 'they are the only accessible place I can think of which give people's addresses. If we take the people on your shortlist and can see that someone of the same name is still living at the address we have for them, then we can be confident that we know where that person is. If we can then get the Electoral Register for that area, then we can confirm that and see who they are living with.'

Jack hesitated, worried that he might seem to be constantly arguing for a different course from Samantha. 'This won't last long if I keep falling out with her,' he thought. Nevertheless, he said what was on his mind.

'We're in danger of going off too soon down the wrong road here. We don't know if we've got all the possible suspects yet. And thirty-five years is a very long time, most people would have moved house more than once in that time. These were blokes who were doing quite well for themselves, and they could have moved upmarket, or moved away with a new job. So we will draw a lot of blanks.'

Samantha looked at him, started to say something, then stopped herself and smiled at Jack.

'I can see why you are on this case now, it's your job to stop me from barking up the wrong trees, isn't it?'

'I'm not sure I can always do that, but I might stop you from doing it too often. How much of a hurry are we in? It isn't as if we have a deadline, is it?'

'Well perhaps not, but when I start something, I like to get on with it. I haven't got anyone really to talk to about it, except yourself, and it is the sort of thing where you need to bounce ideas off someone,' she said.

'It's a wild goose chase at the moment isn't it? We need to eliminate some of the geese first, as many as we can, otherwise we will be flying all round the country after them, chasing shadows,' said Jack, mixing his metaphors.

'OK, so what's the next step, then?'

'It would be great if you could find the missing receipt books, there is no reason to think that she would have deliberately thrown them away, is there? And we could then look out to find more of her regulars, who had been coming for a while.'

'You're right, we need a shorter shortlist. Here, have a look at the address book. Your entry is here, work backwards, are there any names there that you recognise?'

For Jack it was a strange feeling, thumbing through Pamela's address book, it felt intrusive, especially seeing his own name there. She had had a careful, neat hand, probably little changed from how she had been taught in primary school, many years before. A couple of the names seemed vaguely familiar, one was a Scotsman, and Jack could remember a whisky salesman with a very broad accent, which made conversation almost impossible. Whether this was the same man, he could not tell. There was also the name that still resonated with him, but he did not yet want to mention to Samantha, thinking that they needed to do more research first. He half-remembered an incident from 1955 but wanted to be sure about what happened Beyond that, he realised it was guesswork.

'I can write down some of these names, but they might be red herrings and I might miss more important ones. Please have another try to find those receipt books, then we can see who came more than once and stayed during that summer. You have to think they were the most likely candidates.'

She again gave him one of her strong steady stares, which Jack found intimidating as he could not meet them and had to look away.

'I still don't know if this is a waste of time or not, do I?' she said.

'What do you mean?'

'I mean that the culprit might be sitting here in front of me, telling me I'm on a wild goose chase to put me off the scent.'

Jack looked around at the people at the other tables. On the next table on one side there was a middle-aged woman in a fur hat with a lot of shopping, who seemed to be bending an ear in their direction. On the other side was an elderly couple, probably even older than him, he thought, whose conversation had stopped abruptly. Perhaps they had been together for so long that they had run out of things to talk about. Samantha seemed oblivious to all of them and maintained her gaze.

'I know,' he said, but could not continue. He knew what he wanted to say, but not how to say it. Silence fell, like a heavy cloud, over their table. He looked back at her, then looked away, and went to take another sip of coffee, only to find that his cup was empty. Still, she said nothing.

'We got on well, me and your mum, I'll admit it, we seemed to be kindred spirits. I could imagine that, if things had been different, if I hadn't been married, then life might have gone in another direction, but it wasn't anything that we discussed. This was the nineteen fifties, remember, some people had played fast and loose in the War, because they thought that they might be dead tomorrow. But afterwards, life was tough, a battle to hold things together, money was very tight, so much was rationed, queuing for everything. I don't think that many folk had much time for a bit on the side, as they used to say.'

Samantha smiled at the reference, and he felt the cloud lift a little.

'I understand that I'm not giving you a straight answer to your question. I was very fond of Pamela, and I can see a lot of her in you. Draw your own conclusions from that. You need help and I am happy to give it to you, if that is what you want. As you say, you need a sounding board, otherwise you've a very lonely journey ahead of you, if you persist with it. There are some things at the back of my mind that I half-remember and I'm not sure how much I can trust my memory. There are other times where I have a much clearer picture, but I'm not sure yet how relevant they are.'

'So you're not going to tell me about them?'

'No, not yet, perhaps later, if appropriate. We've enough red herrings as it is.'

'Then I have to accept that, do I?'

'Yes, please.'

'And you still think that it is worth us carrying on?'

'Yes, I do. For me, it is good to have a project, I don't want to be just drifting along.'

'Fair enough, then that is what we will do.' Another pause.

'I've got a bit more information, although I am not sure if it takes us any further. I have been chatting to the next-door neighbour, Mary Barthorpe, she's lived there as long as Mum. She's a right old gossip and I know Mum didn't really trust her. She was always careful with what she said to Mary, as it soon got round.'

'I know the type,' said Jack, 'we've got one of those in our road.'

'I think there's one on every street,' said Samantha with smile. 'Well, she says that she clearly remembers Mum being pregnant with me. "Bit of a shock," she said, as they all knew she was a good respectable woman. Mary said there had obviously been a lot of men at the house, coming and going, but in the neighbourhood there was a lot of respect for her, as she was making the best of a difficult situation. There was plenty of sympathy from the women from round about. “Good for her” they had said.

‘Mary remembers Ken coming round to see her, to go courting as Mary puts it, she baby-sat me so they could go out sometimes, but of course that was later on. But there was also another man that Mary had seen. I think she’d had plenty of amusement, peering from behind her net curtains. She thought this man was local, grey-haired, quite smart, “a business type” said Mary. He came on foot and would stay an hour or so, then walk back towards the city centre.’

‘Blimey, did she time him in and out?’

Samantha laughed again. ‘Not quite. But you could always rely on Mary to know what was going off up and down the street.’

‘Could he have been a solicitor or accountant or someone like that?’

‘Yes, he could have been, but I don’t remember anyone like that being around at all.’

‘Do you believe this Mary?’

‘Erm, I think so. I don’t think she is malicious, and she’s always been good to me. I had to prise the information out of her a bit. I didn’t want to say anything to her about looking to find my father, but I did push her to tell me more about the time before I was born. She has no real idea of timing, not after all these years, so it could have been well before I was born, or well after.’

‘Is there any correspondence you could see that might tell us more, legal or financial letters perhaps?’

‘There’s a lot of stuff I haven’t been through yet. I have to be careful because my sisters are rather suspicious of what I’m doing.’

‘You haven’t said anything to them either?

‘No, not a word.’

‘But you don’t want to involve them with this?’

'Not at all, anyway they don't have any information that would help us, and it's not their father that we're talking about.' said Samantha very firmly. Jack waited again for a natural pause.

'Will you tell me a little more about yourself, please? I don't know much, you said that you were married but separated from your husband, is that right?' asked Jack.

'Yes, that's correct.'

'So do you live on your own?'

'Just me and my son.'

This was something else that Jack had never thought about. A son! Who would be his grandson if…

'A son? I didn't know that. How old is he? What's his name?'

'He's called Adam and he's eight now.'

'And your husband is his father?'

Samantha gave him a filthy look which answered his question and he found himself waving in apology again.

'Sorry, I do put my foot in it sometimes. Do you have your own house?'

'I do, it's just like my mother, talk about déjà vu all over again. We took out a mortgage which I now am paying off while he has gone off with a much younger woman. Not that I know that Norman did that to Mum, but I wouldn't be surprised. Men, a lot of them just cherry-pick what they want for a while and then chuck it aside when they have had enough.'

'Not all men, but I do understand. What you've said makes me even more determined to help you.'

Samantha looked back at him, her eyes filling up.

'I know. Bless you Jack, I know I'm snappy sometimes, but I really do appreciate it.'

With that she reached across the table and collected up their plates, cups and saucers, fetched a tray and took them all back to the counter, then did not sit down again, signalling an end to the conversation.

'I am going back to Jenny's now and then home on Sunday. Next weekend I'll go back to the house and have a more thorough search for the receipt books and have a sort through all her papers, see what else I can find. Perhaps something that will tell us more about Mary Barthorpe's mystery man.'

'OK, let me know how you get on, good hunting.'

'Thank you Jack.'

They left the café and walked along Albert Road towards Watford Junction station, but little more was said until they arrived at the station.

'OK, I will be in touch, thanks again.'

Another awkward parting and she headed for the ticket barriers. Jack watched her go and waited a while before going for his own train. During the ride back to Kenton, he pondered on his situation. Life was steady, his health was normally good, making a good recovery from the operation. Money was not a problem, he had always been prudent, and he had his pension from Gladwin's as well as from the State. He was sixty-six, how many years he might have left, nobody could tell him, nor how long he might stay independent. He did miss Margaret, but he was adjusting slowly to living alone. He regretted that, when he had achieved something or had some interesting information, she wasn't there to tell any more, she'd been a good listener. After all those years together, returning to an empty house wasn't easy. He had to admit to himself that his life was dull.

What did he want to do with himself? More than mere survival, that was for sure. He had never involved himself much in charities or organisations like Round Table, which his son supported, he hadn't felt comfortable in that sort of society. He did bits for the church, but wasn't drawn to do more for them, there was a tight clique there which kept you firmly on the outside. Too many patronising, self-confident do-gooders for his liking. But he did want to feel that he was a useful member of society, not just another pensioner in God's Waiting Room. He had never forged many close friendships, his life had revolved around Margaret and his work.

From the first meeting with Samantha, after overcoming the initial shock and hearing that Pamela had died, he had glimpsed a worthwhile project that would absorb his time and perhaps lead to a satisfying, successful outcome. Something to get up for each day, to measure progress against a plan, ticking jobs off a list to confirm progress, that was what he liked to do. However, he realised that it was Samantha who had come away from their meeting with the to do list, whereas he had nothing on his, and that did not sit well with him. He wanted to find a way to make a bigger contribution.

CHAPTER 12

Nottingham, Easter 1990

SAMANTHA KNEW THAT she now had to put some time aside to investigate the files and documents that her mother had left, so on Easter Sunday, soon after her return from Watford, she said to Adam, 'You're not going to see your Dad today, he's away for the weekend, so we are going to Granny's to sort out some stuff there that I need to do. You can give me a hand.'

'What sort of stuff?' asked Adam, without looking up from his book of football stickers.

'Papers, clothes, some of her odds and ends.'

'That sounds boring.'

'It doesn't have to be, we can make some fun out of it. I've made us some sausage sandwiches, how does that sound?'

'That sounds better already.'

'Right come on then, bring your football.'

AS THEY GOT out of her car, she could see Mary Barthorpe's curtains twitch. Samantha waved, to let her know that she had been spotted, and the nets were drawn aside as Mary waved back. Her mother's house felt musty inside, it was a few weeks since she had been there. There was a pile of post behind the front door, mainly general circulars, although there were a couple for her mother, addressed to Mrs. Charlton. She unlocked the back door to let Adam out on to the back lawn, which she was pleased to see had received its first mowing of the year.

She went upstairs to Pamela's bedroom, at the front of the house. She looked out of the bay window; not much happening on Sunday morning in the street, a man washing his car, another had his Morris Minor up on blocks, working underneath it. Mary Barthorpe had decided it was time to do some front garden weeding, they would have to negotiate a way past her when they came out.

Samantha still could not face going through Pamela's clothes, opening the wardrobe door and closing it again. Emma and Rachel had already taken a few things they wanted, but she really would have to sort out with them if there was anything else they fancied. She sat down on the padded stool in front of the dressing-table. She had seen her mother there so often, it felt to Samantha like an intrusion for her to take her place. She had already gone through the small central drawer with her sisters, dividing up their mother's jewellery, what there was of it, so that was now empty. On the right-hand side she found underwear and cosmetics. There were bottles of various tablets, all out of date, which Samantha dropped into a carrier bag she had brought, so she could safely dispose of them at home. She had already put in the letters she had picked up on their way in.

On the left hand-side, more of the same until she came to the bottom one. There were some photographs, which she recognised as the ones she had once shown to her mother when she was in the nursing home, not long before the end.

'Of course, I've been meaning to show these to Jack, then I forgot about them. It would help for him to see these now,' she said, realising that when she was in that house she still spoke to herself out loud, as she had done as a child. She lifted out the photos and saw underneath there were some large brown envelopes, full of documents. They were all addressed to her mother, so she put those into the carrier bag with the photographs for further investigation at home.

As there was nowhere else in the bedroom to look, she checked round the other bedrooms to see that all was in order, then went back downstairs and looked out of the back door. She couldn't see Adam at first, and started to feel anxious, but he emerged from the bottom end of the garden, the old vegetable patch, which was now overgrown. He was carrying his football.

'Have you finished?' he asked.

'No, not yet. Are you ready for a sandwich and some chocolate biscuits?'

'Yes, please.'

They sat down at her mother's kitchen table, which had been there for all of Samantha's life. It bore some scars from various knives over the years and marks had been made by injudiciously placed hot saucepans and mugs.

'I wonder what we'll do with this table,' said Samantha, 'it goes back a long way, but we haven't got room for it so I suppose it will become firewood.'

'It's a bit grotty, isn't it? It wouldn't look nice in our kitchen,' declared Adam.

'No, you're right, no point in being nostalgic about it.'

'What does "nostalgic" mean?'

'It's when you get sloppy about old bits and pieces that don't mean anything to anyone else. It's not very productive, it just sends you off down the Memory Drain, which is literally a dead end.'

'What are you doing now?'

'I need your help. I am looking for some things which ought to be here but which I can't find.'

'What are they?'

'Some little blue booklets, books of receipts that you give people when they pay you money. I have some of them, but I couldn't find them all. Shall we go look see?'

'OK, where are we looking?'

THEY WENT INTO the dining room to Pamela's bureau, where again she could picture her mother sitting, writing cheques and checking her bank statements. She pulled down the flap, which formed a writing surface. Inside were lots of little pigeon-holes, in which were paperclips, pens and pencils, envelopes and stationery. She found some postage stamps, which she dropped into the carrier bag.

'Nothing of interest there, let's look in the drawers.'

She started with the top one, pulling it out almost as far as it would go.

'This is mainly bank stuff. There are statements here going back years. I might as well take them all, they are of no interest to anyone else. I'm running out of room to put everything, can you please look in the kitchen and see if you can find another carrier bag anywhere, maybe in the kitchen cupboard?'

Adam came back quickly with a large canvas bag into which Samantha put the bank statements. There were other papers in the drawer, gas, electric and water; Samantha carefully checked that there was nothing significant, then pushed the drawer back in. It was in the second drawer that she had previously found the receipt books, so it was nearly empty now. Another quick check and she closed that. The third drawer was the bottom one, and when she pulled it out, it stuck at first, so that when given a sharp tug, it shot out on to the floor, narrowly missing her toes as she sat on the chair.

'Oops, careful now, that was close.'

It didn't seem that this one had been opened for a long time. It was heavy and there was a layer of dust on top of some parcels of fabric.

'Look, Mum, at the back there, are those what you are looking for?' shouted Adam, who was still down on his knees at floor level.

Sure enough, right at the back of the compartment, were three more receipt books.

'Well spotted Adam, I wouldn't have seen those, they must have fallen over the back of the drawer. They're what I was looking for. Well done. There's nothing else of interest in here so we can put this drawer back and go now. It wasn't like Granny to let that happen. I guess my sisters have been in here furtling about and they pushed some of them over the back.'

As they left, Mary Barthorpe was still out front, trowel in hand, chatting to a passer-by.

'Hello Sam, are you all right? Your boy's growing up, isn't he?'

Samantha waved back and the presence of the neighbour enabled them to make it to the car without further interrogation, putting the two carrier bags into the boot.

'Thanks Adam, that was very useful.' She drove them back home with a sense of relief.

IT WAS THE next evening when Samantha rang Jack.

'Jack, I've made some progress, I've found the missing receipt books. In particular, I've got the one from end May to early September that year. They had fallen down the back of the bureau, into the space behind the drawers. It was lucky that my son spotted them, I might not have seen them.'

'That's Adam, isn't it?'

'Well remembered,' said Samantha.

It was taking time for Jack to become accustomed to the idea of Samantha as a mother and he tried to picture Adam. He remembered David at that age, bright, inquiring, good company, and he guessed that Adam would be similar. He would love to meet him one day.

'Well, what you have found is great, am I in the books?'

'Oh yes, I can track you down now, I can tell you exactly when you were there. It is what you said, you were there all summer, apart from a week in June, when you said your daughter was born. Otherwise, you were there pretty well every week, Monday to Friday. There's more.'

'Go on, then.'

'I have found some photos that I had forgotten about, which I had shown to my mother while she was still in the residential home. She recognised you on two of them, that's when she seemed to give me the message that you were someone special to her. There's a picture of you outside a pub, with a pint in front of you and her drink on the table as well. There are some others of men I assume were some of her lodgers and you are on one of them. You might remember some of the others. I will try to photocopy them and send them to you, together with a list of the new names I have found.'

'I can't say that I remember any photos being taken, but let's have a look by all means. Are you going to go through some of those older receipt books as well, to see if we can properly identify who were her regulars?'

'Yes, I will add them to the new list I'll send you.'

'She had a lot on her plate, didn't she?'

'She did. So, stand by for another package from me. Another list, more names and addresses and copies of photos, are you ready for that?'

'No problem, I can update the long list, so to speak, and try to highlight the most likely suspects.'

'I reckon if you can do something to narrow them down a bit, that would be great. If we got it down to half-a-dozen names, that might be manageable.'

'It could be, yes. OK, I'll wait for the package and come back to you.'

'Thank you, Jack.'

ALL WAS QUIET in Samantha's house and around about, a suburban Sunday evening. Adam was soundly asleep after his interesting day, which was how he had described it as he went to bed. Samantha settled down to look at the pile of correspondence which she had collected from her mother's house. The documents were in four large brown envelopes, although it was not obvious how they had been sorted. They seemed to mainly consist of letters to Pamela, some addressed to Mrs. Charlton, up to 1958, later ones to Mrs Townsend, so they covered a number of years. All very formal, on printed letterheads, in the format of the 1950s: – "Dear Madam", "I refer to yours of the 5th inst.", "I am your obedient servant" and so on. Some from different firms of solicitors, others from a Private Investigation Agency.

She made herself a cup of cocoa and brought a packet of biscuits to her chair in the lounge. She put the papers in piles in front of her on the coffee table, remembering the new letters that had arrived. The next day was Easter Monday, a Bank Holiday, so she settled down for a long night.

CHAPTER 13

Kenton, Late April 1990

AFTER HIS MEETING with Samantha in Watford, Jack was still thinking that he ought to be doing more to help their quest but could not work out what that might be.

One morning soon after, while on his way to go shopping in Kenton, he happened to see an old school friend with his wife who were on their way back from the shops. Normally, Jack wasn't keen to encourage conversation in such situations, especially when it was with a couple like them. They were certainly kind and friendly, that wasn't the problem, it was more the opposite, they were too much that way inclined. Jack was embarrassed when the conversation would include Margaret, her death and whether he was lonely on his own; he was embarrassed and speechless in the face of such concern. On this occasion however, a light suddenly flashed on in Jack's mind, and he went over to Derek and Janet.

He and Derek had been good friends in secondary school, while Janet had been in the year below them. In his teens, before he was called up, Jack had taken her to the pictures a few times, but they had never really clicked, she was too dour for his taste. Whenever he met her out on her own now, she had complained about Derek's obsession with his model trains.

'Hello, you two, how are you?'

It was Derek who answered, putting down their shopping bags to indicate a willingness to chat. He had always been a big man, but now his extra weight had become very apparent.

'We're OK, thanks Jack, usual aches and pains of course, but nothing serious, touch wood.' He tapped the side of his head, laughing. 'How are you, coping all right?'

Jack gave a non-committal reply, and for a few minutes the conversation followed a typical course, with amiable inquiries about the progress of each other's children and grandchildren. Janet and Derek had a son in Australia, ("Melbourne, it's lovely there, he's doing very well in IT") to compare with Jack's daughter in New Zealand ("Christchurch, they say it's very nice, but Margaret and I never went").

When they left school, Derek had taken an engineering apprenticeship with the G.P.O., as it then was, at their local telephone exchange and he had stayed with them all his working life until retirement a couple of years ago, around the same time as Jack, at the age of sixty-five.

'Actually Derek, there's something that you might be able to help me with.'

'I will if I can.'

At this point Jack had to think quickly to concoct a cover story for his inquiry.

'I'm trying to track down the family of an Army pal of mine. We were good mates for long time, but then he was killed after El Alamein. I've still got a few things of his I would like to get to his family. They're up in Yorkshire somewhere, but I'm not sure where. He had an unusual surname, Kenworthy, so they might not be too hard to find, but I don't know where to start. I wondered about telephone directories, but I might need to look at quite a few round the Yorkshire area. I have tried our libraries, but they only have the local ones from round here, do the G.P.O. have a place where you can see all the directories from all over the country?'

'Oh yes,' said Derek with enthusiasm, 'Of course, it's all BT now but Telephone House, in the City, is still the same. They have them all there in like a sort of Library Reading Room.'

'And can anyone go in there?'

'Definitely, we'd lost the phone number of one of Janet's cousins in Plymouth and we went there and found them.'

Janet, who never said much and was still hanging onto Derek's arm, nodded confirmation.

'Whereabouts is that then?'

'Telephone House, grand building it is, in Temple Avenue, near Temple and Blackfriars tube stations, just up from the river. Easy to find.'

Having secured this precious piece of information, Jack was conscious that he was now impatient to bring the conversation to a swift end, but he was too polite to do that. Together they drifted off into reminiscences about their school years. Derek asked if Jack knew that George Prentice had been killed in a car crash on the M1 when he was with someone else's wife. No, Jack didn't know, how awful it must have been for all concerned. They continued in this vein for a few minutes until Janet started to show restlessness, tugging on Derek's arm. At last, she spoke.

'Come on Derek, it's nearly lunch-time. Sorry, Jack but we've got frozen peas in the shopping, we need to get them in the freezer.'

'Yes love, let's go,' replied Derek. 'Well, it's been good to see you again Jack, you're looking well. Good luck with your search, I'm glad I could help.'

'Yes, it's been great to have a chat again, see you around soon.'

Jack was elated, it felt like a breakthrough, something positive that he could tell Samantha. He headed off home, quite forgetting to do his intended shopping. He had to go out again in the afternoon, fearful that he would be embarrassed by bumping into Derek and Janet again, or Mrs. Hodges.

ONE MORNING SOON afterwards, around nine o'clock, Jack took the Tube from Kenton, the Bakerloo line direct to Charing Cross. Across the carriage he saw two men, casually dressed, one in his fifties, the other called him 'Dad'. Arsenal supporters, they were concerned at their recent form and feared that they were not going to win the First Division this year. Jack noticed how the younger man listened respectfully to his father and didn't argue with him, even when Jack could see that he didn't agree. Jack compared their relationship to his own with David.

From Charing Cross, he enjoyed the walk along the Embankment. The river Thames was never something that he thought about and, when he saw it, it always seemed so big and wide, busy with assorted traffic. 'Where have they been, where are they all going?' he wondered.

With help of his A to Z, he found Temple Avenue and was immediately overawed by the grandeur of Telephone House, a most imposing building, perhaps built before the First World War. It was at least five storeys high, with high chimney stacks. Jack, who knew a bit about building materials, recognised that it was constructed of Portland stone. He was impressed.

A terse uniformed commissionaire guided him towards the Directories Room. There a smiling middle-aged lady, smart in twinset and pearls, pointed him towards a chart on which all the Directories were listed, in alphabetical order, giving their directory number. Remembering his story to Derek and Janet, he located the Leeds book and took it to one of the tables. He looked under Kenworthy and found there were about twenty of them listed. Taking a note-book and pencil from his pocket and aware of the attention of the smiling lady, he noted down their initials, addresses and phone numbers. He felt that he should appear as if he had a serious purpose, knowing that he would never use them. There was little other activity in the room, a few people came in, took a directory to a table, jotted down a note or two, then left.

After a suitable interval, Jack also headed for the exit. He hadn't learned that much but did know now that if they had some firm details of any individual, they would be able to find if he was still in the phone book at the same address. It felt like some progress, however minor.

The reception lady, comfortable and secure behind her desk, made him think of his years behind his counter at Gladwin's. He had been the King of that particular Castle. He always knew his stock, what he had, what he didn't have, what was on order and when it was due. He could advise on the best materials for a specific job, based on his customers' experiences. He knew his staff, his suppliers and most of his customers and how to manage all of them. They all trusted him, his knowledge and his honesty. That was where he had felt in charge and in control, ever since he came back from the War. Outside of work and his home territory, he had never felt the same self-confidence. He was often hesitant and shy in unfamiliar surroundings, especially if there were others, more assertive than himself, who appeared to be in control.

LATER THAT WEEK, another envelope arrived from Samantha, again bearing the name of Amber Valley Borough Council. As promised, it contained more copies of pages from the receipt books, a list of new names and now some photocopied photographs. These photos had not copied very well and were cloudy; Samantha had sent all the ones that she had shown to Pamela, including their family pictures. Jack was interested to see these and felt an uncomfortable pang when he realised that Samantha had had a resemblance to his own daughter, Elizabeth, at the same age. Pamela's husband, Ken, wore a harassed, distant look, in keeping with Samantha's description of him.

Jack was amused to see the picture that Pamela had taken of himself outside the pub.

'Blimey, you look a bit younger there, Jack,' he told himself. 'And you do look very relaxed.'

When it came to the other photos, there were three of them, of men coaxed into smiling groups on Pamela's front doorstep. The group photo featuring Jack had him alongside two older men. He remembered them as being from Liverpool, insurance men, he thought. None of the four faces on the second picture was at all familiar to him. Those in the group of three, however, were. One was Barry from Cardiff, the traveller in ladies' underwear and another was strange silent Cedric, from the West Country. It was the third man who immediately took Jack's attention. Taller than the other two, smart and confident, looking directly at the camera with an amused smile and a raised eyebrow.

'Well, that's him all right, I knew he would crop up eventually,' said Jack. 'I just wonder, could it be him, Bob Dawson, who turns out to be the Mystery Man?'

Jack remembered him as a smooth talker who gave little away. If asked what he did or where he was from, there was never a straight answer. He would say that he was 'In Commerce' and from 'Down South', implying to Jack that what he did would be well over the head of simple fellows like him. He recalled Bob being there for more than one week, perhaps with gaps in between. And there was one incident with him which Jack still could not get clear in his mind.

He took out his original list and updated it with additional names from Samantha's information which seemed relevant, so that his list of potential suspects had now expanded to twenty-five names.

'Too many, some pruning needed, I think,' said Jack.

With all of the information from the receipt books now to hand, he went through the list again. The critical period was around September 1955, nine months before Samantha's birth, give or take a month or two. He put a 1, 2 or 3 by each name, according to their likelihood as culprit: 3 was for those who had only stayed for a few odd days; 2 was for men who had stayed at least for a full week; 1was for frequent stayers, 'my regulars' as Pamela would have called them.

He judged that those who had stayed with a colleague were not credible suspects, but the loners were much more likely. That reduced his list to eight '1s', and he made detailed notes about them; name, address, employer's name where known, any comments Pamela had made, and when they stayed, and if that coincided with Jack. Some of them had paid cash, others had presented a cheque from their employer.

He had a range of names, with addresses from North, East, West and South. On the list of 1s was Bob Dawson, who had given an address in Sheffield, not that far away from Nottingham.

CHAPTER 14

Nottingham, June 1955

I WAS HAVING another really busy day when I saw the car draw up, mid-morning. It was becoming very hot. I had just finished dealing with an uninterested young man from the *Evening Post* who had called in and thought they 'might' include a feature on our opening 'soon' in their Business section.

The building was coming on, but not as rapidly as I would have liked. The shell had gone up quickly but having different trades teams to fit it out took some co-ordinating, and time was moving on. A gang of plumbers were working on the toilets and kitchen. I was happy with them, they were a good bunch who got on with their jobs and knew what they were doing. However, the carpenters hadn't turned up again. They were the proverbial pain in the arse; stroppy, bloody-minded and their quality had to be watched carefully. I could hear them going on behind my back about 'bloody Cockneys criticising our work'.

We were still open to the elements, which wasn't so bad as it was summer, but a problem when it was either wet or windy, or both. My 'desk' was an upturned packing case, my 'chair' an oil can with a grubby old cushion on top. There was always dust in the air and drills hammering away. I had a ten-minute walk to a phone box if I wanted to contact anyone and then sometimes had to wait in a queue. That afternoon, a representative from a hardware company was coming in to take our stock orders, so I was working hard on the inventories that I would require from him.

You didn't see that many Jags on the Colwick Industrial Estate (the locals pronounced it 'Collick') and I recognised this one straight away, not only by the personalised number plate, but also the deep shade of maroon: my boss Brian Gladwin.

He stopped a moment to have a brief word with the young red-headed woman in the passenger seat, before emerging in a cloud of cigarette smoke. She wound down her window and I could see her lighting up a fresh one.

'All OK, Jack?' he asked as he strolled across the yard.

I stood up quickly.

'We are getting there, should all be ready on time.' I still couldn't bring myself to address him as "Brian" as he liked us to call him, making us sound like good pals.

'I can see it has come on a bit since I was last here.' One of the plumbers peered round the doorway to see who it was, then ducked back inside.

'Have you driven up this morning then?'

'No, no, came up yesterday afternoon,' he said, nodding towards the woman and the car by way of explanation. I changed the subject and brought him up to date with progress.

'Shouldn't there be some chippies here?'

'They haven't turned in today again. I rang their office, but I only got the boss's secretary. She said he was out on a job, so I said it was a pity that it wasn't our job. She was sure they would be here tomorrow, but I don't think she'd know that for certain. I'm not happy with their quality standards, but the foreman gets aggressive if I complain. I told them last night that the finish on that counter wasn't good enough, but he said he couldn't see anything wrong with it.'

I rubbed my hand down the edge to show him the rough patches.

'You're quite right, that's really poor. Stick to your guns, lad, only the best is good enough for Gladwin's.'

I knew that wasn't always true, but I let it go. He wandered around for a while, poking his finger into a few corners and testing the door handles. He looked in on the plumbers with a breezy 'All right, lads?' and stubbed out his fag end on the concrete floor, leaving a black mark, which is something I would never have let the carpenters get away with.

'Well done Jack, keep up the good work. Are your digs still OK?'

'Couldn't be better, thank you,' which was enough for him to raise an eyebrow and grin.

'See you soon. Drop in at the yard on a Saturday morning when you are home, it would be good to see you there.'

I had done just that most Saturdays when I was back, but usually early, around nine o'clock, so I had never seen him there. With that he was away with a wave, lighting another cigarette before getting into the car, having a quick word with his passenger and roaring away, probably a country pub lunch next stop. After that, who knows?

The plumber's foreman came out again.

'Bit of a wide boy, your gaffer, isn't he?' I smiled but did not answer.

'Nice motor, though.' They would have seen it from the toilet windows which hadn't been glazed yet.

'Do you ever get a lift in it?'

'Certainly not.' I went back to grinding through the detail of the hardware catalogue.

As I ARRIVED back at Pamela's that evening it was past seven o'clock. She called out from the kitchen to say that dinner was ready, so I had a quick wash and went down to the dining room. My meal was already on the table, a fresh ham salad.

'Have Frank and Ernie been in and gone out again?' I asked as she came in, tea towel in her hand.

'No, you are the only one here tonight. They came back in a hurry around ten o'clock this morning. They'd had an urgent call from their office in Liverpool telling them to go straight back for a meeting this evening. They paid me for tonight, which was good of them.'

'It sounds ominous,' I said, 'that sort of message is usually bad news.'

Frank and Ernie were a couple of amiable Scousers who worked for a big insurance company. They had told me they were doing some sort of audit on their Nottingham branch. It now occurred to me that this would be the first time that Pamela and I had been in the house on our own. She was so busy there was usually someone else there, even at weekends.

'Have you had a good day?' she asked.

'To be perfectly honest, I've had a bugger of a day. My boss turns up out of the blue, which was OK, but without any warning. You panic for a moment in case there is something wrong. That shower of a team of carpenters didn't show up again, which has put us behind and the fellow who came to see me this afternoon was an hour late and didn't apologise. That's why I am late back because we had a lot of detail to sort out.'

I paused. 'Are you sorry you asked?'

She laughed and said, 'I haven't seen you as worked up as this before.'

'And it's my birthday.'

'Oh Jack, happy birthday, but that is too much. I'll bring you your pudding to compensate.'

She came back with a piece of her apple pie with custard and a cup of tea in her other hand. She pulled up a chair and sat down, which I hadn't seen her do before.

'Have you been away from home before on your birthday?' Pamela asked me.

'Oh yes, in the war, nineteen forty-two on Salisbury Plain, then forty-three and forty-four, my twenty-first, in North Africa. I didn't get back to Blighty for nearly three years.'

'That was before you were married?'

'Oh yes, I didn't meet Margaret until nineteen forty-eight.'

Pamela gazed out of the window. 'It's a lovely evening,' she said, which sounded to me like an invitation.

'Would you like to go out for a drink?' She immediately looked me in the eye.

'Ooh… yes, please, I think that would be very nice. Give me fifteen minutes to tidy up and I will be ready.'

SHE DIDN'T KEEP me waiting. She had changed into a summer frock and heels and put on some lipstick. She was carrying a smart handbag and I saw her pick up a camera and drop it in.

'Where's the best place to go to take a lady for a drink?' I asked.

'Not down on the corner, too many locals in there, it will get folks talking. Let's walk up the Dale, there's a decent pub at the top with tables in the garden. At least it's downhill on the way home. Is that OK with you?'

'Sounds good to me, I'm ready for a pint.'

Pamela continued her gentle probing as we walked up the hill. I remember it as one of those beautiful midsummer evenings, shirt-sleeve weather. As we walked up the hill the houses became more substantial and better kept, some men were still out mowing their lawns, the pleasant smell of new-mown grass in the air. No motor mowers in those days.

'How's the baby?'

'She's coming on fine, thank you. Very quiet and settled compared with her brother, thank goodness.'

Pamela's heels made a reassuring click on the pavement.

'How's your wife managing?'

'She makes it clear that it would be better if I was there, but she's got her mum and sister close by, although she gets a bit exasperated with them at times.'

'I didn't realise that you were away for so long in the War. Your parents must have been worried about you?'

'Ah well, that's a bit complicated. I lived with my aunt and uncle in London from when I was twelve. I was born in Lancashire, but my mum was poorly for a long time, in and out of the local asylum, so my Dad sent me to live with his sister and her husband, it was the Depression then and he said I would have a better chance down South.'

We were still climbing the hill and I started to think that I was not as fit as I thought I was, but Pamela didn't seem to be having any difficulty in keeping up.

'That must have been a big change for you, did that work out OK?'

'It did, they've been great to me. They couldn't have children of their own and I think I was a bit spoilt.'

'Are they still around?'

'They are, but they moved out to a cottage on the Chiltern Hills, near Whipsnade Zoo, when Tom retired from the Post Office. They love it out there.'

'So you have been used to looking out for yourself then?'

'I have.'

We arrived at the pub, which from the outside looked like an ordinary town place, but it opened out into a nice garden at the back. Pamela chose us a table outside and asked for a Babycham. I had pint of one of the local beers, Shipstones, which I found to be something of an acquired taste. The pub garden was quiet, apart from the birdsong, nicely shaded by trees. She told me about wartime in Nottingham, spending nights in an air raid shelter, waking up to find that nearby houses had been bombed.

'Did you like being in the Army?' she asked.

'I did. When I joined up, there was this big older fellow, a Sergeant Major in uniform. He asked me what I did for a job and, when I told him, he seemed very pleased. "The Ordnance Corps for you, my lad, just the sort of chap we need." We were responsible for all supplies, guns, ammunition, uniforms, tools, you name it, so the job was similar to what I was used to, it really suited me.'

'So you weren't in the front line, then?'

'No, but we were dive-bombed and machine-gunned a few times, once by our own planes. It was damn hot in the day but cold at night. It could be very chaotic. My best pal, Ted Kenworthy from Yorkshire, was killed when one of our trucks reversed into him. I saw that happen.'

I realised that wasn't a subject for light conversation, so I went in and bought myself another pint, but Pamela would not have more than the one drink. When I came back she took a small camera out of her handbag and took a photo of me, which was a bit of a surprise.

'Was Norman in the war?' I asked.

'Reserved occupation, he was a toolmaker at Raleigh Cycles. He said he was too important to be cannon fodder. You can see what sort of a man he was.'

After that we lapsed into light chit-chat about nothing in particular. It was still warm and neither of us seemed in a hurry to end the evening. Eventually we wandered back down the hill. As we arrived back at her house, Pamela said, 'Jack, that's been a lovely evening, thank you for the drink.'

'My pleasure, thank you for coming. I think we both needed that.'

'We did. Goodnight.' She headed off to the kitchen, probably to get the breakfast things ready. I could hear the clatter of crockery and cutlery as I went upstairs.

Suddenly a penny dropped with me, I hadn't rung Margaret, and on my birthday! I knew I would be in trouble for that. It was gone ten o'clock by then, far too late to ring her, she would only panic if a call came in at that time. It had been such a day that she had completely slipped my mind. As it was a Thursday, the next evening's call would be very short and sharp, from the station, to tell her which train I was on. It would be along the lines of 'Oh, you are still alive then?'

I was usually a good sleeper in those days, but my mind was too active that night, thinking about the busy day, Brian's visit, and the pleasant evening we had just had. After about half an hour, I heard Pamela come upstairs, firmly closing her bedroom door.

Next morning it was business as usual. My alarm went off at six, breakfast at half-past. Pamela did a good substantial breakfast to set you up for the day, but she could never manage to get the bacon as crispy as I liked it. Then it was off to catch the bus to Colwick by seven, wondering if the carpenters would turn up.

'Thanks for last evening, Jack,' said Pamela, as I

breakfasted alone. ‘It made a nice change.’

‘It did, didn’t it? Thank you for the pleasure of your company.’

She gave me a warm smile.

CHAPTER 15

Kenton, May 1990

WHEN JACK RANG Samantha, she sounded slightly surprised to hear from him, which disconcerted him.

'Oh, hello, it's you.'

'It is, am I convenient? Time to bring you up to speed on what has been going on down here, I thought, if that's OK with you?'

'Yes, it's fine, all quiet here. Well, what have you got to report, then?'

'I'll start at the beginning.' He went on to describe how he had created his list of twenty-five names, dividing them into the three categories.

'On what basis have you done that?' she asked.

'Not very scientific. I've included the most regular visitors, the blokes who were on their own, not with colleagues, also noted the comments Pamela made, any other clues I could find.'

'How many Number Ones have you got?'

'Eight at the moment. They are somewhere to start, but we shouldn't forget the others completely.'

'OK so far.'

'Good. I looked at the photos that you sent. They are not very clear because they are just photocopies. I enjoyed seeing the ones of you children together, they gave me an indication of how life was then for you.'

'What about the other photos?'

'On one of the group pictures I didn't recognise anyone in the four who are there. I am on another one with two fellows who I do remember, but they are Number Threes on my list. Two nice chaps from Liverpool, probably in their fifties, who came together for a couple of weeks. No reason to think they are of interest to us. On the other one, three of them on that, I remember them all, two unlikely, one is a strong possibility.'

'Oh yes, why is that?'

'He was a man I never took to, had a superior air about him, didn't seem to give you a straight answer. Charming, I'm sure, but not trustworthy.'

'Which one is he then?'

Jack could hear the rustling of documents, so he paused for a moment.

'He's on the right of the three. On the left is Barry, the Welshman in ladies' underwear, who I know Pamela didn't care for, his humour was too crude for her taste. In the middle is Cedric, he was from Somerset, you can see how strange he looked. I don't think he is a candidate, I never heard him string more than half-a-dozen words together.'

'And the other one, I am looking at the photo now, and I can already see what you mean,' said Samantha.

'Bob Dawson. If you asked him what he did, he would say that he was 'in Commerce' and from somewhere in the South. Yet the address that Pamela had for him was in Sheffield. That's not so far away, why would he need to stay all week?'

'No, it's not that far, although this was before the M1 was extended north.'

'True. But you would wonder why he needed to stay in Nottingham all week, it's still only an hour's drive away. We don't have any information about who he worked for. Just something that doesn't ring true for me with him.'

'What about the picture of you outside the pub, Jack, very presentable looking young man, if I might say so, I can see why Mum was happy to be seen out with you!'

Jack was glad that she could not see him blushing, such compliments were rare, and he was quick to change the subject.

'That's very kind, I do look a lot younger, don't I? I also have something else to tell you.'

'Oh yes?'

'I've found out where I can go to see all the UK phone directories, a place called Telephone House, near the river. I met a bloke I was at school with, who was a GPO telephone engineer, he told me about it. I went and had a look last week, it's like a reading room. I am going again tomorrow, see what I can find about my Number 1s.'

'That's a real breakthrough, Jack, well done. I am still going through all the documents that I brought back from Mother's, but I won't jump the gun on those yet, but there will be more to tell you from those soon.'

'Fair enough. Well, it's a start, let's see what I can find.'

IT WAS WELL after nine o'clock when he put down the phone. When it rang again soon afterwards, Jack had a feeling who it might be at that time, his daughter Elizabeth, calling from New Zealand, she would usually ring him as soon as she had taken her children to school.

After the usual pleasantries, she asked,

'Have you been on the phone, I tried earlier, and you were engaged?'

'Yes I was.' Jack wasn't sure what else to say at this point.

'Was it my Aunt Brenda?'

Jack was tempted to tell a lie, but he did not like to do that with his children, he had always drummed it into them to tell the truth.

'No, it was someone else that I believe David has talked to you about.'

'The lady that thinks you might be her father?'

'Yes, that's her. What has David said to you?'

'You know what he's like Dad, he gets very worked up about things and straightaway he is on his high horse, isn't he?'

'Yes, he is,' said Jack with a laugh. 'Has he told you to talk me out of it?'

'Look, I'm not going to try to do that. I was shocked at first when David told me, but I know you as well, you'll only dig your heels in and carry on regardless, won't you? Tell me about her.'

'She turned up on my doorstep a while back.'

'What, out of the blue, just like that?'

'Yes, just like that, a bit of a shock, as you can imagine. Her name is Samantha, she is around the same age as you, lives near Nottingham. She's the daughter of the lady I used to lodge with in 1955, when I worked up in Nottingham for a while.'

'I've never heard anything about that, how did that come about?'

Jack told her about Brian Gladwin's ambition for market domination.

'And tell me about Samantha's mother.'

'Her husband had cleared off and left her with a big house and a mortgage, she felt that she had to take in lodgers to make ends meet. Her name was Pamela, I was there most of the summer, and we got on well. She was very efficient and organised, didn't feel sorry for herself, just got on with things.'

'Not quite like our Mum, then?'

'Different, shall we say?'

'Has Samantha got a husband, then?'

'She's had one, but they are separated. She has a boy of eight.'

'I see, she hasn't had it too easy then either, like her mother?'

'No, that's why I want to help her.'

Jack expected more questions about his possible parenthood, but they were not forthcoming. He sensed that Elizabeth was going to be more diplomatic and supportive than her brother.

'OK, I won't ask any more now, perhaps you can tell me more some other time. The real reason that I rang is to say that we are definitely planning to come over later in the year, perhaps in September, you will be around then, won't you?'

'Oh, that would be lovely to see you all again, it really would, to catch up with your girls again.'

'We have of course been invited to stay at David's, he is adamant about that.'

'I am sure that you will be well looked after. Louise was very kind to me. Are you OK with staying there?'

'I really would like to know her better, there always seemed to be tension with her when Mum was around. Quite a big age difference as well between my two and Simon and Lucy, not sure how that will work out now.'

'Yes, I was shocked at how much those two had grown up since I had last seen them, it wasn't that long ago. To see Fiona and Kelly again will definitely be something to look forward to. It must be two years since you were here, for Margaret's funeral.'

'That's right, and that obviously wasn't a very happy time. We will, of course, be going up to Yorkshire to see Howard's parents, but I'll be sure to have enough time for you.'

'How long do you think you will be here?'

'At least a fortnight.'

Jack paused while he took the plunge with what he wanted to say next.

'Great. Look, I've had a thought at the back of my mind for a while that perhaps, when you next came, I could come back to New Zealand with you, I would love to see where you are.'

'Oh Dad, that would be brilliant, Howard and I would love you to come.'

'That's really something for me to look forward to.'

'OK, Dad, see you quite soon then. I'll confirm our dates and let you know. Look after yourself and good luck with your project.'

JACK SAT DOWN in his chair, but not before pouring himself a small whisky and water, which the occasion seemed to call for, there was much to think about.

He was thrilled at the idea that Elizabeth and family would be visiting soon. She was a steady and calming influence on everyone around her, some of which he hoped would rub off on her brother. Unlike David, she had gone to University, where she had studied Modern Languages. After a lot of European travel, she had settled down to teaching at a comprehensive in Kent. Jack had a high regard for Howard, his son-in-law, he had studied hard in medical school and was now a GP in Christchurch. Jack would be very happy if Howard were his doctor instead of the strange woman to whom he was now allocated at his surgery. Elizabeth had jumped at the opportunity to go with him to New Zealand ten years previously, soon after their marriage and their girls had been born out there. He was excited about the prospect of going out there with them.

He was still becoming accustomed to the idea of Samantha as a mother, and to understand why he had never thought of that before. After all, she had been married and was in her mid-thirties, so why was that such a surprise? She must have had to make special arrangements for the lad when she came down to Watford, that would have been asking a lot of someone, a friend probably, as there seemed to be no-one from her family around to help. That showed to Jack how important this quest was to her. He sensed that she was cautious, wary of giving away too much personal information.

He picked up Samantha's package again and took another look at the photographs. In particular, he wanted to look again at the two of their family. It was good to see pictures of Pamela again, looking happy. The one of the whole family, Pamela, Ken, Samantha, Emma and Rachel, at the seaside, must have been taken when Samantha was about fifteen, so in the early seventies. She was frowning slightly at the camera, as if not entirely comfortable, fashionably dressed in a T-shirt and mini-skirt, her younger sisters were wearing bathing suits. Jack wondered who had taken the photo, was someone else with them or had they just prevailed upon a passing stranger to take it?

Jack looked again at Ken, who was wearing shirt, tie and a sports jacket, not what most would not call ideal beachwear. He had what used to be called a Bobby Charlton hair-style, a big comb-over job. Surely Pamela could have done better than him? Jack was disappointed for her, but she appeared to be happy enough in the photo.

The other picture was probably taken a couple of years later, outside their house. Samantha looked much more relaxed in a head and shoulders shot of the three girls. Emma was definitely growing up and adopting an attitude, while Samantha had a really nice smile for the camera. Now if David had brought her home to

Margaret and himself, he would have had their full approval, compared with some of the heavily made-up, under-dressed items he had escorted, before he went decidedly upmarket with Louise.

He sipped his whisky. Interesting times ahead, he thought.

CHAPTER 16

Kenton, May 1990

WHEN JACK RETURNED home from searching for addresses at Telephone House he was weary, it had been a tiring day. It had not been as straightforward an exercise as he had hoped. The phone directories often covered a wide area; for instance, the one he wanted for Norwich extended over much of the whole county of Norfolk. He realised that the address that lodgers had given to Pamela might have been their firm's address, while they lived some miles away. Jack's knowledge of UK geography was patchy, and he had no idea of the precise location of many of the place names that he saw.

There were different ways of presenting a name. When looking for George Bell, he could have been Bell G., Bell Geo., or Bell George. It made the job time-consuming as he did not want to miss anyone. It was also tiresome trudging through over three hundred Smiths in the Shrewsbury, Hereford and Mid-Wales book.

It was now mid-afternoon, and he did not feel ready to analyse his notes, such as they were. To be active he decided to mow his lawns and trim his hedges, even though he had only done them the previous week. While he was doing that, he let his mind ramble over many thoughts, about Pamela, Samantha, Gladwin's and the Army.

By the next morning he felt more energised, and he sat down with his notes and drew himself a chart, starting with his Number 1 choices, then going on to the Number 2s. He had not bothered with the 3s:

Category 1.

NAME	TOWN	EMPLOYER	LOCATED ?	NOTES
Keith Walker	Enfield, London	Tesco	Yes, same address	
Bob Dawson	Sheffield	Not known	No	36 R Dawsons found in Sheffield and Rotherham
Malcolm Turton	Birmingham	Cadbury Brothers	No	7 M. Turtons found in Birmingham
Ron Kennedy	Bristol	Not Known	No	J. Kennedy found at same address
Graham Horrocks	Nantwich	Albert Jones & Co.	No	No person or company of that name found
Bob Bullimore	Newcastle	Rank Hovis	Yes, same address	
Brian Jenkins	Norwich	Norwich Union	No	No name found
George Bell	Glasgow	Bluebird Cycles [Nottingham]	No	60 G. Bells in Glasgow

Category 2.

Dennis Smith	Shrewsbury	Salop Agricultural	No	100 D. Smiths. Company not found
Tom O'Neill	Belfast	Not Known	No	70 T. O'Neills and 10 Thomas O'Neill
Brian Wyatt	Blackpool	Blackpool Borough Council	Yes, same address	
Jeff Cunningham	Reading	British Railways	No	K. Cunningham at same address
Adrian Dennison	Bradford	Yorkshire Electricity	No	No A. Dennison found
Tony Bird	Middlesboro	ICI	Yes, same address	
Peter Davie	Tunbridge Wells	Davie Finance	No	Business found. One P. Davie found
Bob Briscoe	Llandudno	Not known	No	2 B. Briscoes and 2 R. Briscoes found

He had made a note that an entry in the 'Located?' column only indicated a possible connection. Sixteen names in total and not an awful lot to go on. Possibly four of them still at the same addresses, two may have relatives still at their old address, others may still be living in the same area. Of the rest, no definite trace, and all randomly scattered across Great Britain. The next day he went to his local Post Office and made a photocopy of his list and sent it off to Samantha, with a brief note attached.

Soon after receiving Jack's update, she rang him again one evening.

'You've made some progress then?'

'A little, not as much as I'd expected. It certainly feels like we have a long way to go. We don't know if we have our target man on this list or not, and it could take ages to work our way through them all and still not have the answer.'

'Jack, this doesn't sound like you, you are normally much more positive.'

He felt a little offended, for him to be accused of a negative attitude was not normal.

'I know, I know. It does start to feel like a tiny needle in a bloody big haystack though, doesn't it? If you think it through, say we find the fellow, what are we going to do, walk up to him and say, "I think you are my Dad"?'

'Not a question I can answer at the moment Jack, it all depends on so many things. I'm not going to be put off now when we've got this far.'

'I'm sorry, that was wrong of me, I shouldn't have said that, but we have set ourselves quite a task, haven't we?'

'Yes, we have. However, I do have something to report from this end.'

'That's more like it! What's that?'

'I told you that I had brought a lot of documents back from Mother's. Well, the short story there is that they are not really relevant to our search, they were all to do with her using a private detective to track down Norman Charlton. He was traced to Brighton, where he was living with another man, relationship not clear. It was to sort out the house ownership, and she was able to buy his half from him at a fairly nominal price. At least I know now that the ownership of the house is clear.'

'That's good for you to know, isn't it?'

'Yes it is. Also, there were couple of envelopes that

had just arrived in the post, which I brought back with me. One was to say that an insurance policy had matured, which is a small bonus. The other was handwritten, addressed to Mrs. Charlton, postmarked Hull, where I don't know anybody. Inside was a scribbled note. I will read it to you.'

'Yes, please.'

'It is not all easy to read but I will tell you what I can decipher.

"Dear Pamela, sorry I have not been in touch for so long, but I have hit hard times. I hope you and your daughter are well, can't say the same for myself." This bit is really scribbled, but I think it says, *"I just wanted to tell you that I haven't forgotten you. Love from B."* That's a capital B. No address or other clues.'

'Wow, what do you make of that, then?' asked Jack.

'It's a real mystery, isn't it? I can't make head nor tail of it, I have no idea who it might be from. Whether it is the man we are looking for, who knows? Or it might be another part of her past we don't know about. Whoever it is seems to know about me, but not my sisters.'

'Hull eh? I've never been there. What I do know is that it seems a long way from anywhere else. He obviously thinks that she will know straight away who he is, if it is a 'he.'

'Oh, I hadn't thought of that, I just assumed that it was a male. Could be an old girlfriend of course, or some distant cousin that I don't know about.'

'It does sound more like an affectionate male, doesn't it?'

'You're right Jack, it does, where he says he hasn't forgotten her, I think that is why I took it for granted that it was a "he".'

There was an extended silence.

'What sort of paper is it written on?' asked Jack.

'Just a piece of lined A4 that has been torn out of a notebook, it's a bit crumpled.'

'Was the envelope stamped?'

'Yes, second class.'

'Well, 'B' is a clue isn't it? The writer clearly expects that Pamela will know who it is. I suppose the nearest suspect to Hull is Mr. Dawson from Sheffield, and he could be a B. I can picture him now, silly moustache and smooth line of chat.'

'That's true,' said Samantha, 'although there are several with a Christian name or a surname, or both, that begin with B. Let's try not to jump to conclusions.'

'Hmm. That period of her life, after you were born and before she married Ken, when was it, from nineteen fifty-five to say, fifty-eight, we don't have much information, do we, and we don't have anybody who can fill it in for us, no brothers or sisters or other family?'

'No we don't,' admitted Samantha.

'But we know Pamela, don't we, that she was never the sort of person to have many hidden relationships, especially if she had a young child?'

'No, you are right. I think it quite possible that this is the person we are seeking.'

'If it is, then it proves that he knew you had been born, although he doesn't use your name. How did that happen, I wonder? We've more questions than answers right now.'

Samantha took a deep breath.

'Jack, there is one of your Number Ones who was in London, Keith Walker, and might still be there. Enfield, I think, I'm not very good on my London geography, is that near you?' she asked.

'Not too far, it's North London, still inside the M25. Is it worth going to look, do you think, what would I learn?'

'Who knows? Keith Walker, he is someone who apparently might still be at the same address.'

'I think Enfield might just be in the London A-Z area, I will check. Same question though, if I go there what am I looking for?'

He sensed Samantha's mind ticking over and he didn't want to criticise her idea.

'I understand what you are saying, but I don't know. It might be nothing, but what type of area is it, how does the house look, is it smart or run down, does it look like the same people have lived there for forty years or so? What sort of car do they have if you can see one? If you saw anyone, just take a note, don't approach them. I know it's not much, but it might make us feel we're getting closer, or you might learn enough to rule him out.'

'OK,' said Jack, 'I'll give it a go. Let me ask you something. The Scotsman, George Bell, he worked for Bluebird Cycles in Nottingham, perhaps he was down on a training course or something. Bluebird are a big outfit, you don't happen to know anyone there who could be able to tell us more about him, perhaps in Personnel or similar?'

Another silence before Samantha answered.

'That's funny, I just might actually. An old boy-friend as it happens, he still works there, I believe. He lives near me, and he is still quite friendly when I see him around. He dumped me, so I reckon he owes me a favour or two!'

'Why would he dump her?' Jack thought.

'Good, we've both got a challenge then, haven't we?'

'Yes, we have, shall we give ourselves a week to follow up, and talk again then?'

'It's a deal.'

CHAPTER 17

Kenton and Enfield, May 1990

DAVID DECIDED TO talk to Jack again but was reluctant to do that while Louise was in the house. He knew what an atmosphere that could create. He waited a few days until Louise had gone to see her parents one evening. He also needed to be sure that Simon and Lucy were safely in their bedrooms, doing their homework. He did not entirely trust them, especially Lucy, to not feedback any overheard conversations to their mother. He felt nervous because, as he reached for the phone, he realised that he did not call his Father that often.

The conversation was not a great success. They had some preliminary banter, in which David asked after his father's health and Jack responded by asking after Louise, Simon and Lucy, by name, in turn. After that Jack, guessing what might be coming, changed tack to ask David his views on the impending reunification of Germany, forcibly expressing his own concerns about the possible risks of a strengthened Germany. A strong European like David was not going to give that much credibility, but it took up a few more minutes and added a certain frisson as he tried to calm Jack's fears of a resurgent united Germany.

'Have you heard any more from that woman, Dad, the one who thinks you are her father?'

'Oh yes, we are in regular contact. We have drawn

up a short list of the most likely candidates and are starting to track them down.'

'For God's sake, what are you getting involved with her for? Honestly Dad, this is only going to end in trouble, you should have more sense.'

David wanted to keep his anger under control, but this was already too much for Jack.

'Don't you talk to me like that, David, you've no right to say such things.'

'But Dad, I'm really not happy about it and I know that Elizabeth will feel the same.'

'Oh, do you? It didn't sound like that when we talked the other night, she was quite sympathetic towards Samantha. She rang me to say that they were hoping to come over later in the year. And I've invited myself to go back with them for a while afterwards.'

David hesitated, knowing that he had gone too far, and that Jack had again successfully diverted the course of the conversation. At a loss to know what to say next, he briefly thought that perhaps he was wrong. He was not comfortable with the idea of being in a minority of one on anything. He could visualise Louise and Elizabeth ganging up together in opposition to him. 'Bloody women,' he thought, but did not say out loud.

Jack took up the running.

'Look, I'm very happy with what I am doing, thank you very much, David. I have no idea about where this is going to take us and that is part of the attraction for me, like a mystery tour. It's a worthwhile project, but we can't say whether we are going to be successful or not. There are all sorts of reasons why we may not be able to track down the man responsible, but we are going to try. And please don't talk to me that way again, you ought to show more respect.'

'OK, sorry. Good night, Dad,' said David and rang off.

JACK PUT HIS head in his hands, it did not make him happy to fall out with his children. David had the ability to upset him, always did have, and now he had become so assured and self-confident. These were characteristics that Jack did not recognise in Margaret and himself. He could only think of Margaret's father as someone who was that way inclined; he had carried himself with a degree of arrogance, usually misplaced in Jack's opinion.

'Oh dear,' he said out loud, 'is it really worth it? I've put myself in a position where I am going to upset someone now, whatever I do.'

Jack had found that he often talked out loud to himself since Margaret died, it made him feel as if he had company. He had turned the TV volume down when David had rung him, and the images were still flickering silently across the screen. He had no appetite for that now and switched off.

'I'm too far in now, I couldn't possibly pull out having taken things this far, I couldn't do that to Samantha, the poor girl is on her own, she would be heartbroken. Whether she is my daughter or not.'

With David living in different world from him, and Elizabeth being halfway across the globe, he could now sense that he was becoming closer to Samantha than to his own children.

'How did that happen?' he thought, 'Maybe she's come along to fill a gap in my life. But I am only a means to an end for her. Say we find her real father, she won't want me around any longer then, will she? And he certainly won't. Would it just be easier to tell her that I am her Dad, I won't lose her that way?'

THE NEXT MORNING, Jack went ahead with his commitment and got off the train at Enfield Town station, buying a local map at a nearby newsagents. The address that he had for Keith Walker was about a fifteen-minute walk away.

The road where Keith Walker had lived, or still might live, was in a very respectable area, made up mainly of semi-detached houses built in the 1930s, nearly all of which he thought would be owner occupied. It ended in a cul-de-sac and had a small parade of shops, with a newsagent and general store, a hairdresser and a launderette. Two young women, with push-chairs and toddlers in hand, were chatting outside the shops. There was little traffic. In general, the houses were well maintained, hedges neatly trimmed, and lawns mowed. On its drive one house had a big camper van and another had a large caravan. 'I'm glad I don't have one of those outside my front window,' thought Jack.

When he came to Keith's address there was nothing to make it stand out from the others. There was a W-suffix registration Ford Cortina on the tarmac drive, clean and tidy, about ten years old. New style PVC windows and doors had been fitted, and a porch added; the house looked well cared for. The front garden was neat but minimalist, a lawn, a low laurel hedge at the front, and a flower bed with a few shrubs under the bay window, which carried a Neighbourhood Watch sticker. Unobtrusive curtains downstairs, Venetian blinds upstairs. A tall fence and a back gate hid the rear of the house from view. You would think that the owners could have lived there for quite a while.

Jack walked past, trying not to stare, and then walked back again, but there was no sign of any activity at the house. Two elderly women, pushing wheeled shopping baskets, came towards him, making him feel uncomfortable in lingering longer. They didn't have any inhibitions in giving him the once over as they went by, ready with a full description for the police if they should be asked if they had seen any suspicious strangers hanging about. He stopped and looked back, only to see that they had done the same. He hurried on.

At the shops, little had changed. The same two women were still talking outside the shops, but their children were showing distinct signs of impatience, pulling on their arms.

With nothing else obvious to do, he walked back towards the station. He found a café and stopped for a bacon sandwich and a coffee, before embarking on his journey home. If he took a taxi he could have been home much quicker, perhaps about fifteen miles, but such an extravagant thought would never cross Jack's mind. Enfield was not an area of London with which he was familiar, but it seemed little different from his home areas of Kenton and Harrow. Similar people were going about similar business. The bank across the road was busy, people going in and out, and he was reminded of David's early days in local banking. You had to give the boy credit, he had come a long way from there. Jack saw a builder's lorry going by, belonging to one of Gladwin's best customers, and he found that strangely reassuring.

'What,' he wondered, 'have I learnt today? Nothing positive really. Only what we already knew that I'm not going to find a bloke standing outside his house asking if I'm looking for him. We have no idea if Keith Walker is our man, but if he is, he may well still be at that address. But he could be dead, his widow might still live there and hasn't chosen to change the entry in the phone book. Some women won't do that, they feel that a woman's name is more likely to attract obnoxious callers or criminal interest, if it looks as if she might be there on her own. Or both Keith and his wife, if he had ever had one, might be dead and their son, perhaps named Kevin Walker, has moved in. Who knows, it's all guesswork, really isn't it? Better not talk to Samantha like this or she will accuse me of being negative again. Can't have that. I wonder how she's getting on with her own little project.'

He caught the train back to Liverpool Street and gazed out of the window. His life had certainly changed, but was it for the better? Or was he too far in now?

CHAPTER 18

Derby, October 1989

WHEN SAMANTHA HAD taken Adam to see Dr. Bhatti at the Royal Infirmary, she was not sure what to expect. Both the doctor who had come to Adam's school and their own GP had been very vague about any problem, if indeed there was one. She was concerned that for him to be referred on to a consultant indicated that there could be something seriously wrong. Frustrated at the lack of information, she carried with her a nagging fear of impending bad news.

It was a typical scene in Outpatients, a hustle and bustle of staff coming and going, people's names being called out. Some were not there, others were there but didn't hear or couldn't understand a Derbyshire inflection on their name, causing confusion. Patients in wheelchairs, others on walking frames, some leaning heavily on sticks. Phones rang constantly and the two prim middle-aged women on the reception desk were clearly exasperated and finding it difficult to keep their composure, ensuring that all patients checked in with them.

Adam tended to go into his shell on such public occasions. He had found a children's book on space travel, and he absorbed himself in that, staying silent. Samantha hid behind a discarded copy of the '*Sun*' from two days before and flicked through it without really taking in any information. This way she avoided eye-contact with any patient who was keen to share their full medical history with her.

Eventually, some twenty minutes after their appointment time, Adam's name was called. A woman in a white coat and black trousers led them down a long dingy passage, past several other consulting rooms, before turning into one right at the end of the corridor. Her name badge revealed her to be Dr. Bhatti, Consultant Neurologist. She was not what Samantha had envisaged. This doctor was a slim, elegant lady, like Samantha in her mid-thirties, with spectacular long earrings, her dark hair held back in a ponytail tied by a purple velvet band. Visible on her desk was a small picture of a good-looking man with two young children.

She introduced herself, her voice was quite low and perfectly enunciated. They both mouthed a 'Hello' in return. She asked Adam to take off his anorak, T-shirt, jeans, shoes and socks and put on a gown. This he did shyly, turning his back on her. She then motioned them into the two available chairs, putting Adam in the one nearer to her. She spoke directly to him.

'You are seven, is that right?'

'Well, I'm eight next week, actually.'

'Oh yes, sorry. Happy Birthday for then anyway.' Turning to Samantha, 'You know that Adam has been referred to us after tests at his school and by your GP. What have you been told so far?'

'Not a lot, they've not been very informative at all,' replied Samantha. 'There seems to be some sort of problem with his reflexes, but nobody has taken the trouble to be very specific with us yet.'

The doctor nodded to acknowledge her frustration, then took from her desk a small hammer with a rubber head. She smiled at Adam.

'Don't worry, I'm not going to hurt you.'

'They've done it to me before,' the boy said.

Dr. Bhatti beat a tattoo on many parts of his body; not just his knees, but his biceps, his elbows and his wrists, followed by his ankles. Adam did not seem to move or react very much. Dr. Bhatti turned to Samantha.

'That's why we think there is a problem, Mrs. Jenkins, the normal reaction is for the hammer to bring some sort of reflex responses and I'm not seeing very much. How is he generally in moving and walking about?'

'Sometimes I call him Camel Foot because he does seem clumsy and he tends to trip over things, but I think that is because he just doesn't look where he is going. You're OK playing football with your mates, aren't you?'

Adam looked crestfallen.

'I like to play but I'm not very good. I'm always about the last one to be picked when we're choosing sides and then they put me in goal.'

'Oh dear, that's disappointing, isn't it?' said Dr. Bhatti.

'Yes,' said Adam, very firmly.

Samantha looked surprised. 'I didn't know that,' she said.

Once again the doctor leant forward to feel around his feet and then lifted them up, one after the other. She stroked his soles and asked if that hurt. He said not.

'Will you please just walk up and down the room for me a few times?'

Adam did as he had been asked, looking very self-conscious as he did so, as if he was walking a tightrope, glancing across at his mother.

'Thank you, you can put everything back on now.'

Adam again turned his back and put on his jeans before removing the gown.

Turning again to Samantha, she said, 'Does he have any decreased sensitivity, such as handling anything very hot or cold?'

'I haven't noticed anything.'

'Does he get restless leg in bed, or leg cramps?'

'I don't think so.'

'Does he complain of any muscle pain?'

Samantha looked at Adam who shook his head but said nothing.

Dr. Bhatti sat back in her chair and looked straight at Samantha.

'Mrs. Jenkins, do you know if anyone in your family has had any problems with their legs or feet? On your side or his father's side?'

This was the sort of question that Samantha had feared.

'On my husband's side nothing that I know of. Not him or his parents, or even his grandparents, although I would have to check with him on that.' She swallowed hard. 'My husband and I are separated, you see. My own mother died from Alzheimer's last year, but she was physically very fit. She didn't have brothers or sisters, and I can't remember her parents having any problems, they had died before I was born.' She paused again. 'I don't know who my father is, so I can't tell you there.'

She looked straight back at the doctor. Adam stared at his mother.

'Oh, I see, I'm sorry.' Dr. Bhatti paused.

'Well, that's how it is.'

Dr. Bhatti cleared her throat and sat forward again. Her right hand picked up the rubber hammer, tapped it on the table a couple of times and then put it back down. She spoke again.

'I am afraid this is still all going to sound rather vague to you, but please let me explain as best I can.

Adam responds to the tests in ways that are not normal, but there can be many different reasons for this. We will take some X-rays and do some other tests today, but I doubt if they will show us much.

'I don't want to alarm you by listing all the possible causes of his condition, because most of them are very remote. However, there is one diagnosis which is very plausible, and that is something with a very strange name, called Charcot-Marie-Tooth disease, CMT we call it. It's nothing to do with his teeth, those are the names of the three doctors who identified it first, over a hundred years ago.'

Samantha took Adam's hand and drew him towards her.

'Adam's not on any medication, is he?'

'No.'

'CMT is a genetic condition, usually inherited. It can cause nerve damage, weakening the muscles, but sometimes may have little or no effect on the person who has it. However, it could also have serious symptoms, although it does not reduce life expectancy. Have you heard of something called "foot drop"?'

Samantha thought she had, so she nodded.

'That is one of the most obvious symptoms, but please don't assume that is going to happen to Adam, we have a long way to go yet. However, he is quite young for any symptoms to be already showing. His feet have quite high arches, which might be significant.'

'Is there a cure?' asked Samantha.

'No there isn't.'

Samantha put her other hand to her mouth and then fiddled with her jacket collar. Dr. Bhatti pressed on.

'But we do have ways of controlling the condition. I do apologise, but I have to come back to this question of your family history. This disease is invariably inherited but can miss out generations and there are often carriers who don't even know that they have it. We are still learning about this disease and advances in genetic testing now give us some hope for better diagnosis in the future.

'If you were able to track down your father and any other children that he may have had, it would be helpful for us to know their medical background. Perhaps we could be able to carry out some tests on them as it comes in many different forms? If we find they have incidences of the disease, that will make it much more likely that Adam has CMT, but it still won't be certain. If there is nobody there with symptoms, CMT isn't necessarily ruled out, but we would also have to look at other possibilities.'

The doctor sat back, as if waiting for a response, which was forthcoming from Samantha, who felt the need to unburden herself of the whole story.

'My mother's first husband left her, and I was born three or so years after. When I was four she remarried and had two more daughters, who don't seem to have any of these problems, and neither do I. Mum would never speak about who my father might be. After her first husband cleared off, she took in lodgers, men such as commercial travellers, who would stay with her for an odd day or a week or longer.'

Dr. Bhatti shifted uneasily in her chair and picked up the hammer again, tapping it against the palm of her other hand. 'I really appreciate you telling me all of this, thank you. If you could track him down and report back to us, that would help us. CMT is not tremendously rare, it affects about one person in three thousand, so there are probably sixty or more sufferers here in Derby itself.'

'I understand,' said Samantha, who was still holding Adam's hand tightly. 'I will try to see if I can find out anything about my father. In any case, I would like to know who he is. If it's inherited, could it affect Adam's children?'

'It might.'

Samantha looked again straight at Dr. Bhatti.

'Not that I am planning anything, you understand, but if I had other children, they could have it as well?'

'Again, they might but it is not certain. And that is only if we confirm that he has CMT. Please, I want to be clear, I am keeping an open mind here. It could be CMT, but I am not pre-judging anything. However, it would simplify the matter, narrowing down the options considerably, to know more of your history.'

'Thank you for being straight with us, Doctor, I do appreciate that.'

'Right,' said the doctor, glancing at the clock. 'We will take X-rays and do some other tests while you are here. We will make another appointment for about a month's time and see what we know then. Adam, just behave as normal. Play your football, get plenty of exercise, that's important.'

TWO HOURS LATER Adam and his mother were sitting in the hospital coffee bar, having a sandwich lunch.

'What did you think of Doctor Bhatti, then?' asked Samantha.

'I thought she was very nice,' replied Adam, 'she was more friendly than some of the others.'

'Yes, and she didn't beat about the bush like some doctors.'

After a brief pause Adam asked, 'Mum, what's a sympump?'

'A symptom. When you have an illness, it's something that shows that you have it. Like if you have the flu, you start shivering, can't get warm. When you had chickenpox, you remember that you came out in spots, they were symptoms of it.'

Adam considered this for a few more minutes. Samantha waited for him.

'You know she asked you about your Dad, and you said you didn't know?'

'Yes?'

'Granny's husband that died, wasn't he your Dad?'

'Ken? No, he wasn't.'

Samantha realised that this could turn into a full-scale exposition of the facts of life before an interested audience in the coffee bar and she was determined not to go down that route.

'Don't you worry about that now, we'll talk about it some other day. Who are Forest playing this Saturday?'

Adam frowned, 'I'm not sure.'

'They're away at Chelsea,' said a little elderly man in a cloth cap, authoritatively, sitting alone at the next table. 'I've got them down for a draw.'

CHAPTER 19

Kenton, June 1990

JACK FELT NERVOUS but could not quite understand why. Samantha had rung him to say that she was coming back down to Watford again. Was it OK to come and see him again and did he mind if she brought her friend Jenny with her? He could hardly say no to either question, but he was uneasy about the addition of Jenny, as he tried to understand Samantha's wish to bring her along. A witness or a chaperone, perhaps? If she had something to tell him that would make him unhappy, would she feel the need to be accompanied? Maybe it was just Jenny's curiosity to meet him: after all, she would have heard quite a lot about him. Or perhaps, she had her own views about their search, good or bad, and wanted to put in her own two-penn'orth?

It had been the briefest of phone calls, hardly a 'how are you?', no questions as to his progress, just 'can Jenny and I come on Saturday afternoon at three to see you? OK, good, see you then.'

Three o'clock, well that was definitely cup of tea time. He had been to Marks and Spencer and bought some of their best chocolate biscuits. And then he worried if that was either not enough or over the top.

On the day he stationed himself in his front bed-room window and, just after three, he saw a neat blue Mini making its way up the road, then pull up outside his house. He realised that coming with Jenny meant that Samantha did not have to make her way from Watford by public transport. He saw a neat, trim figure in jeans climb out briskly from the driver's side and skip round to the pavement in the time that it took Samantha to vacate the passenger seat. They stood and looked up at his house for a moment and he had to step away sharply from the window.

He was still coming down the stairs when the doorbell rang, so he did not keep them waiting long.

'Hello, Jack how are you doing?' asked Samantha. 'Meet Jenny.'

He was never sure how to greet Samantha when they met, they did not make any sort of physical contact or show of affection. With Jenny he reverted to his failsafe mode and shook her hand, which seemed to surprise her.

'Welcome,' he said, 'please come on in,' and stood aside to usher them into his lounge. 'Please sit yourselves down. Cup of tea, girls?'

'Yes, please,' answered Samantha briskly for both of them, 'one without milk, no sugar in either.'

'Coming up.' He could hear them talking softly to each other while he was in the kitchen, without being able to hear anything specific. He took in a tray with three cups and a plate with some of the chocolate biscuits.

'Oh, you are honoured Jenny, chocolate biscuits, I don't usually get these.'

The two women had seated themselves side by side on his settee, leaving him his favourite chair. He and Jenny studied each other unobtrusively. She was shorter and slighter than Samantha, with blue eyes and a blonde ponytail.

'How long have you two known each other?' he inquired.

Jenny answered, 'Since primary school, Mrs. Slack's class, wasn't it?' Her Midlands accent was not as pronounced as Samantha's.

'It was many, many years ago,' said Samantha.

'How long have you been in Watford?' asked Jack.

'Coming up for five years now, I think.'

'Do you like it?'

'Watford's not bad, but I love my job there, I am a theatre nurse,' said Jenny, with some pride.

Jack winced inwardly, thinking of his own recent hospital experience, he had great admiration for people who could do such work.

'Good for you,' he said. He waited to see if they were going to speak first. He glanced at them and saw that it was up to him.

'Jenny, are you up to speed with what she and I are working on?'

'I am.'

'And what do you think about it?'

'I support it one hundred percent, I think it is really important for her to find out what she can.'

Jack quickly told them what he had found in Enfield, looking for Keith Walker, saying that it had been very inconclusive, but they should not rule out the possibility that he might still live there.

'Did you have any joy with your old boyfriend, if you'll pardon the expression?'

Samantha smiled, while Jenny looked surprised.

'Tell me more,' said Jenny, 'she hasn't told me about this bit.'

'Do you remember Darren Thompson that I used to go out with for a while, dropped me for Tracy Wass?' Jenny nodded.

'Well, I forgot to tell you that I'd rung him. He's done all right for himself and Tracy, and he doesn't live far away from me. I see him round the local market sometimes on a Saturday morning with his three kids. When he left school, he took a job in the offices at Bluebird Cycles, got some qualifications and he has worked his way up the management ladder, he is now someone important in Personnel, or Human Relations as he likes to call it.'

Samantha took a big sip of tea.

'Jack found out that one of our possibles was a Scotsman, George Bell, who worked for Bluebird. You thought that he might have been down on a course, didn't you Jack?'

'I did.'

'Well, I plucked up courage to ring Darren. Tracy answered, which was a little unfortunate, when you're landed with three kids, you don't want old girlfriends ringing up, do you?'

'I always thought she was bit stuck-up, Tracy, didn't you? I wondered if Darren would be good enough for her,' said Jenny.

'She was all right about it, passed me straight over to him. I told him the background and asked him if he knew the name of George Bell. He made a feeble joke about it possibly ringing with him, at least I think it was a joke. He said he didn't know, but he could check the files, as long as I didn't make a habit of it.'

'That was noble of him,' said Jenny. She gave Jack a knowing look. 'She hasn't told me about this bit, I wonder why?'

Samantha blushed and put her tongue out at her.

'Anyway, as I was saying, that was fair enough. A couple of nights later, he rang me back and it's a really sad story. George Bell joined Bluebird as a salesman in the spring of nineteen fifty-five, came down to Nottingham for training for two weeks and was then killed in a car crash when he was driving back to Glasgow. Apparently they said at the inquest that they thought that he had fallen asleep when he was nearly home, he hit a lorry head-on.'

'Oh blimey,' said Jack, 'cross him off the list then.'

Jenny was not ready to let the subject of Darren drop.

'What does he look like now then, young Darren, has he lasted well?'

Samantha smiled. 'He still a good-looking guy, keeps himself fit, but I am sure he and I would not have worked out in the long run. I think he would irritate me no end.'

There was long silence and Jack wanted to bring the conversation back to the job in hand.

'Where does that leave us then?'

Samantha reached into her rucksack and pulled out an envelope, taking out the message inside and laying them both on the coffee table. It was the letter addressed to Pamela from Hull, which Jack had not yet seen. He picked up both envelope and letter and studied them closely.

'What do you make of that then, Inspector Clouseau?' asked Samantha with a mischievous grin. Jack responded by pretending to pull out a magnifying glass to peer at them and grinned back at her.

'Very interesting,' he said, 'you don't know anyone in Hull?'

'Can't think of anyone,' replied Samantha. Jack compared the envelope and the note.

'The envelope is written with a different pen from the note, blue ink and not black. Makes you think they were written at different times. They are both in the same hand, although the envelope is all capital letters.'

'Do you think that is significant?' asked Jenny.

'I've no idea,' replied Jack. 'The note looks scribbled, as if it has been written in a hurry, or perhaps he, if it is a he, had been drinking. I am no expert, but it does look more like a man's writing than a woman's. You didn't see anything else like this in the papers you found?'

'No,' replied Samantha.

'So, if there had been previous notes, it does not seem that Pamela thought them to be worth keeping, does it?'

'It's so frustrating because we need to know for your Adam's sake, don't we?' said Jenny.

'What do you mean, for Adam's sake?' asked Jack. Samantha grimaced and glanced at Jenny.

Samantha briefly gave him Adam's CMT story.

Jack got up from his chair and stared out of the window for a while.

'I see,' he said, 'thank you for telling me that.'

'Does that change anything for you?' asked Samantha.

'No, I think it makes it even more important to sort this out. Is his condition serious?'

'Not at the moment, but there could be problems for him in the longer term. He can be treated but it would help to know if anyone else in the family tree, as it were, has suffered and, if so, how they fared.'

'I understand even better now why you are so keen to find out who your Dad was,' said Jack.

For a while it had appeared that Jenny was becoming impatient, with something on her mind, and she could not hold back any longer. She sat up straight and put her hands on the knees of her jeans.

'Jack, I must ask you this direct question, is it physically possible that you are Samantha's father?'

Now Jack understood why Jenny had come, it was to ask that question, he thought they had worked out their tactics in advance. Samantha had looked away from Jenny while she spoke but did not appear surprised. Whether it was also planned to make the disclosure about Adam's condition was not so clear, it felt as if that had slipped out accidentally.

Jack shifted in his seat, took off his glasses to wipe his right hand across his brow, then put them on again.

'Fair enough,' he said, 'you've been open with me, so let me tell you the story as much as I can remember. Just bear in mind the fact that it was a very long time ago, before you two were born. This is how I remember things, right or wrong.'

CHAPTER 20

Nottingham, September 1955

THERE'S THIS CHAP Bob Dawson staying at Pamela's, who is someone that I have taken an immediate dislike to. This doesn't happen very often. I try to give people the benefit of the doubt, but there are a few who put you off straightaway. He's arrogant, what I would call smarmy, super smooth but with a wicked glint in his eye. Good looking, tall, dark and handsome, you might say. Definitely a bloke who thinks he is a cut above the rest of us, but still not a man you would trust enough to buy a second-hand car from. I asked him where he was from and he just grinned and said, 'Down South'. I asked him what line he was in, and he grinned again, saying that he was in 'Commercial Business'. He's never asked anything about me.

Back in May he had only stayed a couple of nights but now he's back for a couple of weeks. I have started to feel uncomfortable about the way he talks to Pamela when she brings us our dinner in the evening. You know, familiar and suggestive, and I could see that she doesn't care for it either. Nothing that you could really take offence at, but what might be called 'innuendo'. I have said something to him about courtesy to our hostess and he called me 'an old prude'. I have spoken to Pamela about Bob, but she just shrugged it off, saying that she was used to people like him, and she knew how to deal with them.

Last Thursday night, I'd gone for a walk after dinner, mainly to get away from Bob, but also to go to the phone box to call Margaret. When I got back, well after nine o'clock I would think, Bob was standing in the kitchen doorway talking with Pamela, and it's very unusual for any of us to go in there. I have always felt it was her private territory.

I looked round the door and caught Pamela's eye. She was putting cutlery in the drawer while she was talking to Bob, sideways on. She made a point of saying 'Hello, Jack, had a good walk?' so that Bob, who had his back to me, knew I had come in. He was leaning against the doorjamb with his arms folded, quite nonchalant and casual. He just looked round at me, but didn't say anything, then turned his back again. Pamela gave me a quick smile, as if to say that she was OK, so I wished them 'Good night' and set off to go up to my room. As I went she just said, 'Usual time in the morning, Jack?' although we had discussed that earlier. It was as if she was just telling me that everything was all right.

It wasn't as if their voices were raised or anything like that. I just had the impression that Bob had gone where he was not wanted, and Pamela was giving him the brush-off.

I'm in my usual room, the back bedroom, next to Pamela's. Bob has been in the room upstairs. I have never had any trouble sleeping here, as I've always had a busy day. So, I was already fast asleep when I was jerked awake by a knocking at my door. I don't know how much time had passed by then. It was Pamela, saying 'Jack, Jack, can I come in please?' quite urgently. I opened the door, and she was standing there with her dressing gown wrapped tight around her. She looked like I had never seen her before, really anxious and flustered. 'Please let me in,' she said, 'I can explain.'

I was a bit embarrassed and grabbed my own dressing gown and shut the door behind her. We both sat on the double bed, opposite sides, and she started to cry, quietly. 'What's up?' I said or something to that effect. 'It's Bob,' she said, 'he won't leave me alone.'

None of these rooms have locks, not even Pamela's. I asked what she wanted to do, and she said it was to stay with me that night. Well, I didn't know what to think, I wasn't sure what she was asking me.

What could I do? I couldn't refuse her. I asked if she wanted me to do anything about Bob, but she said she didn't want any trouble. So, I told her to stay round the other side of the bed, so that I was nearer the door. We got into bed, she snuggled up to me, just for a moment, told me that I was a true gentleman and then I'm sure we must both have turned our backs on each other. A few minutes later, I heard Bob come downstairs and open Pamela's bedroom door, switch on the light, curse in a very foul way, and slam the door shut again. I was terrified that he was going to come into my room, but he waited for a moment and then I heard him go back upstairs. I was awake for a long time, worried that Bob might come back. I couldn't tell if Pamela was asleep or not.

I AWOKE WHEN my alarm went off on Friday morning, and she was already gone, still warm on her side of the bed. I could hear her, as normal, preparing breakfast in the kitchen below. At breakfast there was no sign of Bob, but Brian, the other fellow staying, from Blackpool I think, was there, so I couldn't have a private conversation with Pamela. I just asked her 'How are you this morning?' like I usually did and got the regular answer that she was fine, although I think she might have added 'thank you very much' to that.

As usual on a Friday I took my suitcase with me to Colwick so I could go direct to the station to catch the train back home to London that evening. I couldn't get her off my mind all weekend, wondering if she was OK, and it now seems that Bob has been here all the time. Margaret was really short with me as she has had another difficult week with David, and I suppose I've appeared distracted. I thought about ringing Pamela to see if she was all right but what could she say if Bob was there?

This morning I went directly from the station to Colwick, like any other Monday morning. So I haven't seen Pamela until I came back here to hers tonight. Bob's here at dinner, silly smirk on his face but somehow showing me a bit more respect than before. Pamela is just the same as normal.

Has anything untoward happened over the weekend? If I ask Pamela, what is she going to say? She isn't going to want to do anything that will affect her business. I just feel awful and helpless about the whole thing. Perhaps I am assuming the worst, and everything is going to be OK. Perhaps.

CHAPTER 21

Kenton and Watford, June 1990

'THAT'S MY STORY, at least that's how I remember it. I've never ever told this to anyone before, out of respect for Pamela as much as trying to protect myself. You'll realise that I couldn't ever have told this to Margaret. Up to you if you believe me or not, but I hope you can see now why I haven't committed myself to anything so far.'

There was now a long silence, deep breaths being taken all round. Jack finished his tea and biscuit. Samantha and Jenny looked at each other and sighed. Eventually, Samantha spoke.

'Thank you Jack for that,' said Samantha, 'I know it can't have been at all easy for you to tell us that. I am going to take you at your word because I trust you and it sounded completely honest.' She sobbed for a moment and put a tissue to her eyes.

Jenny picked up the flow.

'My first thought is, was a crime committed against your mum that weekend and are you the result of it?'

'That is what I have been thinking all along,' said Jack.

'Bloody hell,' said Samantha and sobbed again. Jenny put her arm around her and looked at Jack.

'Yes, thank you Jack,' she said, 'I don't know what else to say. That was very brave of you.'

Even Jack had to brush away a tear now.

'Look at us lot,' said Samantha, 'what a bunch of cry-babies we are.'

NOTHING WAS SAID for a while, until Samantha spoke.

'What do you think Jack? This was nineteen fifty-five after all, if something violent had happened to her, would my Mum have just stayed schtum and not said anything to anybody? Would she have not wanted the police involved because it might affect her business and they might not believe her anyway?'

'I think it is very possible, especially knowing her,' replied Jack.

Samantha went on. 'I am going to say this because I don't think that you will, it is also possible that if something did happen that weekend, it was with her consent. Either way, she was very unlucky if she got pregnant as a result. Of course, no such thing as the Pill then and no reason for her to be on it, if it had existed.'

Jenny said, 'Now she's gone, there's only one person who can tell us about events that weekend, when you weren't there. And he might still not be the answer to our quest.'

'No,' said Samantha, 'that's true. And if it was Bob who has sent the letter from Hull, it implies that he believes there was a sort of friendly relationship between them, doesn't it?'

'It does, at least from his point of view,' chipped in Jenny. 'I can really see Jack why you haven't committed yourself about this, or not denying that it just might have been you, am I right?'

'Yes, I don't think it was, but it just could have been. Certain things that happen in your life that you just try to erase from your memory, if you can. Others stick with you, but you can't be sure that you are remembering them right.'

Samantha had a way about her that made it clear when conversations were at an end. She collected the cups and saucers, and the few remaining biscuits, and took the tray out to the kitchen. When she came back she said, ‘You’ve given me so much to think about, Jack, I need to collect my thoughts. I’m wondering now if I still want to pursue this. I don’t want to say any more for the moment.’

There was no hesitation about how to say goodbye this time. Both girls flung their arms around Jack and Samantha even gave him a peck on the cheek.

‘Thanks so much Jack. I will be in touch soon, I promise,’ she said.

Jenny lingered longer to say, ‘It might not seem like it at the moment, but I think that helps us to understand your position, thank you.’ She squeezed his hand.

He stood on the doorstep to watch them go and waved them off as Jenny turned her car round to head back to Watford. With her usual perfect timing, Mrs. Hodges happened to be just going past, out on patrol, walking her horrible little yappy dog this time. She stopped and turned to watch the car go by.

Jack closed the door and slumped back in his chair, a load off his mind. He had mixed feelings; anger that he been provoked into telling his story before he was ready, but also a sense of relief that he had finally told it to someone. He felt totally exhausted by the episode.

AS JENNY DROVE Samantha back to her flat in Watford, they were both silent for a while until they came to a halt at some traffic lights.

‘That was a stunner, wasn’t it?’ said Jenny, ‘poor bloke, he has been living with that story for thirty-five years.’

Samantha still didn’t speak.

'You do believe him, don't you?' persisted Jenny.

'I don't think he would invent a story like that, not when it might incriminate him or someone else. Is it "The Whole Truth and Nothing But The Truth," as they say? Is it really the whole story? Is he leaving something out, is he putting something in? Can we fully trust his memory? It's a story with so many implications.'

She fell silent again and Jenny drove on. All that Samantha added was, 'I need a drink.'

'Shall we go round to the pub when we get back?' asked Jenny.

'I think that's a good idea,' replied Samantha.

JENNY BOUGHT TWO large white wines. It was now early evening, and the pub wasn't crowded, so they could settle themselves in a quiet corner. Still Samantha did not speak, watching the traffic on the busy road outside.

She took her time to answer when Jenny asked her, 'What are you thinking now?'

'My mind is still in a whirl. Don't quiz me on this one yet, but part of me is still saying that perhaps Jack hasn't told us the whole story. He hadn't told us this before, is there anything else that we still haven't heard? Did she really spend the night with him? He was a married man, and now he is saying that he can't distinguish between what did happen and what might have happened. Or what he would have liked to have happened, come to that.'

'OK. What else?'

'As I see it now, the main alternatives are: One, that this man Dawson forced himself onto my mother, she didn't go to the police for whatever reason, and I am the product of that. Two, she consented to him making love to her unprotected and was unlucky to become pregnant. Three, something else happened that weekend, or thereabouts, and someone else, who could be Jack, is responsible.'

'We know from the timing that it must have happened around that time, give or take a week or two, either way.'

'Correct, so the most likely is Dawson, option one or two, but also the third option, but probably only if it is Jack. I've looked at the receipt books and Dawson did stay over the weekend. There was someone else there that Thursday night, but that was the only night that person ever stayed.'

'If we find the right man, he is unlikely to admit to rape and will claim that it was consensual.'

'Yes, the only witness we have is Jack with what he says happened that night. Nobody's ever going to court about this, it's too long ago and, in the end, probably just one man's word against another's. And, shocking though it is to think of my mum in that situation, that is not what I want to happen, I just want to know who my Dad is, or was.'

THEY BOTH TOOK a long sip of wine.

'I have a really good reason to continue.'

'Adam?'

'Yes, my Adam,' replied Samantha. 'I am so worried about what the future might hold for him, and for me, come to that. I just hate to think of him struggling and being potentially a cripple.'

'That's a plenty good enough reason. So, what's next?'

Samantha realised that Jenny's persistent interrogation was helping her to clarify her feelings.

'Look, first of all, thank you so much for taking me

over today. As we thought it might, it moved Jack on a step. Just the fact of you being there. I doubt if he would have revealed what he did if you hadn't asked him outright, not yet anyway. You've been an absolute brick so far. Without my Jenny and my Jack, I wouldn't have got anywhere yet, I know that. But, as to where we go from here, I need more time to think, suddenly it has all become deeper and darker.'

Samantha took her mother's photographs from her handbag and pushed the one with three men across the table.

'Have a look at that.'

'Which one?'

'Guess.'

Jenny looked closely. 'The one on the right?'

'Why did you pick him?' asked Samantha.

'Because he looks like the sort of man that every girl's mother warns them about. Smooth, too confident of his attraction to women.'

'Yes, that's Bob Dawson, the man we are talking about.'

Jenny studied the picture again, and then at Samantha.

'I don't see any great resemblance to you, to be honest. He's conventionally handsome, like a man on the cover of a Mills and Boon, and you can be a very good looking girl, when you put your mind to it, but he doesn't leap off the page as being your Dad. Perhaps if you met him, and could see his mannerisms, the way he walks and so on, it might be different. And don't forget, he is now thirty-five years older, so he won't look like this. I also can't say that I see any great resemblance to Jack in you, either. Did you say that you had a picture of him from then as well?'

Samantha showed Jenny the photo of Jack at the pub. She looked at it, then at Samantha, then back at the photo.

'It's hard to realise that he was around the same age there as we are now. He looks such a decent guy, doesn't he? Open and straightforward, I quite fancy him myself. If I had to choose a boyfriend from between him and Dawson, I know which I would pick,' said Jenny with a grin.

'And would it be the same one that you pick to have as a father?'

'Hmm, yes, I see what you mean. One could be a short-term fling choice, but you would like to settle down with the other. Is that what you are thinking?'

Samantha nodded positively. They finished their drinks and went back to Jenny's flat.

BACK IN KENTON, next morning, Jack was also reflecting on their meeting and wondering how much to believe of what he had been told about Samantha's son's condition. He had not intended to tell his story at this stage, and he realised that Jenny's direct questioning had been a factor in prompting him. Whether that had been Samantha's plan or not, he had no way of knowing. He could not think of any other reason why she had set up the meeting in the way that she did. The previous night, he had been quite angry, to think that he had been provoked into spilling the beans, as it were, but now he felt some relief at a burden, if not completely lifted, then at least now shared. He just hoped that they accepted what he had told them.

He had been very moved by Adam's story and hoped that was true. For him it certainly made Samantha's intensity in pursuing her mission much more credible. It was understandable that for her only child to have the potential threat of a serious illness was a great motivator. Jack related it to his own feelings if one of his grandchildren had a similar problem. Now it seemed that his life had gone from being empty to being overfull. From having nothing much beyond the mundane to think about, his mind was now crowded with many thoughts, some swirling away from him before he could get a proper grip on them.

As he often did at such times, he escaped out to his workshop, at the end of his garden. One advantage it had was that neither the phone or the doorbell could be heard from there, and he wasn't ready for a call from anyone right now: not Samantha, and certainly not David or Brenda, and it wasn't the right time of day for Elizabeth to call. Margaret had used to tell callers, 'He is down in his shelter, I don't know when he will emerge again, but I expect to see him for his lunch.'

'Where do we go from here?' he asked himself, 'We aren't any further forward than we were a week ago, not to find the man we are looking for, anyway. Going to Enfield didn't tell me much that I didn't know already but seeing Keith Walker's house made it all seem more real. I could have knocked on the door and who knows, if he still lived there and had come to the door, I could have had the answer five minutes later.'

'Yes,' he thought, 'and I could also have come away with a punch on the nose!'

He switched on the power and took a length of oak and started to saw it into the right size pieces to make more of his engines.

CHAPTER 22

Kenton, July 1990

A FEW DAYS later, in the evening, Jack's phone rang again, it was his daughter Elizabeth calling from New Zealand. After an initial conversation, checking that everyone was well, she confirmed the dates for their visit to the UK, two months ahead.

'We come in to Heathrow, David will pick us up and we will stay with him and Louise for five days and he says he'll bring you over during that time. Is that all right with you?'

'Oh, definitely, it will be lovely to see you again and for us all to be together. I think your Mum would be pleased to know we have done that, don't you?'

'Yes Dad, she would. I want Fiona and Kelly to get to know England better. Who knows, they may want to come over there to study at some time.'

'That's a nice idea,' said Jack, 'I hadn't thought of that.'

'Anyway,' continued Elizabeth, 'after that we are going up to Yorkshire to Howard's parents, where you'd be very welcome. You're invited, Dad, as Norma and Trevor would love to see you again, they are asking us to take you up there when we go.'

'Really? That's very nice of them, I would like to see them as well. I didn't get to spend as much time with them at the wedding as I would have liked, so that would be good. I thought Trevor seemed to be a really good bloke.'

'Yes, he says he'll take you to his local.'

'Great, tell him it's my round first.'

'We can all stay with them for a week, then come back to David's for a couple of nights before we fly back. Now the big question, are you still wanting to come back home with us?'

'Yes, please, if you'll have me.'

'Of course,' replied Elizabeth, 'now the second big question, have you got a passport?'

'Oh, blimey, I've never thought about that. No, I haven't.'

'Well, you better get a move on and get one or they won't let you into New Zealand. Or you won't be able to get back in to the UK afterwards. I will book your tickets from this end, you'll be our guest, is that understood?'

'You don't have to do that, love. I can get my own ticket.'

'Dad, it's a wonderful country and we want to show it to you. Be our guest. The girls are really excited about the idea of you coming to see us.'

'It'll be a big thrill for me, too. Is Howard OK with all of this?'

'Of course he is, he wants you to see where we are as well, although he will be back at work some of the time. As you know, we've had Norma and Trevor out a few times now, so it'll be great for me if you come as well.'

'I'd better come now, before I am past it,' laughed Jack. 'I've always wanted to come, such a shame that your mother was so nervous about flying.'

JACK DID NOT like to festoon his home with family

photographs, all those eyes watching what he was doing, so he had taken many down after Margaret died. He did have one picture of which he was particularly fond, of Elizabeth and Howard on their wedding day. While they were talking he had taken it out of the telephone table drawer, where he normally kept it. Howard at six-foot-six, head and shoulders above her at five-foot-three. To Jack she looked so beautiful and contented, it was a special moment captured. He also was reminded of her resemblance to Margaret, her mother, triggering memories of their own wedding day, now forty years ago, back in 1950. A spartan affair, a Church Hall reception, without alcohol, and then by train for a weekend honeymoon in Margate.

Louise's parents had splashed out in a big way to make an event of the reception for her marriage to David, at a posh hotel with a band and many guests. Margaret had resented it, as she thought they were doing it to show off their wealth and she had been very tense and on edge for the whole day. Elizabeth's wedding was much simpler, he and Margaret had made all the arrangements. Jack had even managed to stumble his way through a short speech.

Unlike her brother, Elizabeth had chosen to go to university, something else of which Jack was proud, the first in their family. She went to Bristol to read History and there at a Folk Club evening she had met Howard, who was reading medicine, her first serious boyfriend. After graduating she had taught in Bristol for a few years, while he finished his studies. Then, ten years ago, Howard had the opportunity to take a position as a GP in New Zealand and off they went, their two daughters being born out there. Elizabeth was now teaching again, working part-time.

THE ARRANGEMENTS SORTED, there was a pause for moment, before Elizabeth said, 'How are things with your new friend Samantha now, are you still helping her to track down her father?'

Jack doodled on his phone message pad before replying.

'Yes, I am, and we are making a bit of progress.'

He paused again but his daughter did not try to interrupt his flow.

'She has now explained to me that her son, who is eight, has what could be a serious medical issue, possibly inherited, and the doctors have asked her to check the grandparents to see if there is any history there. Her husband's parents are fine and so is she, so finding her father becomes really important for her. It's not just a question of knowing who he is.'

Jack waited for Elizabeth to respond, which took a few more moments.

'Oh, my word, Dad, that's really sad.' She waited again. 'I do feel for her. She's on her own, isn't she?'

'Yes, there isn't anyone else but me who can or would help her. She's a nice young woman, I think you'd like her. We've got a few ideas to follow up, but there is still long way to go.'

THERE WAS ANOTHER pause before Jack spoke again, rather hesitantly,

'Love, there is something I want to tell you. I have told Samantha and her friend Jenny, the nurse, who came with her last time. I don't think I could bring myself to mention this yet to David, but now that she knows, I want to share it with you. Have you got a few minutes?'

'Of course, Dad, what is it?'

JACK PROCEEDED TO relate to Elizabeth what he had told Samantha and Jenny about his night with Pamela. He had by now sat down on the stool by the little table in the hall, the phone in his right hand, Elizabeth's wedding photo in front of him, while running his other hand through his hair. For some reason he had his eyes closed. Elizabeth heard him out without interrupting until he said, 'That's it, end of story.'

There was a long silence, until Elizabeth said, 'It's all right, I am still here. So, you don't think that you are her father, but you have some idea who it could be and that is why you can help her? You didn't open up about this at the beginning?'

'To be honest, it was really embarrassing for me to talk to two young ladies about such things, it is such an intimate story. I find it hard to tell you. But this Jenny, she is quite a strong character, perhaps it's her nurse training, she doesn't beat about the bush. She asked me a straight question and somehow it seemed right not to lie but to give her a straight answer. I think that is why Samantha brought her, to ask the direct question.'

'Yes Dad, I can understand that. It still leaves plenty of other questions to ask though. Is this man Dawson her father? Did he do something against her will? Did she consent to have sex with him?'

Jack grimaced at hearing his daughter use the word 'sex'.

'If you find him, will he accept the fact? Will he agree to have the medical tests? Hmm, you're right, best not to broach this with David just yet. Is it OK for me to tell Howard all this, he might have an input on the medical side of things?'

'Of course, I trust him completely. And look, I don't want all of this to overshadow your visit, if we are not careful we will end up with it dominating everything.'

Elizabeth laughed, 'No, you're right, we don't want that to happen. Thanks for telling me Dad, it really helps me to understand the situation better. David does have a point though, you are taking a bit of a risk as you don't know where it will lead you. What happens if you find this man and he is aggressive? And you are just there to help her, not fall in love with her, aren't you? It is her search, not yours.'

Jack felt himself blush and was glad Elizabeth couldn't see him.

'I understand. Only you could say that to me and get away with it! I will be careful. If it comes to a crunch she may want to go ahead on her own.'

'Dad, I'd better go, I'm due at the school soon. It has been lovely to talk to you. I can't wait to see you again in a couple of months.'

AFTER THEY HAD said their goodbyes, at first Jack sat in his rocking chair, gazing out at a beautiful summer's evening. Then he put on his jacket and walked down to the Preston to enjoy a pint, to sit quietly on his own with his thoughts. He felt mellow, happy that he had plenty to anticipate and that he had shared his story with Elizabeth. He made a mental note for the next day to go to the Post Office and inquire about obtaining a passport.

CHAPTER 23

Nottingham, July 1990

As Emma and Rachel are my sisters, well, half-sisters anyway, I should really love them dearly but, somehow, I can't quite feel that way. Emma was born when I was six, Rachel two years later, so it isn't even as if we were ever in the same school together. I had left primary school by the time Emma started, and I finished at the comprehensive after the fifth form, so same again there. They could be fun sometimes, but also a real pain when I was trying to do homework or read quietly. You can imagine the sort of sniggering that went on when I was sixteen and started to have boyfriends, so I never brought anyone home, I always thought that they would be put off. When I left home to be married in 1979, they were both still living with Mum.

I felt quite nervous to be opening up Mother's house ahead of their arrival this Saturday morning. It was strange, sitting there waiting for them to arrive, as if I was interviewing them for jobs, wondering if they would be suitable candidates, but fearing that they might not.

They both live in London now, but separately, one with a boyfriend, the other with a girl. I am not sure of the relationship there; it's like, please don't ask. I have to remember that Emma is twenty-eight and Rachel twenty-six, but I find it hard to think of them as grown-ups and there are occasions when they certainly don't act that way. Deep down for me they are still 'the kids'. I've done my share of baby-sitting for them over the years. They always played me up if Mum and Ken had a rare night out at the pictures.

Emma did a Fashion Design course at the local Polytechnic, while still living at home, and managed a middling sort of pass. She thought she could walk into a design job up here in Nottingham with Paul Smith or someone like that, but the reality was very different. Disappointed when she had no luck locally, off she went to London. She did some odd bits of freelancing and modelling for a while, even some photographic modelling, although she was always rather coy about what that involved. That is where she met Tony, her now long-term boyfriend, who is a photographer of sorts. She eventually found work in a small fashion studio as a Pattern Cutter and that seems to be her level. At least that gives them one steady income, as he is still freelance.

Rachel is different, very different. She was always obsessed with make-up and jewellery. While still at school she went to work as a Saturday girl at Jessop's department store here, on one of those cosmetic concession counters, going full-time as soon as she could. Having always hankered after living in London she found herself a similar job at Selfridges on Oxford Street. That is where she met Angelique (who I think was originally christened Angela) and moved into her flat, where she has lived ever since. They both work now somewhere in Knightsbridge, Harvey Nichols or similar, not sure where as they have moved around a lot. Angelique is like the Pied Piper, wherever she can go, Rachel is sure to follow.

As you can tell from that, we don't have a lot in common. I can't work out who they take after. Emma has Mum's slim build, but her features are more like Ken, her Dad, who didn't have film star looks. Rachel looks more like Mum, attractive rather than pretty, but altogether more solidly built, size 14+. If you saw the three of us in a crowd, you would never pick us out as sisters.

WHEN I ARRIVED at the house, picking up the junk mail that had accumulated, for the first time I noticed a mustiness in the air. The house was starting to feel unloved, would they notice? They came from the station by taxi, as London girls would. I am sure that Mary Barthorpe next door would have noticed that. Emma in denim jeans and jacket and a black punk band T-shirt, with short, cropped hair. Rachel in high heels, fishnet tights, short black skirt and a yellow jacket. Long flowing dark tresses, changed from her original mousy brown. Me left behind in fashion terms, in fleece jacket and jeans.

I made them coffee while they wandered around the house, I could follow them by the sound of Rachel's heels on the uncarpeted top stairs. Then we sat at the kitchen table with our drinks. I didn't offer biscuits. At least the aroma of the coffee made it feel a little more homely. A heavy summer shower was beating on the window.

'It's been a long time since we three sat around this table,' said Rachel.

'I don't think that we've ever done it as adults,' I replied, 'it's eleven years since I left to be married and you both headed off south soon after that.'

Rachel glared back at me then stared out of the kitchen window at the rain. I guess that dark brown lipstick must be fashionable in London now. Emma had her head down, studying the kitchen tablecloth. Silence reigned. I kept my nerve and waited for one of them to open a conversation. Young Tommy Barthorpe next door began his saxophone practice, 'Baker Street', which made me smile, given the place from which they had just come. Eventually Rachel spoke again after a heavy sigh.

'All right then, what are we going to do with this house? What do we think it's worth, eighty thousand?'

'You'll be lucky, you're talking London prices there, I think thirty-thousand is top whack round here, one similar down the road has been on the market for thirty-two since February, but it hasn't sold yet.'

Emma looked up now. 'If we split that three ways, that is around ten thousand quid each.'

'You would have to reckon on no more than nine each, after estate agents' and solicitors' fees,' I said.

'Couldn't we convert it,' offered Rachel, 'into flats or two maisonettes? I quite like the idea of having a retreat up here. And the money from renting the other flat would be nice.'

I waited to hear Emma's response, but none was forthcoming, so I dived in.

'Flats wouldn't be easy in a house like this. There would have to be a second front door to make two maisonettes and also a second bathroom down here. How much do you think that would cost? We'd have to finance the work, I don't think any of us has got that sort of money, have we? Once it was done, we would have to pay an agent to let the other one for us.'

Emma did chip in now. 'Well, you're up here, you could do that, couldn't you?'

'Oh yes, with a job and an eight-year-old, I've always got time on my hands, haven't I? Anyway, what is the use to me of a flat half-an-hour away from home? I'm never going to use it. I say let's put the house on the market and get rid. I had enough to do looking after

Mum when she was in the home and then sorting out all the stuff here. You're not saddling me with a lot more work while you both watch on from the side-lines.'

More glares from Rachel, while Emma went back to studying the tablecloth.

'That's not fair,' said Rachel, 'we would share the work between us.'

'Like we did when Mum was in Oak Tree House? How many times did you two come up to see her? Once, twice?'

Rachel blushed behind her heavy make-up and shifted uncomfortably in her seat, while Emma found a stain on the tablecloth to remove. I tried to put space between them.

'What do you think, Emma? Wouldn't nine thousand now come in handy for you and Tony? You've only got one steady income, haven't you?'

Emma bristled, perhaps I should have been less direct. 'I'll have you know he's just got a commission from *Clothes Show* magazine,' she said, 'don't keep putting him down, he's doing OK.'

'Huh,' said Rachel, 'how long's that going to last?'

'It's for three issues, but it could be extended if it goes well.' Emma seemed close to tears, and we stood off her for a while.

'That's good,' I said, desperately trying to recover lost ground, 'but a sum of money like this would really take the pressure off, wouldn't it?'

'Yes it would,' she replied and sat up straight for the first time. 'Rachel, I know we talked on the train coming up about keeping a place here, but I can see now that it would cost us plenty, and it could be a long time before we got any money back. I say sell it.'

We both looked at Rachel, who shrugged.

'OK, if that is how you feel, don't say that I didn't

suggest an alternative,' indicating that this could be a grudge that she would carry for some time.

'Is that a definite,' I asked, looking them both in the eye, 'is this the final word on the matter? I can go into Frank Innes this afternoon and ask them to put it on the market without anyone changing their mind?'

'Yes,' sighed Rachel, 'do you want it in writing?'

'No, that's fine. You can leave it with me, and I will start the ball rolling and I promise to keep you posted. The house was left to the three of us jointly, so we would all have to sign for it to go through.'

I could feel the tension easing away. Emma even smiled at me.

'Thanks, Sam.'

I HADN'T BEEN sure if I wanted to broach the next subject with them, but it felt like now or never and, after the conversation we had just had, I didn't want them saying that I hadn't told them about it.

'There's something else I want to tell you.' Even Rachel looked interested now. Nothing else was said, they were just staring at me, eyebrows raised, as if I was going to tell them that I had got myself a new man or had decided I was gay or was planning to emigrate to Canada.

'I'm trying to find out who my real father is or was.'

Simultaneously their heads swivelled to look at each other, then back at me. I carried on.

'I know it might be a needle in the haystack job, but I have got a real reason. The doctors think that Adam has a rare disease, Charcot-Marie-Tooth, which might cause him problems in later life. It's usually inherited, so we've checked out his father and his parents and also me, and there are no signs of it. Too late to check out

Mum, but to be sure the medics would like to test my father.

'It does not take a mathematical genius to work out when, approximately, I was conceived, around mid-September 1955. Before she was too far gone, I showed Mum photos she'd taken of some blokes who stayed here. One in particular stood out, someone she seemed to have fond memories of. After some prompting, it emerged that he had taken her out for a drink one or two evenings, I don't suppose that happened often back in those days.'

They were still staring at me. Neither of them seemed to have twigged that Adam's diagnosis might affect them, and I wasn't going to spell it out.

'She told me his name and from her address book and receipts I could tell that he was here for the whole of summer nineteen fifty-five, so he fits the timescale. His address was in Kenton, North London, and my old friend Jenny, who now lives in Watford, was able to find him still there in the local telephone directory.'

I paused for effect.

'So, I've been to see him.'

They both gasped. Emma said,

'Kenton, that's only a couple of stops on the Tube from us in Neasden. You could've called in to see us.'

One sharp look at her dealt with that idea.

'What did he say?' asked Rachel.

'He's a really nice old bloke, name of Jack, nearly seventy now and widowed. He lives on his own, he's got a son and a daughter, some grandchildren. Back then he was already married, with a young family. He says he was sent up here for work on a project in the summer of fifty-five.'

'And?' inquired Rachel.

'At first he didn't give me a straight answer. You know, "Oh it was a long time ago, memory playing tricks" and so on. Anyway, I took Jenny, and she gave him the third degree and he told us this story, saying that he had been too embarrassed to talk to young women like us about such a topic. You can tell that Mum meant something to him, I think he was hoping I had a message from her for him.'

I told them what he had told Jenny and me.

'Do you believe him?' asked Rachel, 'It sounds far-fetched to me.'

'I think I do now, I wasn't sure at first, but he has already gone to a lot of trouble to help me, so, on balance I do.'

'Bloody hell,' said Emma. 'Do you think that perhaps Mum was assaulted by this man, or consented to having sex with him?'

'Wouldn't she have said something to someone, if he'd attacked her, gone to the police or told her GP?' asked Rachel.

'She might, but don't forget this was thirty-five years ago,' I said, 'what sort of assistance would she have got from the police in those days? Even now it wouldn't be easy. The bloke would only have had to say that she'd seduced him, and he would've been believed. Knowing how Mum was, needing the income from her business, she would have just got on with her life. Even when she fell pregnant, she would've just gone to her GP and said that the father wasn't around. It hadn't been that unusual in the War, lots of illegitimate children born round here, of all colours, thanks mainly to the Yanks.

'There's something else. We've also had a couple of strange letters come here, addressed to Mum, postmarked Hull and just signed "B," which hint that something had gone off.'

'Ooh, can we see them?' asked Rachel.

I was glad to be able to answer honestly and say

they were at home.

'Yes, but what do they say?' Rachel persisted.

'Not a lot, just that he hadn't forgotten her, so a suggestion that they had some sort of relationship.'

'You don't think that our Dad, Ken, was involved with her then?' asked Emma.

'No, I don't, she didn't marry him for another three years or more, and you two were born well after that.'

There was another silence until Rachel said, 'Well, good luck with that.' No-one seemed to want to extend the conversation further.

AFTER A BIT more chat and another wander round the house, they called a taxi and left, without making any plans for us to meet again. After lunch I went into town to see the estate agents, before anyone could change their minds. They will come to see it and take photos next Saturday. When I came away from the agents, I was overcome by a surge of relief.

CHAPTER 24

Kenton, July 1990

WHEN SAMANTHA NEXT rang Jack, he told her about the arrangements for the visit of Elizabeth and family, their trip up to Yorkshire and then his journey to New Zealand. She asked about his previous travel experience.

'I haven't been abroad, apart from the war, of course. That was a special case, but it did show me how different things are in other countries. Not just the weather and the landscape, but the way people live, their attitude to life.'

'They do say that New Zealand is like Britain was thirty odd years ago, don't they?'

'Well, perhaps that isn't a bad thing,' said Jack, his mind momentarily flashing back again to 1955.

'Tell me some more about your children, what's your son like?'

Jack launched into a resumé of David's CV.

'Yes, but what's he really like?' asked Samantha.

Jack took a deep breath.

'Ah, yes. He's been a handful, to be honest. Head-strong, you might say, like a bull at a gate sometimes, although I think Louise has now got him where she wants him.'

'Who does he take after then, that doesn't sound like you or Margaret?'

Jack laughed. 'Margaret's Dad was like that, you

couldn't tell him anything, bullied her mother something rotten. I can't say he and I were close.'

'And do you get on with David OK now?'

'By and large. He is very money conscious, and he still needs to learn there's more to life than that.'

'Does he know what you are on to with me?'

Jack paused, then thought it was always best to be straight.

'Yes he does, and he isn't keen on the idea at all. Says I don't know what I am getting myself into. Which is right to certain extent, I suppose.'

'Has he tried to stop you?'

'Oh, yes, he's tried all right.'

'And...?'

'We had a few words about it, but I told him this is what I'm doing.'

There was a long pause.

'Jack, I don't want to cause you any trouble with your family.'

'Don't worry about that. As it happens, because I had told my full story to Jenny and yourself, I decided to tell Elizabeth when she rang last week, and she is much more understanding. As a mother she appreciates your worries about Adam and why you would want to find your father. I told her that I think she and you would get on well.'

'Tell me a bit about her then.'

Jack gave a potted version of Elizabeth's story and her family, saying that he hadn't seen them since Margaret's funeral, more than two years ago.

'That's enough about me, how've you been? You said you had a few things sorted.'

'The main thing is that I have persuaded my sisters that we should get on and sell Mum's house. It wasn't easy, but in the end they could see that there wasn't really any other option. It would cost us far too much to turn it into two maisonettes, although that is what I guess a buyer might do these days.'

'It's left to the three of you equally, is it?' asked Jack.

'Yes, I don't have any problem with that. I've been to the estate agents, and they are coming to see it and take the photos on Saturday. They seem confident of getting a good price for it, but they always say that don't they?'

'I suppose so, I've only ever bought one house, this one, and that was about forty years ago. I don't reckon on ever buying another.'

JACK PAUSED, ABSORBING again just how alone and isolated Samantha was. Separated with a child, perhaps to be divorced, mother now dead, distant from her sisters, no mention of anyone else in the family that she could lean on, like he used to have his Aunt Edna and Uncle Tom. Apart, of course, from her friend Jenny. He understood now just how important she was to Samantha.

'JACK, I'VE THOUGHT a lot about your story since Jenny and I came to see you. We had a long chat about it, and we do believe you.'

'Thank you for that,' replied Jack.

'Knowing my mum, spending the night with you would have been the sort of practical way to deal with a tricky customer. Except, of course, that if something happened with this guy Bob over that weekend, it didn't solve the problem. I still don't like to think what might have happened to her, though. It could have been very horrible, but she was in a vulnerable position. Any accusation of assault back then, would have been her word against his, with little chance of her being believed.'

'Wasn't there anyone she could have confided in, not a sister or an aunt?'

'No brothers or sisters.' Samantha laughed. 'I don't know what you would have made of her aunts, Maud and Elsie, they were a couple of old battle-axes. Long gone now, they would have just told her to pull herself together and get on with it. For them this was how women's lives were. They'd not had it easy themselves, both widowed young with big families, then living through the War. Maud's house was bombed.'

'I see, said Jack, and then, 'Right, we need to get a move on now, don't we?'

'We do.'

THERE WAS SILENCE for a few moments before Samantha spoke again.

'Jack, I may be way off-beam here, but you have set me thinking.'

'Go on.'

'You said that you would like Elizabeth and I to meet, or words to that effect?'

'I did, yes.'

'Well, if you are driving to Yorkshire from down there, the way most people would come is up the M1, past Nottingham. Why don't you all stop off to see us, Adam and me?'

Jack sat down quickly on the stool, looking at the bruise on his thumb where he had dropped his hammer on it. His heart had leapt at the idea.

'Are you still there, Jack?'

'Yes, I am. Blimey, I hadn't thought of that, ...what, come to your mum's house?'

'Yes, I think that would be the best way to do it.'

'Golly, I'd have to think about that for a bit. It would feel very strange coming back there after all these years.'

'Like re-visiting the scene of the crime?' laughed Samantha.

'Now steady on, don't let's have any of that sort of talk. I do think it would be nice for you and Elizabeth to meet. And I really would like to know Adam, very much. After all, it's him we're doing this for, isn't it? He's a similar age to Elizabeth's girls, isn't he?'

'Yes, he'll be nine in October. You see, my original thought was that David and Elizabeth could be half-brother and sister to me. I don't think that now, but we could still have a sort of bond, through you, couldn't we?'

'I think so, yes. It'd mean that you become a real person to some of my family, rather than just some anonymous being that I've told them about. Let me ponder on it a while. Of course, Elizabeth and Howard would have to agree as well.'

While sounding doubtful, Jack was already thinking about practicalities.

'Would it have to be a weekend for you to make it?'

'No, I've got lots of holiday due, going nowhere in a hurry, and I would take Adam out of school for the day, if they're back after the summer when you come.'

'When did you say you will be back down here?'

'In a couple of weeks or so, I'll tell you when.'

'OK, see you then. Goodnight, Samantha.'

'Goodnight, Jack, see you soon.'

JACK WENT BACK to his chair in the lounge, rocking back and forth, staring at the ceiling and noting a few cobwebs for tomorrow's dusting. For the first time, he started to worry that his life was spinning away out of his control. Elizabeth's visit, staying with Norma and Trevor in Yorkshire, then the long flight to the other side of the world. He wasn't used to staying in other people's houses. All out of the ordinary events, outcomes unpredictable. Was he taking on too much, or had he become too much addicted to his routine, stuck in a rut? Having led such an ordered, uneventful life, he wondered if this was now all more than he could cope with at his age. He was now venturing into unknown territory, and it unnerved him.

Added to all that, now to go back to Pamela's house again. How would that feel? Would Elizabeth want to do that? And yet... It was exciting as well, something positive to look forward to when he woke up each morning.

He spoke out loud.

'Too late to change it now, Jack. I've started, so I'll finish.'

CHAPTER 25

Kenton and Reigate, August 1990

JACK WAS BECOMING accustomed to his phone ringing in the early evening, even to the expectation that it could be a woman calling him. However, on this occasion, when the voice said, 'Hello Jack,' he was at a loss at first to identify the caller. Not Samantha, the most likely candidate; he knew her voice well by now, too southern and posh to be her. Not Elizabeth, wrong time of day. Not even sister Brenda from Preston, some cause for relief there.

'Hello,' replied Jack, as assertively as he could manage.

'Yes Jack, it's Louise.'

Now that was unexpected. In fact, Jack could not remember his daughter-in-law ever calling him before. His first thought was that there might be a problem.

'Ooh, it's you, that is a surprise. Is everything OK?'

'Yes, all well here, thank you. I'm not surprised that you're surprised, I had to look up your number in our address book. Have I ever rung you before?'

'No, I don't think you have.'

'Well, I thought that it was about time I did. We haven't spoken since you stayed with us after your operation back in March and I have the chance now, so here I am. David's in Athens this week, that's new ground for him, Simon is at Scouts and Lucy is round at a friend's house. I know we're all going to meet up soon anyway when Elizabeth and her family come over, but I wanted to have a chat with you first.'

Jack laughed. 'And the coast is clear now then?'

'Yes it is. How's your recovery going?'

'Very well, thank you. An occasional twinge now and again if I bump the scar but I am feeling very fit. I'm really looking forward to seeing Elizabeth again.'

'And you're going back out there with them, that's even more exciting, isn't it?'

'Yes, the idea of me being over on the other side of the world is hard to imagine.'

'I'm sure you will love it. It must be eight years since we went, Fiona had just been born. I think you will feel at home out there.'

'Yes, I've had to go and organise my passport. I didn't need one with the army in nineteen forty-three.'

Louise chuckled and sounded more relaxed.

'Of course not. Look, I just wanted you to know that David has told me about your project with the young lady, Samantha.'

'Oh no, where's this going?' thought Jack.

'And David does not approve.'

'He's made that crystal clear,' agreed Jack.

'I am sure he has. As you know, he tends to form opinions quickly and he then sticks to them, regardless. He is genuinely concerned for you, do please understand that. I haven't argued with him about it, I've just heard him out. It really isn't about the money, you know, but he is worried that you might find yourself in a situation which is compromising or even dangerous. That's fair enough, I think.'

'Yes, it is,' agreed Jack.

'But she doesn't have anyone else to help her very much, does she?'

'No, she really doesn't. Her mother died two years ago, she is separated or divorced, I'm not sure which, from her husband. She does have two half-sisters, but they are much younger, and she isn't close to them.'

'But you are not her father, or there would be no need to track down someone else?'

'No, as far as I can remember, I'm not.'

Louise chuckled at his choice of words.

Jack sat down on the stool in the hall, as he often did when searching for words.

'It's not an easy subject for me to talk to you about, but I told Samantha and her friend, and I've told Elizabeth now, what I can remember of what happened back then. The answer to your question is that I don't think that I could be her father, but I have a good idea of who might be. We have a name and a photograph from nineteen fifty-five of a chap I can remember, but we don't have much idea about where he might be now. That is what we are trying to find out. There's more to it than just wanting to know who he is and where he is now. Samantha has an eight-year-old son with a serious health problem and tracking the man down could be helpful in his treatment, as I understand it.'

'Oh, my word.' Louise caught her breath for a moment. 'David hasn't told me that.'

'I don't think I've told him, I didn't know that myself when I was staying with you. He might ask, how do I know that's true, and of course I don't for sure, I have to take her word for it. There is a lot of medical stuff these days that is beyond me, what they can find out, it's amazing.'

'To convince David it might help to know a bit more about that,' said Louise. 'Jack, I wanted to ring you to let you know that I am sympathetic to what you are doing and, from what you have just told me, it's very noble of you. It isn't going to be easy though, is it?'

'No, I call it a needle in a haystack job, but we do have some clues, so we might be lucky.'

'What did Elizabeth say when you told her?'

'Much like you really, she was very sympathetic towards Samantha. I told her that I thought they would get on well together. You mothers find it easier to put yourselves in her position, I think.'

'Well, it does make me wonder how we would cope if one of our children was seriously ill. Sometimes you worry that things are going too well, that there must be something nasty lurking round the corner. You feel that to go through life without some serious setbacks would be too good to be true. Right, Jack, here's Lucy being brought home, so I better ring off now. She and Simon were asking if they would be seeing you again soon,'

'That's nice of them. It will be great to see all of my grandchildren together,' said Jack, thinking, 'well, I believe that those four are *all* of my grandchildren.'

CHAPTER 26

Kenton, August 1990

IT WAS TWO weeks later when Samantha was back with Jack again. He was a little disappointed to see that Jenny was not with her and Samantha sensed this.

'No, she's working today. I reckon you've taken quite a shine to her, haven't you?'

Jack was embarrassed now. 'Oh no, not really, but she is a nice girl, isn't she? I can see that she's a good friend to you.'

'Yes, she's a good mate. I've helped her through a few things as well. She had a rather nasty boyfriend near home that we had to warn off. That was one reason why she moved down here. Her home life hasn't been too stable, either.'

'I see,' said Jack, 'you don't know what has gone on in some people's lives, do you?'

'True. She always seems on top of things, so well-organised, but I don't always know what she is thinking. She's found a good bloke now, he's very reliable and laid back. It does me good to spend some time together with her, she's the one friend I really trust to keep stuff to herself and to be straight with me.'

'What happens with Adam when you're down here?' asked Jack.

'Sometimes he stays with his friend whose Mum says it is easier to look after the two of them than her son on his own, as they entertain each other. This weekend though, he's with his Dad.'

Jack would have liked to ask more about her husband, but it didn't feel as if this was quite the time to do it.

SAMANTHA DIDN'T WAIT to be invited but sat herself down on the settee in her usual place. Jack had already made himself a cup of tea and he brought her a glass of water.

'There's been a development,' she said, delving into her rucksack. 'I only found it yesterday when I called in at Mother's. Another letter.'

'Same man?' asked Jack.

'Same handwriting anyway and signed 'B' again.'

'What's it say?'

'I'll read it. Postmark is Hull again, same sort of paper. *"Dear Pamela, thought I'd write again. I do hope you are OK. It does seem a long time since I stayed with you, is it around thirty-five years now?"*

'He's put twenty-five and crossed it out,' explained Samantha, before going on,

"It's been up and down for me since then. I'm on my own now, life is a bit quiet here. I haven't forgotten you. Love B."

That's it,' she said, 'what do you make of that?'

'It's odd, isn't it?' answered Jack. 'On the one hand it is almost like he is asking to come back, but he doesn't give her an address to reply to.'

'That's what I thought. It does suggest some sort of warm relationship between them, from his angle anyway. There must have been something special for him not to have forgotten and to keep writing to her. And to believe that she would know who "B" was.'

'If it is Dawson, I think he would have been older than me, quite a bit, so probably well into his seventies by now. Perhaps he is losing it, a bit confused. Using a brown envelope and not proper writing paper seems strange to me. I would have used Basildon Bond to write a letter like that.'

Samantha smiled at the thought. 'He's not like you though, is he?'

'No, I suppose not. It doesn't help us much, but we do know he's still around, that's all, no more information as to where he is or whether he is Bob Dawson or not. We can't rule out this being someone else that we don't know about.'

She sighed and passed the letter and its envelope over to Jack who studied it but passed it back without a word. She put it back in her rucksack and changed the subject.

'Have you thought any more about calling into Nottingham on your way north with Elizabeth?'

Jack put his hands together in front of his face, almost as if he was praying.

'I think it's a really nice idea for you to meet her. I'm going to feel a bit emotional, to go back there, but I think it's the right thing to do, meeting Adam as well. You will still have the house then, will you, you are selling it aren't you?'

'Oh, I'm sure we will. There have been a couple of viewings, but no great interest yet. The agent says to leave the house furnished until it is sold, it will look more attractive that way. It's only been on the market for about six weeks now.'

'Let me confirm with Elizabeth and Howard, to see that it would fit in with their plans. We would just drop by for an hour or so, I am thinking?'

'Yes, and it would be around middle day, I assume?'

'I'll check. I guess that they will be having a hire car, so that will need to be sorted out. So, back to the job in hand, what next?' asked Jack.

'If we assume that these letters are from Bob Dawson and that he is in Hull, then that's a start. Could you go back to Telephone House to look again through the directories and see if he is in the Hull one? It's a long shot, he probably hasn't got a phone at all, but there might be an old address, or his wife, if he's got one, still living there. What do you think?'

'Yes, I can certainly do that,' said Jack.

'Dawson's not that common a name. He might be under "B" or "R", assuming his actual first name is Robert.'

'Perhaps. If he had been christened Cyril or Cecil, it might have suited his image better to be called Bob. I reckon he made up a lot of stuff. Once you are accustomed to lying, it becomes your second nature. I will go and look by all means, see how many Dawsons I can find.'

CHAPTER 27

Kenton, August 1990

AS HE HAD promised Samantha, Jack made a return journey to Telephone House, now more confident, as he knew what to expect. The same uniformed commissionaire directed him again down to the basement where the same smiling lady sat safe behind her desk, giving no indication that she recognised him from his previous visit, back in April.

He found the Hull Directory and took it to a vacant desk, taking a notepad and a pencil from the pocket of his jacket. When he turned to the Ds, he was surprised to see so many entries for "Dawson". He had never known anyone else of that name, so hadn't judged it to be very common but he was now looking at a list of well over one hundred and fifty names. In general the addresses were in streets that appeared to be within the city itself, but some were in places of which he had never heard: presumably villages further out, such as Kirk Ella, Sproatley and Swine. Who would want to live in a place called Swine, he thought.

He also noticed that one or two lived in Beverley, home to his daughter's in-laws, Norma and Trevor. He had not realised that the town was so close to Hull. And he would be going there soon! A plan started to shape itself in his mind.

He went back to the job in hand. He found eleven "R. Dawsons," three "B. Dawsons" and two "Robert

Dawsons". A sudden surge of excitement swept through him. He felt as if he was a hunter closing in for the kill, or Sherlock Holmes conclusively identifying a murder suspect. Suddenly things were coming together!

He carefully copied down all of the names, addresses and phone numbers, all with the code "0482". He then saw that there was also one "R. Dawson-Jones", so he added that name to his list. He carefully replaced the directory in its place in the racks, said 'Thank you' to the lady on the desk. He climbed the stairs and stepped out into the London sunshine with a feeling of exhilaration.

'Just wait until I tell Samantha about this,' he thought, as he headed back to the Tube. When he changed trains at Baker Street he went into WH Smith's, where he considered himself fortunate to find a Hull A-Z street map that he could buy.

'I don't suppose you sell too many of these down here,' he said to the young man behind the counter, who could only manage a bemused stare in reply.

On his return home he located all of his addresses in the A-Z, adding the page numbers to his list of names and marking the streets on the maps with a red pen. He realised that the information meant little to him because, as yet, he had no knowledge of the city at all. But he had hopes there was someone who he would soon meet who could tell him more.

THAT EVENING HIS phone rang and he leapt to his feet, thinking that it might be Samantha.

'Hello Dad,' said David, 'how are you?'

Jack was annoyed to feel so disappointed when his only son rang him, and it took him a moment to gather his thoughts.

'Oh, I'm OK, thanks David, everything alright

there?'

'Yes, all well here, thank you. I'm just back from a trip to Athens. God it was hot there, over ninety degrees and half of the country was on holiday.'

'Oh, dear, that doesn't sound very pleasant.'

'It wasn't, but I did some good business there.'

David started by confirming the arrangements for Elizabeth's visit the following month. The date of arrival and the Saturday when he would collect Jack to take him over to his house for them to all be together. The following week Jack would go to Beverley with Eizabeth and Howard.

'It's really nice of his parents to ask me to go up there. I take it that Howard and Elizabeth will have a hire car?'

'All sorted, Dad, I've got a contact in Round Table who is in the trade. It'll be big enough to take the five of you.'

'Great.' Jack made a note of the dates on his phone pad, so he could tell Samantha when they would call in at Nottingham. 'I've got that all written down, thank you.'

'Excellent. Everything all right with you, no twinges after your operation?'

'No, I feel good. Thanks again to you and Louise for having me afterwards, coming straight home from hospital would have been a bit too much for me.'

'It was good to have you, we all enjoyed it,' said David, not sounding totally convincing.

Jack waited for the inevitable question. He sensed that David was still deciding how to phrase it.

'Erm, is anything happening with this woman who contacted you?'

'Samantha, do you mean?' replied Jack.

'Well, I hope there's only the one of them,'

'Yes, just the one. We are making some progress. In

fact, I've been to Telephone House up in town this morning, doing some research in the Hull phone directory. That's where we think her father might be now.'

'Oh, Dad, where's this going?' David sounded less antagonistic now, more resigned to the situation than he did before. 'It's pointless, isn't it, and there's no reason for you to be involved?'

'No David, it's not pointless. She's got an eight-year-old son who has a serious medical problem, which might be inherited, so she needs to track the man down if she can and she's got nobody else to help her.'

While Jack had not told David this before, he assumed that it could have been relayed to him by Elizabeth or Louise, or both. David did not appear to be surprised.

'Do you know that's all true, Dad?

'I trust her, that's the point. And I want to help her, it's not as if I've got too much else in my life now. It feels good to be doing something useful.'

'So, what happens if you find this chap and he's difficult or violent or something?'

'David, I'm well aware that is a possibility, but not all that likely, he's probably even older than me. We'd just have to beat a hasty retreat if that happened.'

'You mean that you'd be with her when she went to find him?'

'If that's what she wants. It wouldn't be advisable for her to go on her own, for the reasons you mention. Don't forget, if this is the fellow we think he is, he's well into his seventies now. I'll have a few years on him. He's not going to pack much of a punch,' Jack chuckled, although he didn't feel as brave as he was trying to sound. He could hear heavy sighs from David's end.

'I shan't say any more, Dad, but please be careful

and don't make any commitments of any sort.'

'What do you mean by that?'

'Um, well, you know.'

'No, I don't know,' replied Jack, 'I'm not signing away your inheritance if that's what you mean.'

'Oh, Dad. Let's just leave it at that, shall we?'

'Yes, David, let's leave it at that. I'll see you here on Saturday the fifteenth, ten o'clock, that's right, isn't it?'

'Yes, that's right. I'll see you then, Good night Dad.'

'Good night, David.'

JACK WENT BACK to his rocking chair. 'Was it David who was difficult, or am I being stubborn? Or maybe both? Why couldn't we have a better relationship?'

Jack thought back to his own father. He had made the big decision that had changed Jack's life completely, sending him down to London from Preston when he was only twelve to live with Edna and Tom, his aunt and uncle. Jack appreciated now what a tough choice his father had made then, leaving himself to cope with a mentally ill wife and a stroppy daughter.

After that he hadn't seen much of his father who had only once come down to London, a year or two after Jack's move. He'd been up to Preston a few times with Edna and Tom, but his father had started to seem like a stranger to him by then. A mild-mannered man, he died just after Jack came back from the war. Only in his early fifties, he had contracted asbestosis from his workplace.

Should I have been a better father to David, Jack wondered, could I have approached it in a different way? There had been plenty of vigorous arguments, which had made Margaret cringe, she just wanted them to be at peace with each other. It had seemed to Jack that David first went through the typical non-communicative teenager phase. Then he became very assertive and opinionated, not someone with whom you could have a reasoned argument. He never appeared to be listening to what Jack said and it sometimes seemed to him that he was being treated by David as an intellectual inferior, and that hurt.

THE NEXT EVENING, Jack rang Samantha, just a brief call, to confirm the date they could call in on her and Adam in Nottingham, which was fine with her.

CHAPTER 28

Reigate September 1990

JACK HAD SPOKEN to Elizabeth on the phone on the Thursday morning after their arrival, but it had been a brief conversation, as she still sounded jetlagged.

'How are they all?' asked Jack as David drove him towards the M25. Before answering, David mildly cursed a cautious driver in a Morris Minor who had stopped sharply at traffic lights as they changed to amber.

'They are fine, good to see them all again. The girls have certainly grown up, and Howard has a beard now. I still think professional men should be clean-shaven, but I suppose it suits him.'

He went on to regale Jack with the details of all the impressive places in Surrey to which he had planned on an itinerary for Elizabeth and family. As a keen gardener, Jack knew about the Royal Horticultural Society's place at Wisley, but the names of all the grand National Trust properties meant little to him.

'Sounds very educational,' he offered.

'Well, they don't have historic places like that out there do they? I thought they would be interesting for the girls.'

To Jack's relief the M25 was clear of heavy traffic that morning, and in no time at all they were pulling on to David's drive. He had seemed quite relaxed, keeping his speed down this time, with only a couple of cars hogging the outside lane of the motorway to disturb him.

David marched up to the house.

'Can I just get my flowers from the boot, please, David?' asked Jack.

Louise opened the front door with Elizabeth, shorter and fairer, standing alongside her. Howard hovered behind them, the children were not immediately to be seen. Elizabeth rushed forward and flung her arms around Jack as he thrust the flowers at Louise.

'Dad, it's lovely to see you again. My word, you are looking well, I was a bit worried when you had your operation, but you're looking really good,' said Elizabeth.

'Oh Jack, you shouldn't have, these are lovely,' said Louise as she gathered in the chrysanthemums.

'You're looking well yourself,' said Jack to Elizabeth.

Howard came forward, neatly bearded as David had described, and shook him firmly by the hand. 'Good to see you again, Jack,' he said.

'Shall we go in?' suggested David.

Elizabeth's children shyly appeared, Fiona and Kelly ushered forward by their mother.

'Hello Granddad,' they chanted in unison. Simon and Lucy hung back but echoed their cousins. As often on such occasions, an awkward pause followed and then everyone started talking at once to fill the gap.

'Coffee, Jack?' asked Louise.

'Yes, please,' he replied, and the group progressed through the lounge to the conservatory, David making sure of his favourite chair as Louise headed for the kitchen, still clutching the flowers. The other adults sat around while the children stood nearby, unsure of what they should be doing.

'Gosh, you girls have grown up,' said Jack to Fiona

and Kelly, who blushed and turned to each other and giggled. 'Well,' he said, 'it's been quite a while since I last saw you.'

Jack asked dutiful questions about the flight (it had been good) and about what they had seen so far. Elizabeth made a comment about 'David's hectic schedule' at which he bristled slightly.

Gradually, they all relaxed, Louise brought Jack's coffee with a chocolate biscuit. Lucy then suggested to Fiona and Kelly that she had something to show them in her room and Simon also drifted away.

It was a lovely late summer day, the conservatory doors were all open and a pleasant breeze wafted through.

'I'm doing a barbecue soon, Dad,' said David, and Jack could see a large shiny machine on wheels outside. Again, trying to impress us all, thought Jack.

'Got my fingers crossed on that,' grinned Louise, 'it's rather new technology.'

'Piece of cake, if you know what you are doing,' asserted David and they all laughed, except for him.

THE MORNING PASSED in desultory small talk, catching up on Elizabeth's teaching, Howard's medical work and their girls' progress in school. Howard had brought a Christchurch guide book for Jack and picked out some of the major sights for him. Jack was content to be surrounded by all his family even if there were certain tense undercurrents. He couldn't help thinking how much Margaret would have enjoyed this, probably even more than he was.

Louise went back to the kitchen while David went outside to start the barbecue, leaving Jack with Elizabeth and Howard.

'Have you arranged it for us to meet up on Tuesday

with Samantha and her boy?' asked Elizabeth.

'Yes, I've said that we will probably arrive around lunch-time, and she said that she would lay on some sandwiches for us.'

'That's nice of her. I don't know Nottingham at all, be interesting to see it,' said Elizabeth.

'Well, where Pamela's house is, I mean Samantha's house, in Sneinton was not the poshest part of town even then, so it probably hasn't improved.'

'I worked in the city around nineteen seventy-five, they were building the Queen's Medical Centre at the time,' said Howard. 'I think it's now one of the biggest hospitals in the country. I really liked it in Nottingham, plenty going on in the city. Good place for sport, with theatres and nightlife.'

'Yes, I think things would have been livelier then than they were in fifty-five,' said Jack.

Exasperated sounds from outside suggested that David was not finding the barbecue to be as straightforward as he had expected. He could be seen frowning as he studied the instruction booklet.

'Should I go and help him?' asked Howard, but Elizabeth thought that would not be wise.

'He probably doesn't realise that we barbecue all summer long at home, but it's best not to tell him that. Just don't complain if the sausages are a bit burnt or raw.'

IN FACT, LUNCH was quite successful, fortified by unusual salads prepared by Louise, not just the standard lettuce, tomato and cucumber. Jack had never tasted olives before and helped himself to several. Like the proverbial curate's egg, the sausages were good in parts and the chicken was also slightly charred, but the burgers came out well. All served up with aplomb by

David in a chef's apron.

Simon told him, 'At least the sausages are better than the ones you did last weekend,' which earned him a scowl from his father.

After lunch, Simon and Lucy, at their mother's firm suggestion, took Fiona and Kelly off to the swings at the local playground. Jack managed to find some time on his own with Howard. He had always liked his calm nature and respected his medical knowledge. Howard's new beard was showing a tinge of grey. He was as unobtrusively dressed as ever, navy jumper, dark blue shirt and black corduroy trousers.

'What can you tell me about this illness, Howard, this Charcot-Marie-Tooth business?' Jack asked.

Howard took off his glasses as he considered the question for a moment.

'Well, it's not that uncommon, although not many people have heard of it. It is usually an inherited disease, but it's often possible to have it without any symptoms. It's over a hundred years since it was identified, but we're still learning about it. I've had a few apparent sufferers at my surgery, although we can't positively diagnose them ourselves and we have to refer them on to specialists at the hospital. How old is this boy?'

'He's nearly nine, I think,' replied Jack.

'That's quite young if symptoms are already showing, it doesn't augur too well for him. However, progress is inconsistent, so it doesn't necessarily mean that he is going to be seriously handicapped physically, or anything like that.'

'But he could be?'

'Yes, he could be.'

'And it would help to know if there is any history in the family?'

'Definitely. If it's possible to go back to his grandparents, that's good. If there is incidence of the disease in others in the extended family, that makes it much more likely that he has it, but it's still not conclusive either way. Whatever problems he has, there could be other causes. It can skip generations, so, as I say, for instance, his mother may have it without knowing.'

'And if she wanted to have more children?'

'They could have it too.'

'And any children of the boy's...?'

'They could also have it.'

'Thanks Howard, that tells me how important it is to know more.'

'Do you want me to discuss it with his mother when we meet them? I guess she is quite concerned about her only child.'

'Not unless she raises the subject first, thank you. They've been to see a consultant at their hospital. Asking you just helps me to understand how serious it is.'

LATER, JACK MADE his way into the kitchen where Louise was now preparing tea, with help from Elizabeth. Their conversation seemed to stop abruptly when Jack entered.

'We saw you have a chat with Howard,' said Louise, 'were you asking about Samantha's boy's illness?'

'About the disease? Yes, I was, very helpful too. I like his bedside manner, he's very good at simplifying things, isn't he?'

'Yes,' said Elizabeth, 'he does make things very clear. You didn't mind asking him, then?'

'Not at all, I was hoping for the opportunity. I'd be quite happy to have him as my GP, I can tell you.'

IT WAS NEAR to dusk when David drove him back home and Jack was starting to doze off when David spoke. 'This Samantha woman, then, you haven't given up on that yet then?'

'No, David, and I won't unless she asks me to.'

'I can't help feeling that it's a big mistake, you know.'

'You've made it very clear that's what you think, and you just might be right, but can you understand that someone has asked me to help them, which I am in a position to do?'

'Yes, but you don't want to get suckered in to helping every sob story that comes your way. You don't want to become a soft touch for people, do you?'

'David, give me some credit, I know what I am doing. I've been around the world a lot longer than you, been in business, I believe I can tell genuine people from those who are putting on an act.'

David sighed. Jack continued, 'You know we are calling in to Nottingham on our way to Norma and Trevor's to see Samantha and her son, don't you?'

'Oh, for Christ's sake, Dad, it just gets worse all the time. Why have you dragged Elizabeth and Howard into this?'

'I'm just being honest with you, not hiding anything. And give them some credit too, they wouldn't be involved if they didn't want to be.'

As ever in the outside lane, David blasted his horn at a dirty white Transit van that suddenly changed lanes in front of him without signalling. As they overtook it, the driver replied with an unfriendly gesture which only added to David's frustration.

Back in Kenton, Jack thanked David for his chauffeuring and for allowing him so much time with his family.

'I really do appreciate it, David, the trouble you go to.'

David looked him in the eye and shook him by the hand.

'We'll see you at Heathrow before you head off to New Zealand, I know you are going to love it there.'

'Thank you, see you soon.'

CHAPTER 29

Nottingham and Beverley, September 1990

IT WAS AROUND noon on the following Tuesday when their hire car, with Howard at the wheel, turned off the M1 at Junction 25. Jack was alongside him, Elizabeth and the girls in the back. They drove into Nottingham along the A52 past the Queen's Medical Centre. Soon they were they were in Sneinton, pulling up outside what used to be Pamela's house. A 'House for Sale' board was attached to the front fence. A small boy's head popped up in the front window, then swiftly disappeared. At the house next door, the net curtains twitched.

'I saw a boy,' exclaimed Fiona.

'And me, I saw him too,' added Kelly.

'Are you ready for this, Dad?' asked Elizabeth.

'I hope so,' said Jack.

After the formal introductions Jack stood on the path and allowed the others to go in first. He took a good look around, it had been thirty-five years after all. The outside of the house looked in good shape, the little front garden was tidy. Did it all now look smaller than he remembered? For a moment he thought he also saw Pamela there to greet him, apron on, tea towel in hand. He blinked and she was gone. He followed the others inside.

'Please excuse the state of everything,' said Samantha, 'As you can see, we are in the process of selling it.

The agents have said to leave it furnished for now as it makes it more attractive.'

'How are you doing with that?' asked Howard.

'We've had quite a few viewings so far and a couple are supposed to be coming back at four o'clock today for the second time. They've already sold their house in London. I'm hoping that you are going to be good luck charms for me.'

'It is a nice house, isn't it?' said Elizabeth, 'It's going to be a wrench for you, having grown up here.'

'Definitely the end of an era for me, although it's more than ten years since I lived here. Back a lot to see my mum, of course. Come through to the kitchen, it's the easiest place for us all to sit. Can I get anyone a drink? Coffee's on. How about you girls, I've got some orange squash?'

Drinks were sorted, then Adam took Fiona and Kelly out to the back garden, where his football sat on the lawn.

Elizabeth took the initiative. 'Well, it's good to put a face to the name,' she said, looking directly at Samantha who returned a not unfriendly but inquiring gaze.

Jack continued to look around him, recognising familiar features and noticing differences, new cooker, new sink unit, walls now painted pale blue. He also noticed changes in Samantha; he had not seen her in a skirt before, now she was wearing a long one in denim, with a crisp white short-sleeved blouse. Lipstick as well, that was new, fresh hairdo and a little work on the eyebrows perhaps, plus discreet stud earrings. It was obvious to him that she had made a real effort and he saw her afresh.

Elizabeth went on, 'It is good to meet you. You've taken on quite a daunting job, haven't you? I am glad that Dad is giving you a hand.'

Samantha swallowed hard and looked away for a moment.

'That is kind of you to say that. I would quite understand if you didn't feel that way. He gives me a push every now and again,' she smiled at Jack, 'to keep things rolling along.'

'I have to say that if my brother was here, his attitude would be different, he's not so convinced. It's not without its risks, is it?'

'No, it's not,' answered Samantha, 'but I need to follow it through for Adam's sake.'

Outside, the children were listlessly kicking the ball to each other in silence.

Howard joined the conversation. 'I do know something about the medical side, it really is important for you to know as much of the family history as you can. It might not be conclusive either way, but it will help the doctors to decide his treatment. He looks pretty fit to me.'

At which point Adam tripped over the ball. Fiona and Kelly laughed at him, as he got up again, red-faced.

Howard noticed and looked away. Samantha smiled.

'He is OK, really. He has always seemed to be bit clumsy, but lads are, aren't they?'

'Yes, I always seemed to have scraped knees and bruised shins,' admitted Howard.

'What do you think the future holds for him?' asked Samantha.

'I'm not a specialist, but I know it could go in different ways. If he is not responding to the knee-jerk and the other tests at his age, that isn't good, but it doesn't follow that it all will go badly. It has to be said though that there isn't a known cure for CMT disease.'

'That's what they have told me at the hospital, the Royal Infirmary in Derby. We're due back there to see the neurologist in a couple of weeks.'

There was a silence until Samantha signalled a change of subject.

'What's New Zealand like, then, you obviously must like it out there?'

'We love it, said Elizabeth, 'although it wouldn't be everyone's cup of tea. It's quieter, even a big city like Christchurch near where we are, and old-fashioned in some ways. It's a beautiful country, we've got the coast nearby, it's very sporty, which we like, good for hiking and climbing. We usually go skiing every winter.'

'You're selling it well, I'm quite tempted myself,' laughed Samantha. 'Jack, are you going to want to come back here after your visit?'

'Well, I'll have to see, won't I? If it's that good, perhaps not.'

THE CHILDREN CAME back in at that point. Jack took the opportunity to chat to Adam, ask about his school and his football, to which the boy responded quickly and articulately.

'Do you mind if we take a look around the house?' asked Elizabeth, 'pretend we want to buy it?'

'Help yourselves,' said Samantha.

'Come on, Dad, give us the tour.'

Jack led the family upstairs and showed them what he called my 'room'.

'And which was Pamela's?' asked Elizabeth, 'It helps to follow your story.'

Jack pointed to Pamela's adjacent room and pushed open the door to 'his room', which still had a double bed in it.

IN HIS HEAD he could hear the sounds he remembered;

the lodgers chatting round the dining table, Pamela dishing up their meals in the kitchen, footsteps on the stairs as someone came down from the top floor. And then the sights, Pamela bustling along the landing with her arms full of clean linen, the vase of fresh flowers that always stood on a table there. His eyes filled up and he had to bring out his handkerchief to dab them dry. Elizabeth put her arm around his waist and hugged him, while Fiona and Kelly looked at him with concern.

'Thirty-five years,' said Jack, 'and suddenly it feels like yesterday.' He blew his nose vigorously.

The germ of an idea that had lain dormant all that time surfaced as he thought that he just might have lived there through all those years, had things been different. He had not been prepared to be as overwhelmed as he was. If only.

They went on up the attic stairs, although Jack could not remember ever going up there before.

'How much is it on the market for?' asked Howard.

'I think she is hoping to get thirty thousand for it.'

'That seems jolly cheap compared with London prices. David was telling us all about the value of houses near him.'

Jack laughed. 'Oh, he knows the price of everything all right.'

'Too true,' said Elizabeth.

WHEN THEY RETURNED downstairs, Samantha had set out the sandwiches for them.

'Marks and Spencer's best,' she offered.

'M&S is one thing I do miss,' said Elizabeth, 'The shops in New Zealand aren't that good. I am going to stock up on clothes for the girls before we go back.'

She went on, 'Can you tell us a bit about your mum, please, Samantha, for us she's the unknown central figure in this search?'

Samantha told Pamela's story, the disappearing first husband, the lodgers, her own birth, the marriage to Ken, and the arrival of Emma and Rachel.

'She sounds a strong character, living through all that.'

'Yes,' answered Samantha, 'but she was fun as well, she had quite a sharp sense of humour. Even at the end, when she went downhill so quickly with Alzheimer's, she could still be funny.'

'How did you get on with your step-father?' asked Howard.

'Ken? Oh, he was OK, not that bright really, you'd have thought she could have done better.' She took a sideways glance at Jack here. He didn't see it, but Elizabeth did.

'He accepted me, that was never a problem, none of the difficulties that I know some women had with their step-fathers. Mum ruled the roost for sure, and he was happy to go along with that. Somebody has to be in charge in every household, don't they?'

Howard and Elizabeth exchanged wry smiles.

'You're right there,' said Howard.

Having finished their sandwiches, the children, by some secret silent means, decided to go outside again.

'If you don't mind me asking, you're separated from Adam's Dad?'

Samantha sighed. 'Yes, I am, and I suppose we should be divorced now, I can't see us picking that up again. He's got too much of a wandering eye, can't keep his hands to himself. He's had a string of younger girlfriends since we split. I think he had some before as well, that I didn't know about. Don't get me wrong, he takes responsibility for Adam, both financially and he has him some weekends. It's still fairly amiable, but there's no future in it.'

'I'm so sorry,' said Elizabeth, and the conversation ended there.

THEY DROVE OFF an hour later, heading north towards the A1 for Yorkshire.

'What did you think, Elizabeth?' asked Jack.

'I liked her. She's not the warmest or most outgoing of characters, quite tough-minded and thick-skinned, I would say, but she made us very welcome. She's not had it easy, has she? I thought she was straight and honest. Trying to do the best for her boy.'

'What did you think of Adam, girls?' asked Jack, which caused more giggling.

'He doesn't say much,' said Fiona.

'He could only talk about football,' added her sister.

A few miles further on, Jack asked, 'Your Dad did well for himself, didn't he Howard? He's retired now isn't he?'

'Started at fourteen as an apprentice on the shop floor of an engineering company in Hull, worked his way up to Sales Director. He still does a bit for them, they pull him in from time to time when they have important clients coming in that he used to work with. Spends most of the rest of his time playing golf. Mum was a hairdresser and still cuts his hair, what's left of it. She had a hard time with me, and either couldn't or wouldn't have any more, I've never been sure which it was.'

'So, it's a big thing for them, their only son and grandchildren being the other side of the world?'

'It is, but they definitely encouraged me to go for it when the opportunity came up. And it's given them the excuse to come out to see us most years.'

AS THEY PASSED a sign saying, 'Welcome to Humberside', Howard said,

'Take no notice of that, that's a government thing, it's still all Yorkshire here as far as the locals are concerned.'

He was on his old home turf now and they soon arrived in the historic market town of Beverley. Jack was interested to see Norma and Trevor's house, a substantial pre-war detached in a comfortable tree-lined road. Howard pulled on to the gravel drive alongside two BMWs, a big saloon and a convertible.

Norma rushed out to grab her granddaughters, while Trevor strode forward to give Howard the firmest of handshakes. To Jack, it seemed that Elizabeth and himself now had just walk-on roles. Norma gave him and Elizabeth both a quick peck on the cheek. Trevor shook his hand, saying 'Welcome to Yorkshire.'

'Hello, lass,' he said to Elizabeth.

Jack had not seen Norma and Trevor since Howard and Elizabeth's wedding, ten years before. To him, they looked alarmingly trim and youthful. He was surprised as to how 'Northern' they sounded to him, he'd forgotten that. He pulled himself up straight and followed his family into the house.

CHAPTER 30

Beverley and Hull, September 1990

ON JACK'S FIRST day in Beverley, he was treated to a tourist's view of the town. The whole party walked along the flat road into the town centre, and admired the impressive Minster, inside and out, which seemed too huge to Jack to be in a small town. Beverley had been very wealthy in its time, built on the wool trade and Jack was struck by the number of handsome private houses and buildings. It seemed a very attractive place to live, given that it was only a few miles outside the big city and port of Kingston-upon-Hull, to give it its full name. They had a sandwich lunch in a posh café, for which Trevor insisted on paying.

'It's not every day I have the chance to take my granddaughters out to lunch.'

They wandered back to the house. Trevor had already shown Jack his highly manicured garden, which he made clear was all his own work. He said he didn't trust jobbing gardeners.

Howard, Elizabeth and the girls went off to see some old school friends of his. Jack, Norma and Trevor sat quietly drinking tea. Howard's parents remembered Margaret from the wedding and wanted to know more about her final years, in a politely probing way. They asked what he did with himself, a question for which he did not have an easy answer. Jack found Norma to be quite direct with her questions and he felt slightly uncomfortable with her. Dressed in twinset and smart trousers she was a picture of domestic efficiency. He was also a little in awe of Trevor, recognising that he had prospered from a humble beginning. His own history appeared inadequate in comparison.

'Jack, do you fancy going for a pint after dinner? asked Trevor.

'On one condition only,' said Jack, 'that it's my round.'

'Fair enough,' replied Trevor, 'I'll let you buy the first one, anyway.'

ON THE FIRST evening, they had brought in fish and chips, but for this evening Norma had prepared a sumptuous roast dinner, beef and, of course, Yorkshire puddings, followed by fruit crumble and custard to which Jack showed his full appreciation by coming back for seconds.

'I hope it's a good walk to the pub, Trevor,' he said, 'I need some more exercise after that magnificent feast.'

'It's only our local, but it's well-kept and the beer's good. About a fifteen-minute walk.'

Jack wondered if Howard would join them, but it seemed clear that Trevor intended it to be just the two of them.

At the pub Trevor was greeted by his first name by the barmaid. Jack got in two pints of Timothy Taylor's Landlord, and they found a quiet table. Jack asked more about Trevor's career and learnt that he was born in Hull and stayed with one company in that city all his working life. He and Norma had moved upmarket to Beverley from their first house in Hull so that Howard could attend Beverley Grammar School.

Jack talked about his own upbringing, born in Red Rose Lancashire, but moving to London to live with his aunt and uncle because his father thought he would have better opportunities there. He then talked about his life at Gladwin's which seemed to give Trevor the chance that he had been angling for.

'Pardon me for asking, and don't tell me if you don't want to, but Howard tells me you've got involved with a young woman who you're trying to help, is that right?'

It was clear to Jack that he was not expected to refuse this opening, and he gave Trevor a potted history of his project with Samantha. Trevor was surprisingly sympathetic to his cause.

'Blimey, they've had it tough, both mother and daughter, haven't they? It makes me mad how some blokes don't face up to their responsibilities. And it's a shame if that lad's going to have some problems. This Samantha's got no one else to help her then?'

'She's got a good friend Jenny, who's a nurse in Watford, near me, but otherwise, no she hasn't.'

He wondered if Trevor was going to challenge him about his possible paternity, but perhaps he had been well briefed by Howard. Jack gave him a brief description of their progress to date, which Trevor quickly summarised.

'So you're looking for a man named Bob Dawson who you think is in the Hull area, right?'

'That's right,' replied Jack, 'I've been to Telephone House in London to look at the Hull phone directory and there are nine possible names in there.'

'Of course, we've got the Hull phone directory in our house as well, so I can find them in there.'

On the off chance, thinking that some opportunity like this might occur, Jack had brought his notebook with him, and he passed it across to Trevor, who scrutinised it closely, moving his spectacles to the top of his forehead.

'OK, I know most of these places. From what you've told me, you think this chap is down on his luck, not likely to be in the smartest part of town?'

'No,' said Jack, 'the notes he sends are on scruffy bits of paper, torn out of an exercise book. I wouldn't expect to find him living in a big house like yours.'

'You can't always tell, some of the people who live around us are unbelievable,' snorted Trevor, 'God knows where they get their money from, it's not by doing an honest day's work.'

Trevor rubbed his hands together briskly and looked ready for action.

'I tell you what, do you want to have a trip out to look at these addresses? Might not tell us too much, I don't suppose that he would be on the doorstep looking out for us, but it will give you some idea of what these places are like?'

'Wow,' said Jack, 'I hadn't thought of that, it would be great, thank you.'

'Tomorrow then, we'll make an early start, nine o'clock sharp. Norma's arranged for us to go a Women's Institute barbecue in the late afternoon, but we'll be back by then. Would you recognise him if you did see him?'

'Perhaps, we've got a photo of him from nineteen fifty-five, but a lot can happen to a bloke in thirty-five years. He was a cocky sod when I knew him, maybe that's been knocked out of him by now. We don't know any reason why he's in Hull. He gave Pamela an address in Sheffield, and he didn't have a noticeable accent.'

'Jack, I admire you for taking this on and happy to help in any way I can. I gather that while Elizabeth understands why you are doing it, your son is less sympathetic.'

'I'm afraid so. I don't understand him sometimes.

Too much obsessed by money and status in my opinion.'

AT EIGHT O'CLOCK next morning Norma had bacon and eggs ready for them. Jack had armed himself with his Hull A to Z, which he had also 'happened' to bring north with him. They set off in Trevor's big BMW. He had mapped out an efficient circular route, which would take them the shortest distance round the locations.

'It's a grey day,' asserted Trevor. 'Hull's not pretty at the best of times, so I don't expect it to look great today. We're starting with the best bits, but it will go steadily downhill from there.'

'I have never been here at all in my life,' said Jack, 'so I don't know what to expect.'

'Well, I can say it as I was born here, but they can be funny folk. Many of them have never been far out of the city, and certainly never to London. Outsiders don't always get the warmest of welcomes. Some of the blokes at our place used to drive me barmy, stubborn as mules, suspicious of any changes, it was hard work making any improvements.'

'I can only say that I've had a very warm welcome in Beverley and that is only just up the road,' said Jack.

'That's good to hear,' replied Trevor, 'but sometimes you could think that we are on another planet. We're supposed to be in somewhere called Humberside now, instead of the East Riding of Yorkshire, lumped in with places like Scunthorpe and Grimsby that belong in Lincolnshire. Harold Wilson panicked when he thought he was going to lose a by-election up here and agreed to the building of the Humber Bridge, which wasn't really needed. It was finished about ten years ago. It looks good, and I have to say that our firm did well out of it.'

THE FIRST ADDRESS on Jack's list was to the west of the city, in Kirk Ella, which seemed a very pleasant place to Jack. The house itself was a big, detached house with several cars on the drive.

'Hm, unlikely,' said Jack, 'if Bob Dawson's down on his luck, I can't see him living here.'

They moved on. Jack was relieved that Trevor's driving style was much more relaxed and courteous to other motorists and pedestrians than his son's. When he commented on this, Trevor admitted to having accumulated 'a few points' on his licence, so that he needed to be more careful now. Jack was asked not to mention that in front of Norma or Howard.

'The next two addresses are in an area we call The Avenues,' Trevor informed Jack. 'A couple of my fellow directors live here, so it might be another unlikely area for your man.'

So it proved. It was another apparently affluent area, which did not fit the bill. Trevor then made a detour down towards the Humber to show Jack the factory where he spent his working life. Jack was a trifle disappointed, he had expected somewhere bigger and smarter.

'Yes, I started there at fifteen and did fifty years. I've even got the gold watch. When we're back home, I'm going to get on to the factory manager, that front fence needs tidying up, it looks a real disgrace with all those weeds growing. That's no way to impress visiting customers.'

Jack compared it with Gladwin's site in Harrow and his own efforts to keep it neat and tidy, and silently agreed with Trevor. They were now travelling through areas which were much more industrial, the houses distinctly smaller, older and generally less well-kept than in the leafy suburbs. On the Hessle road, close to the city centre, Jack had an address which turned out to be in a poor street of terraced houses with derelict cars parked. This seemed to be much more feasible Bob Dawson territory.

They travelled out from the centre, along the Beverley Road and one address there also appeared to be probable as a location for Bob Dawson, an old house converted into many flats.

Then there was an area known as the Orchard Park Estate, where Jack felt intimidated by the huge tower blocks and some empty houses, graffiti and signs of vandalism. An address there was also ticked as a possible. After that, there was the big Bransholme estate, where the picture was similar.

'Seen enough?' asked Trevor, after they had found all of the locations.

'Brilliant, thank you,' replied Jack, 'It's given me a real feel for the area. It's really flat here isn't it?'

'Oh yes, definitely. I know a nice pub in Woodmansey, we can stop there now for a pint and a pie, my round this time.'

Jack was more at ease with Trevor now and they spent an amiable lunch-time in the quiet pub, with just a few regulars at the bar. Trevor had not been in the war as he was in a reserved occupation as an engineer, so he was interested to hear about Jack's experiences. Jack of course was only too ready to tell him. He was content that he now had a lot more information to give to Samantha. There was also something else, much more problematic, that he needed to explain.

CHAPTER 31

Harrow, January 1956

I REMEMBER IT now as being on a late winter afternoon, usually the quietest part of our day, especially at that time of year, as our builder customers would knock off early as soon as it started to get dark. Having finished in Nottingham the previous autumn, I had settled back into my old routine.

Not much had changed. Brian's big plans for more new branches appeared to have stalled and were never mentioned again. Fred's retirement was planned for the coming July, but nothing had been said to me about his replacement. I had picked up where I had left off, standards had slipped in a few places, and it had taken me some time to restore them to how I thought they should be. The building of new houses in the area continued, with several new estates being planned. We were busy enough, but I missed the excitement that my job in Nottingham had brought. Sometimes stressful but full of variety.

WHEN THE PHONE rang, it was Elaine from the office, as usual, who was putting through the call.

'Jack, there's a woman on the line for you, she won't give her name, but says it's definitely you she wants to speak to, do you want to take the call?'

I couldn't think who it might be, most of our calls

were from customers or suppliers and their secretaries knew to ask for me by name if they wanted to know what was happening.

So I said, 'I suppose so, let's see what it's all about.'

The staff were putting away the deliveries we had received that day, so I was on my own at the desk, and there weren't any customers in. I started in my usual way.

'Hello, Jack Rodgers speaking, how can I help you?'

I immediately recognised the voice on the other end of the line.

'Hello Jack, how are you? It's Pamela here, from Nottingham.'

This was a shock, we hadn't had any contact since I had finished up there the previous autumn. I was stunned, not knowing how to respond, but my heart also leapt as I wondered what was coming. I was well aware that Elaine could be listening in. Private phone calls were not really approved, except in the direst emergencies.

Eventually, I managed to stammer out something along the lines of, 'I'm OK, thank you, how are you?' She said that she was 'not too bad'. She apologised for ringing me at work, then went on to ask me about someone else who had lodged with her around the same time, name of Bob Dawson. She said that he had paid her with a cheque, which had bounced.

'Was I in contact with him at all?'

I'm afraid that to start with I was a bit brusque with her. I was offended that she might think that he'd be a friend of mine. I said he was not my type, I certainly wouldn't be in touch with him, and was not surprised if his cheque was a dud. I was rather disappointed that she would expect me to have kept contact with a man like that. I then realised I needed to be friendlier.

'How's business?' I asked.

'Oh, it's fine, still keeping me busy,' she said, 'although I think I might be giving it up soon.'

'Is it getting a bit too much for you?'

'Yes, you could say that.' she replied, 'How's your company's business doing up here at Colwick?'

I went on to say that it had started quietly but now seemed to be going well. The chap I had recruited was doing a good job.

'Don't you ever come up to see him, then?' she asked.

I said that it hadn't been necessary and that there had been talk of opening another depot in Birmingham and I might have to go there next, although I knew that was probably never going to come to anything. She then went on to ask about my family and I said that they were doing fine.

It was her final words that struck me as strange.

'Well, don't forget,' she said, 'if you come up any time, do drop in and say hello. You know where to find me.'

I had to finish the call then as a customer came in.

I said, 'I'm sorry, I'll have to go, thanks for ringing, it's good to hear from you,' and I hung up. I wondered what Elaine would have made of that. She never said anything to me, but for a few weeks afterwards, whenever I saw her, I got the dreaded knowing smile and wink from her. I wondered if she ever said anything to Brian. Not that he would have really been bothered, more likely to say, 'Fair play, mate, good on you'.

AT THE TIME it felt like an odd call. Pamela did not sound relaxed, but we had never spoken on the phone before. Many people were uneasy on the telephone in those days, as they didn't have calls very often. I couldn't help thinking that the question about Bob Dawson was just a pretext to ring me. Was the mention of his name telling me something? She knew that we both stayed with her at the same time. Would she really have thought that he was someone I would have been friendly enough with to keep in contact?

Her last sentence was said in a sort of pleading way, as if she was asking me to go to her. And, of course, I now realise that she would have known by then that she was pregnant, what was she going through? If she closed her business, she would have to go on the dole, unless there was a new bloke on the scene to support her. And with a kid on the way, would anyone be interested? With hindsight, I suppose that is what had caused her to call me like that, out of the blue.

I thought of that Nottingham film from the 1960s, *Saturday Night and Sunday Morning*, where the Albert Finney character got a married woman pregnant and tried to arrange an illegal backstreet abortion for her. I hate to think of her now even considering that way out of her predicament.

I must have looked a bit shaken because Fred came over and asked me if I was OK. The memory of that call stayed with me for a long time afterwards, it was as if she was trying to give me a message with the tone of her voice but couldn't bring herself to put it into words. I can only think now that she was offering some sort of an invitation. Even if it wasn't my child? Or was her memory playing tricks as well?

CHAPTER 32

Kenton, September 1990

'SAMANTHA, I'VE GOT a confession to make.'

It was usually Samantha who instigated the telephone calls, not Jack, and when he rang her, she expected that he was going to be full of news about his time in Yorkshire. She was not prepared for what came next.

'Go on, then,' she said, hesitantly.

'It must be my age, you know your memory can play funny tricks because suddenly an image can pop into your mind that you had totally locked away somewhere and forgotten about.'

'Come on Jack, come out with it, what are you trying to tell me?'

'It was when we came to Pamela's house the other week, I mean your house. Just for a moment I thought I saw her there, standing on the step with you and Adam, which must have brought it back into my mind.'

'Jack, you're beating about the bush again, what are you telling me?'

'Please believe me, I haven't been deliberately hiding this from you.'

'Jack!'

'I'm sorry, here goes. After I had been in Nottingham for that summer in fifty-five, I finished in mid-October, didn't I?'

'Yes, Jack, we know that from the receipt books.'

'It must have been the following January when it happened. One afternoon, quite late in the day, I think, Pamela rang me at work.'

'She did what? And you've only just remembered? I don't believe this. You can't suddenly come out with this now.'

'Oh Samantha, please you must believe me, it's the truth.'

'It just seems so important for you not to have remembered this before.'

There was a long silence before she went on. 'What did she say?'

'Best as I can remember, she started by asking me if I was in touch with Bob Dawson at all, as a cheque he had given her had bounced. Well, I could believe that part all right because I wouldn't have trusted him as far as I could throw him, but I was really miffed she might think that I'd want to be in touch with a bloke like him.

'I don't think she believed it either, afterwards it just felt like a ploy, an excuse to ring me. Look, I've never thought of myself as God's gift to women, I have never been used to having them chase after me.'

'Was that it or did she say anything else?'

'I felt bad straightaway, really thought that I had been too sharp with her, saying I would not want to be in contact with Dawson. So, I asked her gently how her business was. She said it was OK, but she was thinking of giving it up soon. That surprised me. I thought she enjoyed doing it and needed the money. I may have suggested that perhaps it was getting a bit much for her, but she changed the subject and asked me how our new depot was doing up there, asking if I ever needed to come up there again.

'I didn't like to tell her that I had been up once, but it was a flying visit to deal with an emergency, I didn't leave Harrow until late morning and then it was there and back in the day. Anyway, I didn't like the idea of dropping in on her unannounced, I didn't know who or what I might find, or even if I would be welcome.'

'So, how did it finish?'

'I expect that we had some chit-chat about my family, and then she really took me by surprise. She always spoke very matter-of-fact, if you know what I mean, not with much emotion. Suddenly, almost as if she was whispering, she lowered her voice and said that well, if I did go up any time, I was to be sure to drop in and see her and that I would know where to find her. She took my breath away, it almost sounded like a come-on, if you know what I mean.'

Samantha waited for a few more moments before asking, 'and what do you think now?'

'That's the thing. I am pretty sure it was in the January, and definitely not before Christmas, it was a quiet time of year when she rang. I understand now that she must have known she was pregnant by then. At least four months on? That's why she was talking about giving up the lodgers.'

'And, what else?'

'Well just possibly she was hoping that my marriage might be in trouble, perhaps I could transfer to the Nottingham branch and live with her? Do you think she might have thought that? She'd have to be pretty desperate to think so, that I'd leave Margaret and the children, wouldn't she? Am I deluding myself here?'

'Hold on Jack, you've got to give me a few minutes now to take this all in. Are you sure this happened?'

'Yes, I am.'

'And you've only just remembered it? It seems bloody important now, doesn't it? How come you haven't thought of this before now?'

Jack squirmed on his stool by the phone. 'I know it sounds very odd, but honestly, it's only just come back to me. Coming back to the house triggered it all. Walking round and expecting to see her round every corner, the penny suddenly dropped.'

'I'm sorry Jack but I need some time to take this all in, you've really thrown me now. I can't say any more now, I'll have to ring you later.'

The phone went dead, and Jack carefully put it down. This didn't happen very often, but on this occasion he went to the cupboard at the bottom of his dresser and took out the brandy bottle.

CHAPTER 33

Ripley, September 1990

IT WAS THE following weekend when Jenny paid a rare visit back to Derbyshire, staying with Samantha, rather than her own family, where she still had problems. On the Saturday evening, having enjoyed a takeaway Chinese and put Adam to bed, the two friends settled down with a bottle of red. Samantha told Jenny about Jack's 'confession', as he had called it.

'Bloody hell, that's a bit much, isn't it?' Jenny exclaimed, 'And he's saying that he's only just remembered it. How come he's telling us this now?'

Samantha did not answer immediately but drained her glass and then refilled it and topped up Jenny's.

'It really shook me, I have to say, and my reaction was like yours. It was so unexpected. It had been so good when they all came to the house, I really thought we were getting somewhere. I'm now really angry with him, I can't decide whether he's only just remembered it, or has been holding it back, or has just made it up. All options seem possible. What do you think?'

'I'm annoyed with him as well, whether it's true or not, just when we thought we were making progress. Still, we don't know what it's like to be nearly seventy, do we, what shape our memories will be in by then, if we get that far?'

'You're right. When I had calmed down somewhat, I thought I could see that returning to the house might have sparked a memory for him.”

‘Yes, I know what you mean,’ said Jenny ‘like blokes you went out with and now you can’t imagine what you were thinking of?’

‘Oh yes, like Dean Wragg, do you mean?’

‘Stop it!’ said Jenny, giggling into her glass. ‘Please don’t remind me. Escaping from him was one of the worst evenings of my life. Who did he end up with, Tina Fern, was it?’

‘Yes. Last time I saw her she had about six kids trailing behind her.’

‘Anyway, back to the matter in hand,’ said Jenny. ‘I hadn’t expected anything like this. How was Jack when he came to your mum’s house?’

‘A bit on edge, not surprisingly, but he relaxed later, although he couldn’t stop looking round at everything. His daughter Elizabeth is lovely, I took to her, very supportive of him and interested in me. Nice children and her husband, well, very good-looking and charming.

‘Jenny, I’ve grown really fond of old Jack, you know. I would still love to wake up and discover that he is my Dad. Adam rarely sees his other Granddad, who isn’t very forthcoming when they do meet. I think him and his wife have always wished that Tim and I had never married, and that our child didn’t exist. Adam told me he liked Jack, and he doesn’t say that sort of thing very often. Since Tim went he’s been cautious about personal relationships. They chat easily about football and his school and stuff. Seeing Jack with his granddaughters, even though he can’t know them too well, you can see that he takes to the part of a Grandpa very easily.’

‘So, you want to believe him, if you can, regardless?’

‘It’s still so very important for me to find out who

my father is, for Adam's sake, to sort out this medical thing. But it is less important now for me personally. I am highly unlikely to get the kind of support and sympathy from my real father, if we ever do find him, that I'm getting from Jack. I don't see the end of our search as being the end of our relationship. Not while he's still around, which I hope will be for a long time yet. The truth is that I don't see any way that I am going to succeed, unless it's with his help. Does that make sense?'

Jenny leant forward and put her hand on Samantha's arm.

'I get that completely, love,' she said. 'All I will say is that we need to stand back from time to time and ask ourselves if this all rings true, don't we?'

'Yes we do,' Samantha replied, 'and I am relying on you to make sure we do that.'

WHEN SAMANTHA RANG Jack again on the Sunday evening, after Jenny had left, at first she said nothing about their previous conversation. Instead she asked him about his time in Yorkshire. That wrong-footed Jack, he had been expecting the third degree. Slowly at first, he told her all about his journey around Hull with Trevor.

'There are some really nice areas, in the suburbs, but it's quite grim in places, old streets near the centre of the city, rundown estates further out. I was a bit surprised to think that some of those houses might even have a telephone, to be honest. They're certainly the type of areas where you'd expect to find someone who was struggling. So, our nine names and numbers are now down to just three most likely. Of course, we have to remember that it's quite possible that none of them are the right person.'

'OK. Well done, it sounds like Trevor has been a great help, doesn't it?'

'I thought it was a real breakthrough. I hadn't planned to do anything like that, and I didn't know him very well at all before. He's what you expect a Yorkshireman to be, very forthright and practical. I think he really enjoyed being part of it all. It also gave him the chance to show me where he'd worked.'

'Right. Thank you for that, very interesting. Now, this confession of yours as you called it. I think I'm going to take it at face value for now, although I still will have some serious reservations.'

'Thank you, I think that's fair enough.'

'There's lots of different ways to take this. Mum might have been trying to tell you that it's your child that she's having.'

'I do realise that. Look, I'm trying to be straight and honest with you and not hide anything now that I'm aware of it.'

Samantha put her hand across the phone's mouthpiece, but Jack could hear enough to know she was crying. He waited.

'Oh my God! My poor mum, what she must have been going through. And nobody around to help her. She must have felt so desperate to call you like that, if that is what she did.'

'I feel guilty now, that I wasn't more helpful to her,' said Jack, wincing as he registered Samantha's qualification at the end. 'But what could I do? I was standing there at our service counter, a customer could've come in at any minute, one of the lads might have overheard me. And the boss's secretary wasn't above listening in if she thought there might be some juicy gossip to be had. Pamela didn't have my home number and I doubt she'd have rung me there anyway. But the middle of the warehouse was no place for a conversation like that. It was the idea that I would have wanted to stay in touch with a bloke like Bob Dawson that upset me. I was just embarrassed.'

'OK, you've told me now. I still need a while to think about all of the implications.'

She took a deep breath.

'When do you fly to New Zealand?'

'Next Wednesday morning, quite early.'

'I suppose I have to bite the bullet now and ring those three numbers. God knows what sort of replies I'll get. Can you send them to me please?'

'I will,' said Jack,' and give me your address again, and I'll send you and Adam a postcard from Christchurch.'

She dictated her address. 'Bon voyage,' she said, 'and tell me all about it when you get back.'

CHAPTER 34

Christchurch, New Zealand, October 1990

JACK SETTLED BACK in his aisle seat on the plane and a rush of emotion swept through him. Relief that he had survived the experience. Happiness that he had been able to spend so much time with his family and could now picture where and how they lived. Joy at absorbing the lifestyle of a different country. Sadness that Margaret had never seen that. Also sad because he didn't know when he would see Elizabeth and family next, if ever. And also anticipation, that he was going home to Samantha and Adam and their quest, which might now be resolved.

There was a woman sitting in the window seat, a space between them, who Jack took to be English, judging by her accent when she took her place after he had already seated himself. He judged her to be around sixty, dressed in a smart turquoise jacket and skirt, a plain white blouse and a considerable amount of jewellery. She was rummaging around trying to find places for her bits and pieces. She then spoke to him, proffering a shopping bag.

'Excuse me, do you mind, could I just ask you to put this in the overhead locker for me, please?'

'Of course,' said Jack. He took off his ever-present grey sports jacket and also put that in the locker before sitting down again and putting his seat belt back on. He was bursting to share his experience with someone.

'Have you been here before?' he asked her.

She did not seem to mind the question.

'Oh yes, I come most years around this time. I come to stay with my sister and her husband. They're at Riccarton, near the university, my brother-in-law, he's retired now, he was a lecturer there in English. I love it here. Have you been visiting family?'

'My daughter and her husband and their two girls. They are out at Sumner, up above the beach. He's a GP there. They've been here for over ten years now but it's my first time over, I think it is a wonderful country.'

'Weren't you tempted to come before?' the woman asked.

'Very tempted, but my late wife would never fly. It's such a shame because I am sure she would have loved it if she had.'

The reference to Margaret put a damper on conversation for a while. Jack noticed that the woman wore a ring on her wedding finger, along with several more on other fingers. After the attentive Singapore Airlines staff had been round with drinks, she opened up the conversation again.

'Do you think you will come back?' she asked.

'I definitely want to, providing I stay healthy enough to make the journey,' replied Jack. 'If I were a younger man, I would think about moving here permanently. Some would say it's old-fashioned, but that suits me.'

'And where do you live in the UK?'

'Kenton, near Harrow, North London.'

'Oh, I'm in Hampstead, not that far away.'

'No,' thought Jack, 'not far at all, but a bit of a difference in the house prices.'

Jack then underwent an extensive interrogation. Did he have other children? How many grandchildren? How long since his wife had died? Was he retired?

What job had he done? It felt rather like a job interview, and he felt reluctant to return the questions. However, she gave him her information regardless.

'I'm divorced myself, over ten years now, just one son and he's in America, bit of a strained relationship since I separated from his father.'

Jack nodded in acknowledgement.

'I'm lucky, lots of good friends and I keep very busy with charity work, Oxfam and Dr. Barnardo's.'

Feeling the need to show interest, Jack asked, 'Is this your only sister that you come to see?'

'Yes, Hazel is four years older than me, but we've always been close, even though they've been out here for more than twenty-five years. My name's Wendy by the way.'

'Pleased to meet you, I'm Jack.'

Having gleaned the information she was seeking Wendy settled back in her seat and picked up a glossy magazine. Jack relaxed and mentally processed all the images of his stay. Cycling with his family; he hadn't ridden a bike for twenty years. The Botanical Gardens, walking on Sumner beach in the sun and in the rain, seeing Fiona and Kelly at their school, their visit to the ski slopes at Mount Hutt. Watching rugby at Lancaster Park, where the All Blacks had beaten Australia just a few months before. Barbecues with Elizabeth and Howard's friends. One picture quickly replaced by another, like a slide show.

He flirted again with the idea of emigrating there. Howard and Elizabeth had made it clear that they would be very happy for him to do that. He thought about David, would he really miss Jack if he did leave England? Probably not very much. Then he thought of Samantha. He realised that to leave now would seem like deserting her, leaving her to finish their search alone. It would look like he was trying to escape from her. The time away had brought home to him just how deeply he was now enmeshed in her life. He regretfully filed the emigration idea away, perhaps to be revisited one day, but not yet.

AFTER THEY HAD left Singapore, Wendy resumed their dialogue, turning in her seat and taking off her glasses to study him. She suggested that he might find living in New Zealand too quiet, after life in London?

'Not really,' answered Jack, 'I live quite a quiet life at home now,'

'You live on your own, I assume?'

'I do, yes.'

'But what about the West End, the theatres and the restaurants?' she asked.

'I never go there, the bright lights have never attracted me. I used to go to Highbury to watch Arsenal and to Lord's and the Oval for the cricket, but that's about it, really. I go to watch Wealdstone FC sometimes.'

The penny was starting to drop with Wendy that Jack's lifestyle was far removed from her own and her interest in him began to wane. She swivelled back in her seat, put her spectacles back on again and picked up another magazine. They both dozed off for a while and there was no more conversation until they were preparing to land at Heathrow.

'Well, nice to meet you,' said Wendy.

'And you too.'

'Who knows, we might meet again in Christchurch one day.'

'Yes, who knows?' replied Jack, thinking, 'not if I see you first.'

CHAPTER 35

Kenton, October 1990

ON THE DAY after his return from New Zealand, Jack now had some understanding of what was meant by 'jet lag', perhaps as experienced by his son David, the frequent flyer. He was surprised by his lack of energy and purposefulness. To stock up his fridge, Jack had been out shopping. He had half-hoped he might see his friends Derek and Janet, so he could boast about having been to New Zealand, but there was no sign of them. He had sorted the post, opened up his workshop to check all was well there, given his lawns a last mow for the year and tidied round the house. He was dozing in his chair after dinner when his phone rang. His first thought was that it might be David and made a mental note to ring him soon.

'You're back then,' said Samantha.

'I am,' he said. 'Recovering slowly, it's a long time to be sitting on a plane, trying to work out what the right time is.'

'Thanks for your card, Christchurch looks very nice. Have you had a wonderful holiday, that's the main thing?'

'Oh I have, it's marvellous out there.' He proceeded to give her a lengthy description of his activities. Eventually he realised that he was monopolising the conversation.

'Sorry, love, I'm going on a bit, aren't I? How are

things with you?'

'No, that's great, it must have been a lovely experience for you. Were you tempted to stay there?'

'Tempted is the word. I definitely feel more comfortable with Elizabeth and Howard than I do with David and Louise, that's for sure. I do admire my son-in-law, he's got his priorities right. I will go back again, God willing, but here is where my home is.'

'Good. Well, there have been some developments at this end while you were away.'

'Go on.'

'For starters, it looks as if Mum's house is sold. We've had a decent offer which I have persuaded my sisters we should accept. The only thing is that the buyers have still got to sell their house, out at Burton Joyce. They are an older couple who want to be nearer the city centre and their son.'

'That's hopeful then,' said Jack, 'You'll be glad to see that go now, I reckon.'

'Yes, I will, it was becoming a saga, other people seemed very interested, and then dropped out. But this couple are very keen. The other news is yet another note from Hull, signed by 'B' again.'

'Blimey, he's getting persistent, isn't he? What does it say?'

'There's a bit more information this time. I'll read it.

'"*I don't think I have got long left now. Life is pretty miserable as I'm more or less housebound, had to ask a neighbour to post this for me. Orchard Park is very bleak now. I just want you to know that you're not forgotten. I should have been kinder to you. Love from B*"'

'Does that mean anything to you, Jack?'

'Oh yes, it does. Orchard Park is one of those run-down council estates that were built in the sixties.

Massive tower blocks, rows and rows of houses, not much in the way of shops or facilities, lots of graffiti. One of the Bob Dawson phone numbers that I gave you was on there, a tower block called Milldane. I hated it round there. Definitely a likely place for him if he is down on his luck.'

Samantha gasped. 'Wow! Well that does narrow it down somewhat, doesn't it?'

'It does. What do you think he means about being kinder?'

'Not sure really, but it does worry me, what might have happened to my mum, what she might have been through. Doesn't bear thinking about. It does seem like a hint that he recognises that something happened that she didn't want, who knows? It's all a bit vague isn't it?'

'Yes, but it seems to point that way, doesn't it?'

'Jack, you sent me those three phone numbers. I have to admit that I have kept looking at them but haven't done anything with them yet. Shall I pluck up my courage to ring that one, then?'

'Well, give it a try, it might be disconnected, but see what happens.'

He then identified which was the relevant number.

IT WAS THE next night when Samantha rang back.

'No luck, I'm afraid, number unobtainable,' she said.

'I'm not surprised, I thought that might happen. At least it doesn't rule that one out, does it? If anything perhaps it is more likely now?'

'Maybe, but where do we go from here?'

'I thought that might happen, so I've been thinking about what our next step should be. We could try writing to him but I'm not sure that will take us any further forward. You know, Trevor quite surprised me. He's rather old school, but he wanted to know all about what we were doing, He was more sympathetic to the idea than I'd expected, said he felt sorry for you and Adam. Very happy to drive me round the area to find all the addresses. I think getting involved made a change for him from playing golf most days and tidying his garden. Relieved the boredom a bit for him, I think. I'm sure he'd try to help us.'

'How could he do that?'

'I reckon that if I tell him the situation he would offer to go and investigate for us.'

'How?' asked Samantha.

'He's very Yorkshire, very direct. He might even go and knock on the door to see who's there. Shall I ask him?'

'If you think that he'll be up for it, why not?'

'HELLO, IS THAT Norma?'

'Speaking.'

'Oh, hello, it's Jack here, you know, Elizabeth's father, how are you?'

'Very well, thank you. Are you OK? What did you think of New Zealand?'

'I thought it was marvellous, thank you. Erm, is Trevor there?'

'No, he's playing golf, as ever. They stop on every Wednesday evening to have a meal, so he won't be back until later. Can I give him a message? Is it something urgent?'

'No, no, nothing like that. Can you just ask him to give me a ring some time when he can?'

Norma wasn't going to let him go at that and he was required to describe in detail what they had done and where they had been in New Zealand. After the call was finished Jack felt quite exhausted.

IT WAS MID-MORNING the next day when Trevor called Jack. Once again he had to give chapter and verse on his time in New Zealand. Trevor was particularly impressed to hear that Jack and Howard had been to Lancaster Park to see the rugby and wanted to know who was playing. Eventually, Trevor asked, 'Anyway, you rang me Jack, can I help?'

'Well, it's like this Trevor,' started Jack, 'You remember when we did our tour of the city. Following up all the addresses I had?'

'I do.'

'We've had another letter from this bloke you see, mentions that he's on Orchard Park. Do you remember that tower block, Milldane, I think it's called? We decided that the address was probably a ground floor flat.'

'Yes, indeed.'

'Well, Samantha's rung the number and its unobtainable, so we don't know if he's there or not, if it is him.'

Jack paused. Trevor filled the silence.

'And you'd like me to go to have a look, would you?'

'If it's not too much trouble. Would you do that?'

'No, I can do it. I wouldn't go on my own, mind you, not to park my car round there.'

He paused for thought. 'I know, I'll take Darren, the young security bloke from the factory, I could borrow him for an hour or two. He's as solid as a brick-built outhouse he is, well over six foot tall, and he knows that area well, nobody will mess about with him.'

'Are you sure?'

'Wouldn't offer if I wasn't, Jack. The way you told her story I feel really sorry for this lass and her lad. If I can do my bit, I will. How do you want me to play it, just march up to the front door and say, *"Are you Bob Dawson?"*.'

'Basically, yes, you'll take him unawares, so best to be direct. What I'll do is to send you a copy of a photo we have which he is on. It's thirty-five years old, but it will give you a clue. I'd just ask him if he was in digs in Nottingham in nineteen fifty-five and if he has been writing to someone there.'

'And if he asks me why I want to know?'

'I would say that you are calling on behalf of someone from Nottingham, leave it at that. He says he's housebound now, so he is likely to be there.'

'OK, Jack. Leave it to me.'

TEN DAYS LATER, Trevor rang Jack again.

'Sherlock Holmes reporting, sir. I've found your man.'

'Really! That's brilliant. What happened?'

'I left Darren minding the car, keeping the yobs away, and there were a few around. You were right, it is a ground floor flat. It's not very nice round about, stinks rather, litter and graffiti. No bell, I knocked on the door, heard nothing for a while, knocked again and then I heard someone shout that they were coming. The door opens and it's this old bloke, on a Zimmer frame. In a dirty track suit with long straggly grey hair, unwashed. I still knew him straightaway from your photo, no doubt who he was. I asked him directly if he was Bob Dawson and he stared at me and said, "Who wants to know?". Quite well-spoken, not from Hull originally I wouldn't think. So I said, "I do".'

'What did he say to that?' asked Jack.

'He asked me why I wanted to know, so I said I was there on behalf of someone from Nottingham. He said, "what, from Pamela?" so I said, "No, not directly". I then asked him if he was in digs in Nottingham in fifty-five and he thought about it and said that he was. I thanked him very much and left him to it. He just stood there with his mouth hanging open. He stayed at the door and watched me walk back to the car. I stood with Darren for a moment, and we stared back at him. He closed the door then.'

'When was this?' asked Jack.

'This morning,' replied Trevor, 'this is hot off the press. I dropped Darren back at the works, gave him a tenner for his trouble and came home. After I had stopped at that pub at Woodmansey, of course.'

'I don't know how to thank you, Trevor, I owe you a tenner for a start.'

'Forget that. I shouldn't have mentioned it. I enjoyed it to be honest, I got a buzz from being involved.'

'Do you think Samantha and I would be safe to go there?' asked Jack.

'I think so, in daylight, just don't go in a big flash car.'

'I don't think we've got one of those.'

CHAPTER 36

Kenton, June 1956

'WHAT TIME DO you call this?'

Margaret could be quite abrupt at times.

'I'm sorry,' I said, surprised to see that it was already nearly seven o'clock.

'This is getting beyond a joke. I always have your dinner ready for six, but it seems like any time now when you get home.'

I was last away from Gladwin's that night, so I'd had to lock up, set the alarms, check all the windows and doors, then lock the gates. That always took time.

'I've said I'm sorry. I found a delivery of nails that hadn't been put away. I couldn't leave it to the morning. We're always so busy first thing.'

'Why hadn't they been put away?'

'It's the new lad, Graham. I can't rely on him to do his jobs. He's going to have to go at this rate.'

'I don't know that it's worth it, this foreman's job. For the little bit extra they are paying you they seem to expect you to work all hours.'

I wasn't going to tell her that the main reason that I was late was because Brian had called me into his office at about ten to five to tell me that he'd done a special deal on a load of bricks from someone who wasn't our regular supplier.

'They're rejects, Jack,' he'd said,' so you might have to go through them and chuck a few out, but most of them will be OK.'

I knew that would be a really painstaking job, sorting out the duds, and I still wouldn't want them to go to our best customers. They could only go to local D-I-Y blokes who didn't know any better and were building themselves a garage at their homes. And they would still be likely to come back and complain. Bad news like that soon travels fast round here and it wouldn't do our reputation any good.

Margaret wasn't going to let up any time soon.

'You know we've got Elizabeth's birthday party tomorrow, don't you? You're not going to be late back then, are you?'

'Seems a bit silly to me to have a party for a one-year-old, she's not going to understand what's going on, is she? And David will be mardy because he won't be the centre of attention.'

'Don't start that again, we've been all through that. You know my Mum and my sister won't hear of us not having a party. Edna and Tom aren't coming because he doesn't want to drive home in the rush hour, so there's no-one on your side to care.'

I usually enjoy lamb chops, but this time they'd been overdone and were too tough. I don't know if that had been done to spite me or not. I was too tired to argue any more, I was struggling to cope with the job, to be honest, since Fred had retired. He'd always seemed so calm and in control and made it look easy, but I'd found all sorts of little wrinkles and tasks that I was unaware of. Mind you, he had been doing it for over forty years. I had taken on this lad, Graham, he was bright enough, but he just didn't care, too slap-dash, spent most of his time combing his hair in front of the mirror in the Gents.

AFTER I HAD washed up and she had put the children to bed, although not without David running up and down stairs about twenty times, shouting his head off, she started off again,

'How much are they paying you now for this foreman's job?'

'They put me up to nine pounds a week when I came back from Nottingham and then to eleven pounds when I was made foreman. So that's more than three pounds a week above what I was on before Nottingham.'

'Yes, but it's still less than you got when you were up there, isn't it?'

That was true. I had hoped that Brian might take me back to twelve pounds when he made me up, so I had been a bit disappointed. I had never known what they had paid Fred, you didn't discuss stuff like that then. He'd have told me to mind my own business if I'd asked.

'Well, I don't think it's worth it. You come home all hours, work every Saturday until quite late and I can hardly get a word out of you in the evenings.'

'What do you think I should do about it then?'

'Well, I think you should be paid more or go back to where you were.'

'No chance of asking Brian for a rise, I'd be out the door in ten minutes flat. And there's no way I am going to work for another foreman if they brought one in. I know how the job should be done. And things are much easier for us now financially, we're actually building up a bit of money in the bank at last.'

'What about going somewhere else? Our Barbara's Richard went for another job and that paid him thirty bob a week more.'

'I don't think your brother-in-law is a great example. He got sacked from his last job and the firm before that went bust. He's only a labourer, he could be out on his neck any time.'

I knew that I hadn't answered her main question. I had now been at Gladwin's too long, it was now eighteen years since I had first joined them from school. I had never worked anywhere else and would find it hard to fit in at a new place. In those days it was quite normal to be at the same place all your working life, from school to retirement.

The signals were that the conversation was now at an end and had not been concluded satisfactorily, as far as Margaret was concerned. She scowled, turned in her chair and picked up her knitting.

SHE WENT UP to bed early, before ten o'clock, and I didn't hurry to follow her. I switched off the TV and just sat in my chair. I started to think about the time, twelve months before, when I was working in Nottingham. It had been hectic, no mistake, seat of the pants stuff, out of my depth sometimes, but quite thrilling in its way. But, every night, back to Pamela's, a meal ready, served with a nice smile and an enquiry as to how my day had been. If her day had been tough, you would never hear about it.

I wondered about who might be staying there that night. And I remembered that evening when we had walked up to the pub, almost like a settled couple out for their evening stroll. Could my life had taken a different turn there? Had I missed an opportunity? Or was I deluding myself, fantasising about something that never could have happened? And I realised that it was too late now to change anything.

CHAPTER 37

Ripley and Hull, November 1990

FOR THEIR TRIP to Hull, Samantha invited Jack to stay with them the night before.

'What, stay at your place?'

'Jack, I've got three bedrooms, it's not a problem. You don't get up at four in the morning or anything daft like that, do you?'

'Oh no, I'm usually a good sleeper. It's just that I'm not used to staying in other people's homes, though. I only stayed at David's because I was recovering from my operation. Of course, I stopped for two weeks with Elizabeth and Howard in New Zealand, but that was different somehow, more like being on holiday.'

'Perhaps it's something you might get more used to, then,' said Samantha.

'Oh right.'

HE EMERGED FROM the crowded train from St. Pancras onto the platform and into the recently modernised Derby station concourse. Samantha and Adam, hand in hand, were waiting for him. She grabbed his small suitcase from him and led him to the car park and her ten-year old blue Mini. He waited while Adam scrambled into the back and then eased himself with some difficulty into the low front passenger seat. The Derby Friday evening rush hour traffic was still heavy but at last they were on the fast A38 dual carriageway and then pulling up in front of Samantha's semi-detached house. She showed him to his room, put down his case, pointed out the bathroom and proposed a cup of tea.

'That would be lovely,' said Jack.

It was a clean plain room with a single bed. He opened his case, set aside his sponge bag and put his alarm clock on the bedside table. Then he nervously went downstairs, uncertain about where to go or sit. Adam was in the front room watching TV, a preview of that weekend's football matches. Samantha appeared from the kitchen with Jack's mug of tea and gestured to him to sit down on the sofa with Adam. She pulled up a side table and put the mug on a coaster, before returning to the kitchen at the back of the house.

Jack and Adam talked easily about football, including Brian Clough's abilities as a manager and the impact that the new Irish player Roy Keane was having at Notts Forest.

'He's a tough nut, isn't he?' said Jack.

'Yes, I love the way he tackles,' said Adam.

'Have you seen him play yet?'

'No, only on telly,' the boy answered, 'I have never been to a match.'

'Never been to see them? Oh dear, that's a shame. I went to see them years ago when I was working up here. I once saw them beat Doncaster Rovers five-nil. Of course, they were only in the Second Division then. Perhaps we could go and see them sometime?'

Adam's face lit up. 'Really, do you think we could? My friend Lee's Dad takes him sometimes, but not very often, because he works most Saturdays.'

Samantha put her head round the door. 'That sounds like a promise that won't be forgotten,' she said. 'Right tea's ready, come and get it.'

They went into the kitchen to eat, giving Jack the chance to go the window and inspect Samantha's back garden. It was rather empty, a stretch of lawn, a path of concrete slabs, minimal flower beds round the edge, and a wilder section beyond, with an old apple tree standing sentry.

'I'm afraid my husband didn't have much enthusiasm for gardening,' she said, 'since he's been gone I've just tried to keep it reasonably tidy. Not up to your standards, I'm afraid.'

'No, but it's got potential,' said Jack, thinking about what he would do with it, if he ever had the chance. He was delighted to find that Samantha's catering was much more straightforward than Louise's, a bought steak and kidney pie, with mashed potatoes and peas. Later there was jam roly-poly and custard.

All three of them cleared their plates.

'That was lovely, thank you, right up my street,' he said.

'I thought it might be. We've got a good butcher, makes his own pies. The pudding was from Sainsbury's.'

'Was it now, I'll have to look out for one of those.'

'There's not an awful lot to see in Ripley, but do you fancy a quick walk round before it's too dark, walk off our dinner?'

Samantha hadn't oversold the town, but Jack found it pleasant enough and noticed the distinct local accent of people they passed on the street.

'Hullo, mi duck,' said one woman who seemed to know Samantha.

'Who's that?' he asked.

'That's Mrs. Dring, she's a dinner lady at my school. She gives me extra helpings,' offered Adam.

When Jack stopped to look in an estate agents' window he was amazed at how cheap some of the houses in Ripley were, about a quarter of the asking price of those in his part of London.

They saw Adam's school, the cottage hospital, and the council offices where Samantha worked. There were a few rowdy youths congregating on the Market Square, limbering up for their Friday night out.

'Time to head back,' said Samantha.

AFTER ADAM HAD gone to bed, they settled down in the lounge. She had two cans of beer in the fridge for Jack, one of which he gratefully accepted, while she had a glass of white wine. She watched a variety show on television while he read his *Daily Mail*, although he had already read much of it on his journey north. By ten o'clock he was starting to doze, so made his apologies and made his way to bed. He was snoring contentedly by the time she came upstairs, some time later.

JACK WOKE TO that most pleasant of Saturday morning aromas, frying bacon. He went to the bathroom, shaved, dressed and made his way downstairs. Samantha and Adam were already at the breakfast table. On the radio, the announcer was just reading the eight o'clock news. He was talking about Mrs. Thatcher being under pressure following Sir Geoffrey Howe's resignation as Deputy Prime Minister.

'Morning, Jack,' said Samantha.

'Good morning,' replied Jack.

'Can I call him Jack as well?' the boy asked his mother. She looked across at Jack with raised eyebrows.

'I mean he's not my Granddad, is he?' continued Adam.

Samantha and Jack exchanged wry smiles as they

considered the hidden implications of which the boy, they hoped, was blissfully unaware.

'Well, that's my name, although I was christened John. Of course you can, as long as I can call you Adam.'

Adam nodded agreement and resumed his attack on his bacon, egg and beans.

'Same for you Jack? asked Samantha.

'No beans, thanks, they don't really agree with me.'

AS HE HAD done the night before, Jack did the drying after she had washed up. Soon after nine o'clock they were drawing up at a house a few streets away, where Adam's friend Lee lived with his mum, Linda. Jack was introduced.

'You've done good service for Samantha, minding Adam for her so often lately,' he said.

'That's OK, glad I can help,' said the overweight young woman, blonde with her hair scraped back. 'To be honest, with my husband at work, together they're less trouble than Lee would be on his own. Come in, Adam.' Lee appeared briefly from behind his mother and the two of them scurried off inside.

'I can see he makes himself at home,' Jack said.

'They're real pals and he's a good influence on Lee. He's bright and works hard at school, so I hope that some of it rubs off on my boy. Can but hope.' She managed a thin smile.

'We won't be late back,' promised Samantha.

Jack did find climbing into the Mini to be hard work, not like David's big cars or Howard's Land Rover in New Zealand. Samantha was a careful driver, not venturing into the outside lane on the motorway and keeping below 60 mph. Jack felt a little tense when some big lorries overtook them, but she seemed quite relaxed.

Soon the Humber Bridge came in sight. Jack had brought his Hull A to Z and his notes in a cardboard folder, and he re-read all the detail that he already knew by heart. He successfully found the right turnings for them to head north, away from the city centre, towards Orchard Park. He felt a sense of relief when the tops of the tower blocks appeared in the distance.

'I need some petrol, shall we make a quick pitstop at this garage?' asked Samantha.

'Good idea,' said Jack, 'I'll pay.'

'No you won't.' After she had refuelled she turned to Jack. 'Suddenly it feels like we might be near the end of a long, long journey. But there again....'

'Yes, fingers crossed.'

Although he had been once before with Trevor, Jack was confused when they pulled on to the Orchard Park Estate and became flustered when he couldn't give her directions towards their destination. To him, one tower block was very much like another. It took a couple of wrong roads and then a U-turn before they eventually found themselves in front of Milldane tower block.

'I see what you mean, it feels like a foreign country here, doesn't it?' she said.

A thick drizzle had set in by now and the wind whipped in from the east. Samantha sat motionless.

'Come on, love' urged Jack, 'for good or for ill, this is what we're here for. Let's go.'

CHAPTER 38

Hull, November 1990

AS THEY APPROACHED the tower block, a skinny youth in a hooded jacket and jeans was standing in the entrance hall, leaning against the wall, smoking something. He eyed them with some suspicion, then averted his gaze. He did not speak. As they passed him, Jack caught a whiff of a strange, sweet odour. The flat they were looking for was straight ahead of them. Jack stood protectively behind Samantha as she knocked with her knuckles on the door. There was a bell-push but, covered in cobwebs, it did not appear to be functioning. They could hear some rustling, but nobody spoke. She knocked again.

'All right, just wait a minute, will you?' shouted an irritated male voice from inside. The youth in the doorway turned to watch. More rustling, a muffled curse and the door opened. Jack moved closer to Samantha. An elderly man in a grubby grey tracksuit stood before them, leaning heavily on a Zimmer frame. He wore a hearing aid, and his lank grey hair was shoulder-length. Although he had changed so much, Jack immediately knew who he was.

'What do you want, are you from Social Services?' he demanded gruffly. Samantha, hands in pockets, put her shoulders back and looked him in the eye.

'We're looking for Bob Dawson,' she said.

'Who wants to know?'

'We've come from Nottingham to see you,' she replied mildly. The man studied her closely and then at Jack, who sensed that there was a glimmer of recognition.

'From Nottingham? Why?'

'To see you, of course.'

The man looked them both up and down again, then sighed.

'Are you from Pamela?'

'Yes, we are,' said Samantha firmly. The man wiped his nose with his sleeve as he continued to stare at them. The smoker across the hall now seemed interested and pulled himself upright for a better view. She spoke again.

'Are you Bob Dawson?'

'I think you'd better come in. It's a bit of a mess but it's the best I can do.' He turned and shuffled his way down a cluttered corridor into a room which other people might have called a lounge. The curtains were closed, and a low-wattage bulb in the centre light gave only a little illumination. More light came from the television, flickering silently in one corner, a bowl with a single goldfish on top of it.

'What a dump,' thought Jack, sniffing the rancid atmosphere. He had looked round for a telephone but couldn't see one.

The man fell back into an upright armchair with his back to the TV.

'Clear that stuff away and find yourselves somewhere to sit,' he said, waving one arm across the room. There were two ancient dining chairs piled high with old newspapers and magazines which they removed and parked on the linoleum floor. There were no carpets or rugs. Jack glanced at Samantha and could see that she was overcome by the moment, so he broke the silence.

'Do you remember me then, Bob?'

'I think so,' he replied, 'can't remember your name. Were you at Pamela's?'

'I was. I'm Jack Rodgers. It's been a long time, Bob.'

'It has, a very long time.'

As Trevor had reported, the man was in fact quite well-spoken, although his voice was hoarse, as if he was or had been a heavy smoker. He certainly didn't sound like a native of Hull, but he didn't have any particular accent.

'Thirty-five years,' said Jack. The man studied the floor for a few moments.

'Yes, I'm Bob Dawson all right. There was a fellow in a posh car, came here saying he was asking for someone in Nottingham. Was he from you? What do you want?'

Samantha cleared her throat. 'I'm Pamela Charlton's daughter and I've come to see you. I've been wondering why you've been sending her these notes.'

Dawson stared at her a while before he spoke.

'How is she?'

'I'm sorry to say she died, getting on for three years ago now. What was she to you?'

Dawson now gazed up at the ceiling. Jack leant forward in anticipation, hands on his knees.

'You see,' said Dawson, 'I've done a lot of things I regret over the years, that's why I've finished up in a hole like this.' He stared again at Samantha. 'Are you really her daughter?'

'That's right, born nearly thirty-five years ago. Does that mean anything to you?'

'Oh my God!' Dawson put his hands to his face and then laughed a hollow laugh. 'Have you come to claim a share of my estate? Then you will be disappointed.' He turned to look again at Jack. 'Were you the fellow who was there that night?'

'Which night was that then, Bob?'

'I think you know what I'm talking about, the night Pamela disappeared into someone's bedroom.'

'Yes, that was me. She was wanting protection from a man who was pursuing her.'

'Huh! What sort of protection did you give her?'

'Just enough to keep you away. No more than that, she knew she could trust me. It is you that has been sending notes, isn't it?'

'Yes, like I say, I've done a lot that I regret. I suppose I wanted to say sorry.'

Jack stared him out and Dawson looked away.

'Samantha and I want to know what happened the weekend straight afterwards, when I think you were there on your own with Pamela. Why did you say in one of your notes that you should have been kinder to her?'

Dawson took a deep breath.

'In those days, in the nineteen-fifties, I worked with a sales agency, based in Bristol, selling whatever we could get our hands on, to whoever we could find to buy it. Sand to the Arabs, coals to Newcastle, I could sell anything to anybody. So I was chasing all over the country. Low salary but a decent commission. I was good at it, everybody said so. No car back then, so I always travelled by train. If I could fix it, I would try to be in Nottingham as often as possible so I could stay at Pamela's. It was nice and central for wherever I had to go next. Lovely lady, attractive of course, even you must have noticed that. But smart with it, intelligent woman you could have a proper conversation with. More than just going on about what was on telly last night. Nice clean house,' he looked around him, 'good healthy food.'

'I always thought you fancied yourself as a ladies' man,' said Jack.

'I'll admit I had some successes. Us commercial travellers, we had a bit of a reputation for it. One of the perks of the job, you might say. But Pamela was special, a definite cut above the normal. Over two or three years I stayed there a few times. Early on, I asked her out for a drink, but she wasn't having that, said she didn't fraternise with her lodgers.'

Samantha had a quick glance at Jack, smiling. Dawson didn't appear to notice and carried on. 'This one night I was chatting to her in the kitchen, thinking I was doing all right when one of the other lodgers came in, spoilt the mood, he did. Was that you?'

'Yes, it was,' confirmed Jack.

'Might have known. That's the night when she disappeared into one of the other bedrooms.'

'That was a Thursday night, said Jack, 'it's what happened after that we want to know about, over the weekend. Were you there on your own with her?'

By now, Dawson was starting to look embarrassed, avoiding Samantha's eye by staring at the floor in front of him.

CHAPTER 39

Hull, November 1990

I FOUND IT hard to believe that after all these years, and all this time working with Jack, that I finally had in front of me the man responsible for my being on this earth. He seemed ready to confess, so I waited impatiently to hear him utter those words.

'I can't forget it, however I try. I went to see a customer on the Saturday morning, somewhere local, we had to work Saturday mornings then. I took him for a couple of beers after I'd done a deal with him, I think it developed into a bit of a session. I tried it on with the barmaid at the pub, but she wasn't interested, so I guess I was a bit frustrated.'

He paused. I had also been staring at the floor up to this point, but now I looked up and stared at him. God, he looked dreadful. Unshaven, dirty and somehow slimy. I couldn't bear to imagine even touching him. If only I'd had a film camera to capture the moment for all time.

'Spare me the details please,' I said. 'If you came back drunk I don't believe my mum would have consented to anything with you. I'm not going to the police about this, don't worry, although I could. I have other reasons for wanting to know what happened.'

He wrung his hands, but I kept the pressure on him.

'I assume that you forced yourself upon her, is that right, knowing that if she called anyone it would be her word against yours? Is that right? Is that how you operated?'

He nodded agreement.

'Did you take any precautions, or wasn't that your style?'

'I might have done, I usually carried a packet with me.'

That expression was just too much for me and pushed me over the edge. I screamed at him.

'You are horrible! Just an awful, awful bloody man. I hate you! And nine months later I was born, that's why we are here. You work it out'.

Silent tears ran down his cheeks while I dabbed a tissue to my eyes. Jack put his hand on my shoulder to comfort me, although he would have realised as he did that it was an inadequate gesture. For what seemed like several minutes there was a total silence. I could sense Jack waiting to say something, but I didn't have any more words.

'It's taken us a while,' said Jack, 'but we finally found you. Samantha thought it might have been me, that's how I got involved. Did you know that she'd had a baby?'

'Some time later, probably a year or more, I needed to stay in Nottingham again, so I rang her to confirm. When she answered, I could hear a baby crying. "What's that noise?" I said. "My daughter", she replied. I panicked and rang off. Never went back again.'

Samantha and Jack looked at each other in disbelief, but before they could say any more, they were startled to hear a key turning in the door. Dawson did not seem surprised. A woman's voice called out.

'It's only me. What I have told you about keeping this place tidy, it's like a bloody pigsty out here?'

CHAPTER 40

Hull, November 1990

A TALL SLIM young woman, ten or more years younger than Samantha, burst into the lounge, dressed in knee-high boots, denim jeans and jacket, with a bright orange T-shirt. She wore her dark hair piled on top of her head, making her seem even taller.

'Christ Almighty, who the hell are you?'

'Calm down, Charlotte.'

To Samantha and Jack he said, 'This is my daughter, I knew she'd be here soon, she comes every Saturday morning to sort me out.'

Charlotte brought a stool from the kitchen and sat near her father.

'Huh, some hopes of doing that. It gets worse every week. What's this all about?'

'I think he's my father as well,' said Samantha, 'it sounds as if we are half-sisters. Pleased to meet you.'

Charlotte gasped as she stared from one to the other. 'Oh my God, I knew his past would catch up with us one day. When did this happen?'

'Thirty-five years ago in Nottingham, when he lodged with my mother. What's more, from what he's told us, I'm sure that it happened without my mother's consent.'

Dawson put his head in his hands and Charlotte's face showed real alarm. She stared at him, and his reaction seemed to convince her to accept what

Samantha had said.

'I suppose you'll go to the police now will you?' She stood up as if ready to leave immediately.

'No, I won't, don't worry about that. I've other reasons for wanting to track him down.'

'If you've come for money you'll know by now that you've come to the wrong place.'

Charlotte sat down again and glared at them. She opened her shoulder bag and lit herself a cigarette, without offering them round. Jack, who was sitting near her, pulled away from the smoke. Charlotte looked at Jack.

'Who are you then? Stepfather?'

'No, I was also a lodger there at the same time as your father. I've helped Samantha in the search to identify and find him.'

Charlotte raised a well-manicured eyebrow and drew heavily on her cigarette.

'OK, now we have all introduced ourselves, let me explain,' said Samantha, 'I've got a nine-year-old boy who has a medical problem. It's important that I know all the family history. I've checked mine, best as I can and my husband's side as well. The doctors have said that I should try to locate my real father to see if he or his children have any similar symptoms.'

Charlotte paused mid-drag and showed interest.

'Oh! I see. What's the problem then?'

'Something called Charcot-Marie-Tooth disease, CMT they call it.'

Charlotte and her father looked at each other.

'Oh bloody hell,' she said, 'do we know something about that?'

'Go on, then,' said Samantha, 'Tell us what you know about it.'

'Well,' said Charlotte, 'my kid brother for a start, he's got a lot of mental problems, but also footdrop, as they call it, is another for him.'

'Any idea who your brother's father is?' asked Samantha with an innocent expression.

Charlotte took another drag and nodded towards her father.

'As far as we know.'

She went on, 'Then my little lad has got real problems with his walking, very flat feet. Bloody doctors are useless, say they can't do anything about it. They call it that CMT name.'

Jack addressed a question to Dawson. 'Bob, when you were staying in Nottingham, were you married then?'

'I've never been married. Fool's game if you ask me.'

'So who is Charlotte's mother?'

'The woman who dragged me up here twenty-odd years ago.'

'Where is she now?' asked Jack.

'Nowhere,' interjected Charlotte. 'She was run over by a bus in town two years ago. She'd been drinking. That's why I'm stuck with looking after him and my brother.'

'Where's your brother?'

'In a home near here. He's got too many mental problems to ever come out.'

'Two years ago you say. That's when you started sending notes to Pamela, isn't it?' asked Jack. Dawson nodded.

'You didn't think she'd take you in, did you?'

Dawson glowered at Jack.

'And what about your boy's father?' Samantha asked Charlotte, cautiously.

'Sailor, on the fishing boats. I see him now and again. You're asking a lot of nosy questions, aren't you?'

'I know,' said Samantha, 'sorry, but I need to ask. My boy is showing symptoms which could be CMT and our doctors, who also say there is no cure, have asked me to see if I can find any family history before they decide if Adam has definitely got it. There's nothing on my side or my husband's side, so I needed to find my true father.'

'Hmm,' said Charlotte. 'I see you don't wear a wedding ring either.'

'I don't, we're separated.'

'Got quite a bit in common then, haven't we?'

'Yes we have. You know it's an inherited disease, don't you? We might be the carriers, you and me, so any children our kids have, they could also pass it on.'

Charlotte frowned, as if this was new information for her. Jack turned the conversation back to Dawson again.

'Bob, have you any idea how many children you might have.'

The man stared back. 'No idea. These two have been quite enough.'

This was too much for Jack.

'You're the sort of bloke who gets us men a bad name. Are you proud of the life you've led, what have you ever done to benefit society?'

'Sod society. What's it ever done for me? Didn't Margaret Thatcher say there's no such thing?'

Jack snorted and folded his arms. He looked across to Samantha. 'Have we learnt all we need to know?'

'Hang on a minute,' she replied, turning towards Dawson. 'OK, we do know more now, and I do believe now that you are my father. I want you to understand that I have total contempt for you and the way you've lived your life. You knew that the police would be reluctant to follow up any complaint from my mother unless there were witnesses. I suppose your morals were no different from a lot of other men in those days, or today, come to that. It's not much comfort to know that your behaviour is the reason why I'm here.'

'She could have had an abortion', said Dawson.

'Huh, like Saturday Night and Sunday Morning, backstreet with a bottle of gin? Do you think that was my mother's style? What I need to ask you both is, would you agree to having some tests, see whether we've got genes in common, or something like that?'

Charlotte quickly said, 'Yes, I'd do that. Might help my boy.' She looked at her father, who hadn't answered. 'Well?'

He shifted uncomfortably again before replying, 'If I must.'

Samantha turned to Charlotte. 'Thank you, I appreciate that.' She turned to Jack. 'OK, let's go.'

Charlotte said, 'Before you do.'

'Yes.'

'It may seem a funny thing to say, but it's good to meet you. I don't have much myself in the way of other family, some on my mum's side, but they are pretty scattered, and I don't see much of them. Could we keep in touch, please, I'd like that?'

'All right with me. I'll have to come back to you anyway, to see what tests the doctors want you to take. Shall I give you my phone number?' She looked at Dawson. 'My mum's house will be sold in a few weeks, so there's no point in sending her any more notes.'

Dawson sighed.

Charlotte said, 'Could we exchange addresses as well?'

'Let's stick to phone numbers for now, if you don't mind.'

They found scraps of paper, Samantha had a pen, and they made the exchange.

Jack and Samantha stood up simultaneously. He

nodded at Dawson but said no more.

'Goodbye,' said Samantha, directing it at Charlotte.

'Goodbye,' said Dawson, 'so sorry to hear about Pamela, I'd have loved to have seen her again.'

Samantha glared at him. 'I don't think you would have been at all welcome. We'll see ourselves out.'

WHEN THEY EMERGED the loitering youth had disappeared, but a couple of young lads were now kicking a football about in the entrance hall. The drizzle outside was heavier and the wind from the North Sea was stronger. They walked back to the car. Samantha waited a minute before turning on the ignition, staring at the rain.

'Thanks, Jack. Thanks for coming and for getting me here. It would never have happened without you. It wasn't easy but we know a lot more now.'

'Glad to have helped,' he replied, 'it's taken us just about nine months from the day you arrived on my doorstep, but we've got you some sort of an answer.'

'I'm hungry,' said Samantha, switched on the engine and drove off the way they had come. When she saw a McDonald's she pulled in to the car park. 'This'll do.'

CHAPTER 41

Ripley, November 1990

McDONALDS WAS A new experience for Jack who needed some guidance through the many available menu options. He settled for a simple burger, fries and a coffee.

'What are fries?'

'Sort of skinny chips.' He did not look impressed, but his attitude improved once had bitten into his burger.

'Oh that's all right. I always wondered what these places were like.' There were some small children running around. 'Noisy though, isn't it? It does feel odd, coming to a restaurant and eating with your fingers. How do you feel now, love?'

'Very mixed emotions. I am so ashamed that such an awful man is my father but there's nothing I can do to change that. I have no feelings for him at all. He is living in absolute squalor, but I have no sympathy for him, it's about what he deserves. I'm glad to know more about the CMT link, but I am worried for Adam as it now seems more likely that it will be confirmed.'

'And Charlotte?'

'That's the really funny thing, I do feel for her, she's another one who's not had a lot going for her, has she? I almost think that I've got more in common with her than my other two half-sisters. We share the same father, rotten dog that he is. I'm touched that she wanted to stay in contact. We didn't ask any more, but it was sad to hear about her brother, and about her boy. I assume she works, that's why she comes to see him on Saturdays.'

'Do you think that you'll follow that up?

'Well, I'll have to go back to her about the tests anyway. After that, it's too early to say but I think I might. I was wary about exchanging addresses as I didn't want anybody turning up on my doorstep.'

'Like you did for me, do you mean? And Bob, come to that?'

She laughed. 'Jack, you do keep a sense of proportion, don't you? I'll see how it goes for a while, but I would like to know how things turn out for her, especially with her boy having CMT symptoms as well.'

She drove them back along the motorways to Derbyshire in silence, noticing that Jack had dozed off. It was early evening when they stopped to collect Adam. He ran straight to Jack.

'Forest drew one-all at Aston Villa,' he announced.

'That's not a bad result after the run they have had, is it?'

'No,' the boy replied, 'but it would have been better if they had won.'

'That's true.'

NOT MUCH WAS said that evening as they both gathered their thoughts. Jack drank the other can of beer she had. On Sunday morning, Samantha and Jack sat at the kitchen table with mugs of coffee while Adam played in the garden, kicking a ball about. A joint of beef roasting in the oven was starting to make its presence felt.

'Jack, I don't want this to be the end for us, you know?'

'What do you mean, love?'

'We're really fond of you, me and Adam, you do know that, don't you?'

'I've grown fond of you two as well.'

'Adam doesn't have a Granddad, Tim's father isn't interested in us, wishes we didn't exist. I can see from the way Adam responds to you, the things he says, that he's really taken to you. There's a place for you with us if you want it. I think he'd miss you if you faded into the background now.'

'He's a nice lad, he's bright and keen, I would like to see what he makes of himself.'

'You're good for me, too. I haven't got anyone else that I can look up to in the same way. You talk sensibly and honestly, that's how I like it.'

Samantha rose from her chair and went to the window, hoping that Jack wouldn't notice that she was welling up. He was staring at his coffee.

'You will understand that it's been quite a weekend for me,' he said, 'one way or the other. Coming up staying here with you for the first time, going to Hull and seeing what had become of Dawson as well. It's been a lot to take in, I need time to sort it all out in my mind.'

'I can appreciate that, I'm not asking you to rush into anything right now.'

'Thank you.' He struggled up from his chair. 'I'll go and kick that ball about with Adam for a bit. It's not that much fun, doing it on your own.'

The doorbell rang.

'Oh blimey,' said Samantha, as she walked through to the hall, 'I bet that's the other half of the story.'

Jack could hear a man's voice in a low-key conversation, and he sat back down again. Then she came back into the room, followed by a youngish man.

'Jack, this is Tim. Tim, this is Jack.'

The man just smiled at him. Wearing jeans and a Metallica T-shirt, unlike Jack he hadn't shaved that morning, nor apparently had he combed his hair. More than six feet tall and well-built, he sat down uninvited at the table, next to Jack.

Tim looked at Samantha for an explanation. Adam was still outside, not realising that his father had arrived. She briefly told Tim about herself and Jack, about which he knew nothing. She also told him about their visit to Hull the previous day. He did know about the CMT, because she had checked with him after she had taken Adam to see Dr. Bhatti.

'You're not her Dad, then?' he asked Jack.

'From what we heard yesterday, I think that I can say pretty definitely that I am not. Although I admit that, up till now, there has been some doubt.'

'You've taken something on though, haven't you, there was no need for you to get involved, was there?'

'I agree, but I felt that there was no-one else who was going to help her.' This with a firm glance at Tim, who looked suitably abashed.

'Fair enough. Thank you for what you are doing anyway. I appreciate that it's for my son's benefit.'

Adam came in from the garden and exclaimed, 'Daddy's here!'

'Yes, he is,' said Samantha, 'although I'm not sure if he's here for anything in particular.'

Tim continued to look ill at ease. 'If you must know, Grant Bowmer saw you driving off yesterday with an older man he didn't recognise.'

'Got your spies out then, have you?'

He threw his hands up in exasperation. 'It's not right, whatever I do, is it? Stay away and I'm criticised, just the same if I'm looking out for you both.'

Adam moved to his mother's side. 'I wasn't being serious,' she said.

'I could never tell when you were, could I?'

He walked across to Adam, tousled his hair, then made his way to the front door without saying anything more.

AFTER LUNCH SHE drove them back to Derby station to put him on his train back to London.

'Forest are at home to Sunderland next Saturday,' said Adam.

'Well, they've got a chance of winning that one, Sunderland are near the bottom of the league, aren't they?' replied Jack.

'Yes they are. I hope Nigel Clough scores again soon, he hasn't scored many yet this season.'

They escorted him to his platform and saw him safely onto the St. Pancras train. He found a seat by the window and waved to them. They waved back as the train pulled away, then walked back to her car in silence. Jack settled back in his seat and closed his eyes.

CHAPTER 42

Ripley, November 1990

AFTER WE HAD seen Jack safely on his train back to London this house seemed strangely quiet and empty, even though he had been no trouble at all. I could see that Adam was thoughtful and I needed time myself to absorb all the events of the weekend.

I had expected there would be plenty to take in from our visit to Hull, whichever way it had gone. We might have had the door slammed in our faces and been none the wiser, back at Square One with nothing to tell the doctors. Or we might have met a charming man who gave me a warm welcome, wanting to reclaim me as his long-lost daughter, while giving Jack the elbow. Both of these possibilities, and many others in between, had featured in my dreams. In fact I was disgusted by what I saw and the man I met, but we achieved our object of answering the key CMT question. We also have the chance now to have tests done on him and Charlotte to tell us more. I was so glad to have Jack with me, I think he helped to put Dawson under pressure.

And I do feel that Charlotte is someone I want to stay in touch with. She's a tough cookie, that's for sure, but also vulnerable as she doesn't seem to have that much support around about her. I can sympathise with her on that. She's actually as much my sister as Emma and Rachel are.

So, I was prepared for a range of outcomes. It was the after-effects from having Jack here that surprised me. When we came back from Hull and picked up Adam from Lee's house, Lee's mother, Linda, caught my arm and whispered,

'Isn't he a nice man? I can tell that Adam likes him. I wouldn't mind having him as my Dad, instead if the useless lump I've got.'

It's true, he is a nice man, but he's more than that. He's sensible, stays calm, just gets on with stuff. And he's got a sense of humour, in a laid-back sort of way. In the car, as we came back from the station, Adam asked me, 'Is Jack coming back soon?'

'Would you like that?' I asked.

'Yes, I would,' he said, in a very determined way.

I don't know what to think now. Jack's got a son, who he doesn't seem to care for very much, and a daughter who I've met and she's lovely, but she's in New Zealand. He's got four grandchildren of his own, although he doesn't appear to see very much of any of them. When all is said and done, he leads a pretty quiet and uneventful life. He has his garden and his workshop, watches a bit of telly but not a lot. Doesn't read that much either, except for his daily paper, although he claims he gets an occasional thriller from the library. And he's not that old, not by today's standards, not even seventy yet. As far as I know, he's fit and healthy, doesn't smoke. He likes a beer but doesn't strike me as a big drinker. Likes his sport but isn't a gambler, so he says. I must sound like a woman who is checking out her daughter's fiancé, giving him marks out of ten.

I guess that politically he's somewhere to the right of me, I've always been Labour. Working in local government you see the impact of the cuts. But he's a moderate man, I think we have plenty of common ground.

He's so good with Adam, that's the thing. He knows how to talk to him. He doesn't talk down or treat him like a little kid. When they start talking football, it's just like listening to two old blokes chatting over a pint in the pub. There isn't anyone else that Adam can talk to like that. Not his dad or his other granddad, no uncles or cousins. I know now that he isn't really Adam's grandfather, but he's a pretty good substitute. Adam certainly trusts and respects him and that's good for him. Let's face it, whatever the feminists say, young lads need a father figure of some sort in their lives, someone they admire and can look up to, a role model I believe they call them nowadays. There are so many bad influences on youngsters now that it would be good for Adam to have a strong man around. And I have found a man I can really trust, for a change.

Adam likes arithmetic, so on the Sunday morning, after Tim had gone, Jack started to set him some sums. He soon realised that they were too simple, so he quickly upped the difficulty level. Jack said that he had needed good mental arithmetic to do his job at the builder's yard place where he worked.

'No calculators or computers in them days,' he boasted, 'you had to be accurate, or the customers would soon catch you out.'

I've never had a father figure for myself, and Jack has made me realise what I have missed. My step-dad, Ken, was okay, didn't give me any problems. But I wasn't his daughter and when two of his own came along, then I was different. Nothing was ever said but that's just the feeling that I had. He wasn't the brightest, so there was never any mental stimulation from him. He was never going to set me any sums to do, he struggled badly with that himself. By the time I was around ten, I was helping him to work out his pools coupons.

I think Jack's good for me as well as for Adam, someone to sound off to. I know I've got Jenny, but she's not going to want to keep hearing about my problems, her family give her enough grief of her own. He's a good listener and stops me feeling sorry for myself. He will tell me straight if he thinks I'm going in the wrong direction.

I don't know what my future holds, that's the trouble. I don't see me settling down with another bloke; been there, done that, and I didn't think it was great, to be honest. Knowing now what really happened to my mum doesn't make the idea any more attractive. And is anyone going to want to take on me and Adam now, especially if he's got serious health issues? Adam has to be my focus now. Having more kids risks them having CMT as well, if that is what Adam has, so I think that is ruled out. It's not an ideal situation, whichever way you look at it.

I marvel at my mum now, how she found a way to cope with what had been done to her. It would have been so easy to give up and feel sorry for herself as a victim. I reckon that she was determined to have more children and to find a man to provide them. Quite cold-blooded in some ways you might say. But she made a new life for herself and gave Ken, bless him, a lot more than he would ever have expected. When they decided to get married, I do wonder who proposed to who!

I am very fond of Jack, it's not just that he has been very helpful for me. We feel comfortable with him, and I am sure he does with us. I just hope that we can keep the contact going somehow. He's filled a real void in our lives, one we didn't know that we had, and it would be very obvious now if he wasn't around. I don't see how I can push it any further just now, it has to come from him. If I push too hard, that son of his could be on my case, saying that I'm after his money, which

I'm not. Mind you, his house down there in London must be worth a bit. I don't know what else he has, pensions I suppose. I guess he's the type of bloke who has been careful with his money, and it doesn't seem to be a problem for him.

We've achieved our big objective all right, but there's a sense of anti-climax now, I'm in limbo, something unfulfilled, wondering where I go next.

I'll give it a week or two now to see what, if anything, I hear from him. What I must do now is go straight back to Dr Bhatti and tell her what I've found out, see if we can arrange for Bob and Charlotte to have whatever tests she wants them to have. We will have to wait a while now to know how all of that works out.

It does feel strange, calling that man 'Bob,' as if I am close to him in some way. I hate him, he's horrible, but he's my father and I have to accept that. I had hoped for someone better than him. Thank God I take after my mother.

CHAPTER 43

Kenton, November 1990

I WAS EXHAUSTED by the time I made it home from Derby, even though I'd been fast asleep on the train. I went to bed early and still didn't wake until nine o'clock next morning. Getting up that late puts me out of sorts for the day. It's a couple of days later now and I am just starting to put my thoughts together.

What I do feel is a genuine sense of success. We have found our man, which was the number one target and, number two, we found that there is Charcot-Marie-Tooth disease in his family. That is a starting point for Samantha to learn more about the outlook for Adam and the treatment he will need. So far, so good, but it seems that there is still a long road ahead of them. When the doctors tell them what tests they want Dawson and Charlotte to have done, Samantha will have to keep on at them to make sure that they happen. It doesn't change anything for Adam, but the doctors could then be pretty sure that it's CMT that he has and what sort it is.

How are the mighty fallen! To see Dawson living like that, in that awful place, that really shook me. He used to be so cocky and confident, pleased with himself. He couldn't have seen this coming for him, thirty-five years ago. What's he got to look forward to now? Nothing, only the way out. If he has got illnesses, that probably can't be helped, but I also think that he's brought it on himself, the way he has lived. And with the attitude he has had, he won't have made too many friends to help him out. Serve the bugger right, I say, I'm not going to feel sorry for him. What he did to Pamela was unforgivable, he's lucky not to have gone to prison for it.

IT'S THE BEST part of a year now since Samantha first appeared on my doorstep. That was a bolt from the blue. Nineteen-ninety has definitely been quite a year. Meeting her and then Jenny and then Adam, all new people in my life. First I had my operation, Elizabeth came over and then my trip to New Zealand, it's not been a normal year by any means. Perhaps next year will be quieter. Is that what I want? This year has just flashed by, do I really want to go back to how it was before? It has made me realise that I am happier when I have got something on, a project or something like that. Keeping my brain ticking over, not just sitting here dozing and reading the paper, doing the crossword, trying to find things to fill up my time.

I do feel sorry for Samantha. She doesn't have anyone to help her, she's definitely on her own. I wonder what happened with her marriage? I know there are usually two sides to every story, but I can't imagine why any fellow would want to leave a nice girl like that. I can't say that I really took to Tim. Something a bit distant about him, I thought, not truly concerned about her and his son. Some of the young blokes today, they've got a bit missing if you ask me. Mind you, look at what Dawson did all those years ago, I suppose these things have always gone on.

With Tim it's not only leaving her but also a lovely lad like Adam. I mean, if he was my son there is no way that I could cut him out of my life like his Dad has. It would be great if she could find a nice bloke to settle down with, someone who would take some responsibility for the boy. However, she seems have set her mind against that. I worry about the future for both of them, it ain't going to be easy. I'm not going to be around for too much of it but perhaps I could help in the short term.

It also makes me think about my own family. I loved being in New Zealand with Elizabeth and Howard and the girls. I felt really relaxed with them, but I have to accept that I'm not going to see them that often. I toyed with idea of going to join them, but that would be just too much of an upheaval for me, at my time of life. David and Louise? Well, they live in a different world. I like her and she tries hard to connect with me, but we don't have too much in common. I don't know Simon and Lucy very well and I sense that they don't feel at ease with me. I can't talk with them in the way I can with Adam. That may sound strange but it's true.

Then there's David. I couldn't admit this to anyone, but I don't like him very much, the way he is now. He's arrogant and aggressive and he's obsessed by making money. His sister clearly isn't very impressed with him. I think I have failed somewhere along the line to get him to see the world the way I do. He's worked hard, no doubt about that, and good luck to him if that is what he wants. It's just that I can't help wondering what's ahead for him, that pride isn't coming before a fall, because I wouldn't want to see that.

It's not that special around where Samantha lives but it's OK. Proper working-class town. House prices are a damn sight cheaper there than down here, that's for sure.

I will leave things for a couple of weeks before I ring Samantha again. There's plenty to talk about. I can ask if she has made any progress with the doctors, if the house sale is going through and to see how Adam is. That should keep the connection alive.

CHAPTER 44

Ripley, Christmas 1990

THERE WAS A tidy collection of wrapped presents waiting under the Christmas tree, but the firm rule was that they must not be opened until after breakfast. As a result that was something of a hurried meal, quickly eaten and rapidly cleared away afterwards.

They looked at each other to see who should go first.

'Come on Jack, age before beauty, you go first,' said Samantha.

'No, that's not fair,' replied Jack, 'it's not right to keep Adam waiting, he should go first. I'll wait my turn.'

ONCE JACK HAD decided that he would be spending this Christmas with Samantha and Adam, and not at David and Louise's, he had agonised intensely about the question of presents. He was greatly embarrassed to think that they would want to buy anything for him. He didn't want them to go to any trouble or expense on his behalf.

Buying for Adam was the easy part: a new football and a football annual. Jack also put in one of his home-made engines, which bemused Adam somewhat until it was explained that Jack had made it himself. But what should he do for Samantha? He had never found it that easy to buy for Margaret, he didn't like going into women's clothes shops, and being approached by one of those snooty, patronising sales assistants. It usually came down to a Size 12 jumper from Marks and Spencer's, some chocolates and what he thought was her favourite perfume. After she had died, he found several unopened bottles stored up in a drawer.

It didn't seem to Jack that Samantha was very interested in clothes, and it didn't feel right to buy her anything too personal. He had noticed that she kept several flowering plants around the house, so he went for a poinsettia for indoors and a healthy hydrangea bush that he thought would improve her garden, either front or back. In the end they were graciously received and put to one side. He planted the hydrangea on Boxing Day morning, where she suggested, where it could be seen from the lounge window. Adam immediately started to read the book that Jack had bought him, exclaiming when he found pictures of Notts Forest players in it.

There were still three parcels under the tree.

'Are those for me?'

'They are,' Samantha said.

'Come on Jack, let's see what they are,' urged Adam, who knew what was in them.

The largest parcel was a cotton twill shirt, similar to several that he already had. Then came a box of toffees and the smallest contained an upmarket ballpoint pen. He was embarrassed and stuttered his thanks.

DAVID HAD CALLED on him the weekend before Christmas, to bring their present for him, still aggrieved that Jack was not celebrating with them that year.

'You were very welcome to come to us, you know, Dad,' he said.

'I know that, thank you David, I know that. It's thinking of them just being on their own, it's not right for that little lad.'

David sighed. 'I haven't got used yet to this Good Samaritan act. If you'd rather spend Christmas with them, that's up to you.'

'Give over, it's not an act, it's what I want to do. And it saves you having to drive me over and back.'

The large parcel that David had brought for Jack, when opened later, revealed a very posh Teasmade machine.

'Blimey,' thought Jack, 'that looks complicated. I like getting up and making my own cuppa first thing in the morning. It gets me underway for the day. I suppose I'm not that easy to buy for.'

Since Margaret had died, Jack had spent two Christmases with David and Louise. It had been OK, but he had never felt entirely relaxed. He found it hard to connect easily with Simon and Lucy. Louise was always very pleasant to him, but David was relentless, not quiet or still for a moment, organising something or holding forth about some topic. Jack found it wearing.

On Boxing morning, before Jack was taken back home, their house was filled up by people that Jack didn't know or feel comfortable with. Some were work colleagues of either David or Louise, many were people they knew from Round Table, mostly couples in their forties, plus the odd elderly parent who had also been dragged along. Apart from exchanging a 'Merry Christmas' or two, there wasn't anyone with whom Jack felt able to hold a conversation. While Simon and Lucy vanished to their bedrooms, Jack found himself a relatively quiet corner of the conservatory.

He felt better about his decision to go to Samantha's after a phone call from Louise telling him that she quite understood his wish to be with them. She hoped she would see him soon in the New Year. Elizabeth had been taken by surprise when Jack rang to tell her.

'That's a big step, Dad, isn't it?'

After a pause she went on, 'I am surprised that you would do that. I think it makes sense though, I reckon you'll be more comfortable there with them than you would be with Louise and David. It's not your scene there is it?'

JACK WASN'T AWARE that any visitors were expected, but at around eleven o'clock on Christmas morning, the doorbell rang. Samantha looked at Adam.

'I think you know who that will be Adam, you answer the door.'

The boy leapt to his feet and ran into the hall. Jack could hear a man's voice, talking in low tones. Adam came running in saying, 'It's Daddy.'

Samantha didn't get up, just swivelled to look at him from her chair and then made the briefest of introductions.

Adam was clutching a parcel which Tim had brought with him.

'Happy Christmas,' said Tim, 'how are we all?'

'I'm very well, thank you.' Jack was the only one to answer, uncertain if Tim knew that he would be there. Adam concentrated on opening the parcel which revealed a large table football game.

'Thanks Dad, that looks great. Jack and I are going with Lee and his Dad to see Forest tomorrow afternoon. They are playing Wimbledon.'

Whether Tim felt any qualms about that being a role he should be taking wasn't obvious. He was staring hard at Samantha.

'Mum and Dad send their best wishes,' he said.

'That's very nice of them. Is that instead of a card

this year, then?'

'I sent you one.'

'Yes, thank you, but they didn't, we're obviously off their list now. One less for us to send next year. Are you staying for a coffee?'

'No thanks, I need to run along soon.'

'Are you having dinner with your parents?'

Tim paused. 'No, I'm with a friend and her family in Chesterfield.'

'Is she a new one?'

'Yes.'

'That sounds like a lot of fun for everybody. You'd better get on then, you don't want to give them the wrong impression now, do you, keep their Christmas dinner waiting?'

There was nowhere for the conversation to go after that. Jack shifted uncomfortably in his seat. Tim stood up.

'I'll say goodbye then.'

'Goodbye,' said Samantha, without stirring. Adam ran to his father and held his hand.

'Thanks for my present, it looks ace.'

'You and Jack can play with it later, can't you?'

With that, he walked towards the door, Adam still clinging on to him.

'Happy New Year to you,' offered Jack.

'And to you,' Tim replied. For a few moments father and son talked in the hall. After he had gone, Samantha looked at Jack.

'I'm sorry about that. I had no idea if he was coming or not, he never tells us. Not very pleasant to put you through that, it must have been difficult to watch, but I'm afraid that's how it is.'

'Yes, it's very sad,' said Jack.

JACK CARVED THE turkey, a role for which he had more than forty years' experience. The meal was excellent, they pulled crackers and wore the silly hats they contained. At three o'clock they watched the Queen's Christmas Message, which was quite sombre that year, talking about the role of British servicemen and women with the threat of imminent war in the Arabian Gulf, following the Iraqi invasion of Kuwait. Then Adam and Jack played with the game his Dad had brought him, but after that Jack dozed off.

That evening, after Adam had gone to bed, Samantha thanked Jack for coming to stay with them. 'It means a lot to Adam, and you both going to the football tomorrow is very exciting for him. He does love having you here with us, you know.'

'I'm looking forward to the match as well, it's a while since I've been to a live game. Nice of Lee's Dad to sort out the tickets for us as well.'

He went on, 'And thank you for having me here with you. The nicest thing I can say is that you both have made me feel at home, different from if I had been at David's.'

'Jack,' she replied, 'thanks for coming, you've made Christmas for us.'

THAT NIGHT IN bed, Jack reflected on their day. The encounter with Tim had shown him a rather different side of Samantha, how hard and unforgiving she could be, in front of Adam as well. He felt for her, how hurt she must have been when they split up. And he also wondered about the effect on the boy who not only had medical problems of unknown severity ahead of him, but also the fractured relationship between his parents. Life was not going to be easy for him. He needed all the support he could get.

CHAPTER 45

Kenton, February 1991

AS HE WALKED home from the solicitors' office, Jack felt relaxed and relieved. Instead of the fusty elderly male lawyer that he had expected to see he had been presented with a glamorous young woman, in a smart business suit with an excess of jewellery and a professional smile. She introduced herself as Miranda.

He had told her the story that he had spent several days rehearsing over and over in his mind, as he wanted to be sure of making himself clear. Even so, he had needed to go back on himself a couple of times, running too far ahead in his eagerness to tell all.

At first Miranda had sat back, making notes on a pad in a professional but detached manner. However, as Jack went through his tale, she was clearly engaged and leant forward, eyebrows raised, as he continued. When he had finished she said, 'Wow, that's wonderful, good for you, Mr. Rodgers, I take my hat off to you. Of course we can help you with both the house sale and the trust. And we can prepare a new will for you, when you are ready to do that. I must say, it'll be a pleasure to work with you on this one. It's not often in this job that I come across a story like yours. How long have you been thinking about this?'

'It's been at the back of my mind for a while, but what I saw at Christmas sealed it for me. I realise now that I've been coasting along for the last year or two.

I'm reasonably fit, healthy and compos mentis, and I've had a good life so far. Time to do something to help others, I thought, without being sure what. Then this came along. They've not been dealt good hands, these two, and I'm in a position to help them, so here I go.'

'Have you told them yet?'

'Erm, no I haven't, not yet.'

'I hope you don't mind me asking, but you are sure that they will be happy with this?'

Jack paused and smiled. 'Good question. I wanted to talk to you first and be confident that what I wanted to do was possible. Now I have my answers, I can do that. Thank you for taking a great load off my mind. I won't do anything more yet, not until I've talked it through with her, then I'll come back, and we can set the wheels in motion.'

'I look forward to that,' said Miranda, now with a big genuine smile. She stood up and gave him a very firm handshake.

WHEN SAMANTHA ANSWERED the phone one evening, the voice at the other end did not waste time with introductions.

'Right, Samantha, are you sitting down?'

It was the evening after Jack had seen the solicitor. He had already made himself comfortable on the stool by the phone in the hall.

'Not at the moment, Jack, no. Should I?'

'Yes, I think you should. Hear me out, I have a proposition for you.'

'Blimey, this sounds important. Hold on a moment while I just finish telling Adam something.' Jack could hear a muffled conversation that did not seem entirely free of stress.

'I hope it's not another shocker about a phone call

that you've just remembered.'

'Ouch,' said Jack, grimacing. 'No it's nothing like that, it's something I hope you'll find positive.'

'Go on, then.'

'I really enjoyed my time with you both at Christmas, you know that don't you?'

'Yes, I do. I was just starting to think that I hadn't heard much from you since then'

'Well, I've been thinking, you see. We've made a lot of progress in the last year, finding your father and setting up the medical tests for him and Charlotte. But I don't want it to end there. Your story has still got a long way to go yet, and I'd still like to be part of it.'

'Go on. You can take a long time to come to the point sometimes, Jack.'

'I know, I know. Here goes. I can't believe the difference between the house prices where you live, compared with those down here in London. How would you feel if I sold this house and came to live near you? I would see much more of Adam and help you out with him, perhaps take him to and from school, that sort of thing. Go to more football matches. Perhaps the cricket at Trent Bridge.'

'Oh, my God, Jack! I didn't see that one coming. But what about your family, your grandchildren?'

'Elizabeth and Howard are well settled in New Zealand, I can't see them ever coming back, not in my lifetime anyway. She has talked about her girls coming here to study later on but that won't be for another ten years or more. David? Well, let's be honest, we just rub each other up the wrong way. I irritate him and he irritates me. We've got different values, he's too materialistic for my liking. I like Louise very much, but we don't have a lot in common, we're from different worlds. And I don't see enough of Simon and Lucy to feel close to them. They'll be off to university soon and who knows where they'll finish up after that? Anyway, the profit I'll have after selling this house can go into a trust for my grandchildren, I've been to see a solicitor today and she says she can set that up.'

'She, eh? Don't tell me you've got another woman in your life?'

'Samantha, stop it. She was very pleasant and helpful, not like your normal solicitor.'

'But you've lived in that area for most of your life, won't you miss it?'

Jack paused, taking in the moment; so far, so good, he thought.

'It's changed a lot. So many new people living here while some I knew have moved further out to nicer areas when they could. Don't get me wrong, I've nothing against the newcomers, good luck to them, but the area looks and feels different. Old shops closing down, replaced by new ones that have nothing for me, Polish grocers and the like. There's not many folk round here now that I would call good friends. Margaret did much more socialising than me.'

He stopped to think what Derek and Janet would think of his idea.

'Jack, I'm not trying to put you off. Anyway, I know one person for sure who would be thrilled if you lived near us and that's Adam. He thinks the world of you.' She laughed. 'He's tab hanging here and nodding vigorously.'

'Well, I think you're exaggerating a little there, but we do get on well. He's a clever lad, I'm sure he can do well for himself whatever physical problems he might have. That's the thing,' continued Jack, 'I feel closer to him now than any of my own grandchildren. I wouldn't make a nuisance of myself, but I would be around if you needed another pair of hands. And I could make something of your garden for you.'

Samantha laughed. 'Ah, we're getting to the truth now, it's my garden that you're really interested in!'

'Look, your mum had a tough life and it's not exactly a bed of roses for you either, is it? I just think that I can help you both, and there aren't many people around who are ready to do that, are there?'

'I can see you've been thinking about this, haven't you, it's not just a spur of the moment thing is it?'

'No, it's not, and Christmas sealed it in my mind. Now that I know that it is all OK legally, it's what I want to do.'

Samantha paused for breath. 'Whew, I must admit that you have shocked me here, I need some time to mull it over. You are entitled to do with your own life whatever you want, it wouldn't be my place to stop you. I do appreciate you telling me first, that's what I would expect from a decent chap like you. It's the impact on your family that I worry about. I'm remembering my mother having to go into a home. What happens if you need that, up here and your son down there? I don't know what David and Elizabeth are going to say to you. Let me think about it first before you say anything to anyone else, will you?'

'Of course. If you thought it was wrong, I wouldn't do it.'

'Alright Jack, speak soon.'

He went over to the dresser and picked out the brandy bottle again. He held the glass of amber liquid up to the light, wondering if this was a celebration or consolation drink.

CHAPTER 46

Ripley and Kenton, March 1991

IT WAS ANOTHER Sunday morning and Tim had dropped by to pay another of his occasional visits to see his estranged wife and son.

'I still don't get Jack and why he's got involved with you,' he said to Samantha. 'Hasn't he any family of his own instead of poking his nose into other people's?'

Samantha had made Tim a coffee this time and they were sitting at her kitchen table while Adam was in the garden with the football Jack had bought him for Christmas.

'Well, first and foremost he's a widower, his wife died so he's living on his own for the first time in his life, and he's lonely. His daughter and her husband emigrated to New Zealand. He's just been out to visit them and their two kids. He has got a son, who lives in Surrey, something in the City. Very materialistic and money-conscious, posh wife and two teenage children that Jack doesn't know very well. Jack's honest enough to say that his son annoys him, and he doesn't feel that they have much in common. He talks down to Jack, which is a big mistake. So, yes, he's got a family, but they are not exactly close. Does that sound familiar?'

Tim shrugged. 'It just seems a bit creepy to me, moving from London to somewhere like Ripley, just to be closer to a woman and her son. I don't get it.'

Samantha glowered.

'No, you wouldn't, because you don't think about other people like he does, you're only bothered with yourself. And don't you dare go putting it about that there's something sinister like that behind it or I shall make sure the world knows what you are like, if they don't already know.'

'That's not a nice thing to say about your husband.'

'You stopped being my husband long ago. I only keep quiet to protect Adam but that wouldn't stop me from dishing the dirt on you if you go spreading lies about us. Got it?'

'Got it.'

Tim left his coffee unfinished and walked out without a further word.

THAT EVENING SAMANTHA rang Jack again.

'I've thought it over. I have to say first that I hope your children take to the idea, but for us it would be great. Adam's so happy about it, that's all that needs to be said.'

'You're sure about that?'

'Definitely.'

'Great, I am pleased.'

'Well, one thing that has certainly come to mind is that I could do more hours at work. They're always on at me to do so but it's been taking and fetching Adam from school, and the school holidays, that have always been the issue, and still likely to be for quite a few years to come. As you know, it's not a fantastic job, just clerical stuff, but I could certainly use the extra money, and no mistake. I still have this idea about getting myself some more qualifications one day, if I can ever decide which. It'd be a big commitment on your part though, Jack, to be available twice a day, entertaining him in the holidays, are you ready for that?'

'You bet. I'd love to have him tell me about his day at school, what he's been doing, see his schoolmates. I might bring my woodworking tools up with me, teach him some skills.'

'Would you like me to send you the local papers with all the Houses for Sale in? Give you an idea of what's available?'

'Yes, please. A terraced place would be quite enough for me. Two bedrooms so Adam could stay overnight if necessary. I'll go back to the solicitors' to tell them to go ahead, and I'd better go and see the estate agents here, I suppose.'

THE NEXT AFTERNOON, while on his way to see the solicitor again, fortuitously, he saw his old friends Derek and Janet coming his way. This time he made a bee-line for them. They had been shopping again and, once more, Derek put down their heavy bags to show that he was ready to talk.

Firstly, Jack told them in some detail about his trip to New Zealand, while they updated him on their plans to go out to Australia again.

'There's something else,' said Jack. Janet, holding on to Derek's arm, as ever, now showed keener interest. 'Yes, I'm selling my house and moving up to Derbyshire.'

'What! Derbyshire! Why Derbyshire?' they chorused in unison. Jack gave them an edited version of the story of the search. This was the sort of conversation that Janet really liked.

'Well,' she said, 'I reckon you'll get a good price for your place on that road. I know you keep it nice. A house near us went for something ridiculous, over one hundred thousand pounds last month.'

'That's what I am hoping for,' said Jack.

‘Bloody hell, Jack,’ said Derek, ‘that’s a big move at your age.’

‘I know but there’s not so much to keep me round here now.’

‘Good luck with that then. Don’t know Derbyshire at all, never been there. It’s near Yorkshire, isn’t it?’ said Derek, picking up the shopping. ‘Let us know if it all goes through. Give us a bell before you move.’

Off they went, chatting animatedly to each other as they went. Jack could guess at their conversation, and he was certain that Janet would spread the news quickly.

‘No going back now,’ he thought, ‘the die is cast.

CHAPTER 47

Kenton, March 1991

JACK KNEW THAT, in principle, first he should ring his son, his older child, when he had news like this for his children, but he just couldn't face it. He hoped that he would have an easier ride with Elizabeth and decided to start by ringing her. She had been really pleased when he had told her the outcome of their trip to Hull. He was in for a shock.

'Oh, Dad, I can't believe what you're telling me, move away from Kenton after all these years. That's our family home you're talking about. When you ring me, I can always picture where you are, what you've been doing and so on, that makes me feel closer and I wouldn't be able to do that anymore. I really liked Samantha and Adam, but it feels like you're ditching us for them. No, I don't think that's the right thing to do at all.'

'Oh dear, I didn't think that you'd feel like that. I feel like a spare part here, drifting along, not doing anything useful, you do understand don't you?'

'There's plenty of voluntary stuff you could do, if that's your problem.'

'I've tried that, at the church and the Red Cross shop, but I didn't feel comfortable there, too many wittering old women, they would rather stand chatting and drinking tea instead of getting on with the job in hand. No thank you. What about the money I'd be putting in trust for your children?'

'That's very kind I'm sure but it isn't the point. You'd be going somewhere you don't really know, no friends there. What happens if you're taken ill, would Samantha be lumbered with you then? David's hardly likely to come charging up the M1 to look after you, is he? When you were over, I half-thought that you might suggest moving out here, be with your own grandchildren.'

Jack was lost for words for a while.

'I won't deny that did cross my mind, I did like it there. That would feel just too big a move. Here I can take my furniture, kitchen stuff, my woodworking tools and so on. I'd have to get rid of practically everything if came out there. I couldn't go that far.'

'Dad, you've really thrown me with this one. I should've known that you might have something like this up your sleeve. I don't want to fall out with you on it, not at all. You have to admit that it is a bit of shock. What does David say?'

'I don't know, I haven't told him yet.'

He could hear Elizabeth sighing.

'Now that is a bit crafty Dad, you thought you'd get me on your side first, did you? Make it harder for him to disagree?'

Bull's eye thought Jack.

'Let me think about it some more first. I'll talk it over with Howard this evening, get his thoughts. He often looks at things from a different angle to me.'

'I'm sorry, your reaction isn't what I'd expected, I will admit. I won't say anything more than that to you for now. Bye love, speak again soon.'

Jack went back to his chair and cried.

BY POST THAT day he received another envelope from

Samantha, this time containing pages from local papers, the *Derbyshire Times* and the *Ripley and Heanor News*, their property sales, adverts by various estate agents. Page after page of properties in places he'd never heard of. Marehay, Shirland, Loscoe and Ironville. There were some really attractive houses in there, taking up most of the space. The cheaper ones only had thumbnail, grainy pictures and minimal details. 'Needing some attention' was a recurring phrase. Nevertheless, their prices were in the range Jack had anticipated from his survey of the local estate agents' windows.

There were several in Ripley itself, which Samantha had marked up for him, as she had promised. Roads with names like Crossley Street, Havelock Street and Alfred Street. She had also sent a brief note with some comments on the ones she had marked as well as a map showing their locations in relation to her home. Jack gained the impression that she had been round the area on foot to see for herself.

NOW JACK WAS in a quandary. He had thought that if he told Elizabeth first, he would receive a sympathetic response, to the extent that she might even take it on herself to tell David for him. Her reaction had changed everything. His fear now was that she might indeed call David, but only to express her opposition to his idea. He had not imagined that his proposed move would alienate both of his children. When he had told David about finding Dawson, while not enthusiastic, he had sounded relieved that it had all gone fairly smoothly, without aggravation.

He still expected David to be negative about the move idea as he thought his motives would not be understood. Jack had already decided that would not dissuade him from his chosen action. For them both to be opposed was a different matter. Of course, he knew that their approval was not necessary but had hoped for some shades of ambivalence.

He felt compelled to call David that evening to at least forestall Elizabeth in case she got in first.

'Hello, Louise, it's Jack here.'

'Oh hello, are you alright?'

'I'm fine, thank you. Is David there?'

'No sorry, he's in New York this week, not back until early on Sunday.'

Just my luck thought Jack, what do I do now?

'Can I help at all, you are OK, aren't you?'

Jack didn't answer.

'Jack, are you there?'

'Yes, I'm here all right. There's something that I want to tell him.'

'Is there a problem? Is it your health?'

'No, it's nothing like that. Have you got a few minutes, I need to talk to someone, can I talk to you, please?'

'Of course you can, please go on.'

AND SO HE spilled out the whole story to Louise – finding Bob Dawson, how he had felt at Samantha's at Christmas, his planned move, Samantha's approval, what the solicitor had said, the money in trust for his grandchildren and, finally, his disappointment at Elizabeth's reaction. It took him a good half-hour, but she had listened patiently, without interruption, although that made it harder for him to gauge her reaction. He waited, fearing the worst.

'Jack, you are a dark horse, aren't you? There's not many men of your age who would even consider such a move. After all those years in that house as well. How long have you lived there?'

'Over forty years now.'

'Well, it is a lot to take in and I can see that you might be apprehensive about telling this to David. I'm perhaps a bit more detached than he is, and I can see both sides, why you might want to do it, but also why Elizabeth should be so unhappy. It is a bit of a life-changer, isn't it?'

'That's true. Do you think I'm wrong?'

'Who am I to say that? As far as I can see, you're doing it for the best of motives. What you have already done to help her so far is brilliant and I can see that it's fired you up with a new purpose in life.'

'I'm so sorry that I've upset Elizabeth, especially after I had such a lovely time out there with them.'

'I understand that. I'm very fond of her and Howard too. They're such a well-rounded, sensible couple and their girls are bright and charming. But they decided to make their home out there, didn't they? They will realise that they can't have the same influence on events that they'd have if they were still here.'

'Louise, you are a comfort to me. The chats that we've had before have done me the world of good. Elizabeth said she'd talk to Howard as he might have a different take on it.'

'Yes, he might, he's a practical man. In his line of work he will hear about a lot of difficult family situations and have to make his own input on them. You'd be surprised, even in a financial advisor job like mine, it's like a confessional sometimes. People feel that they trust you enough to unload all sorts of stuff that isn't directly relevant to their financial affairs. You're learning that you can't please everyone, aren't you?'

'I'm learning that,' said Jack.

'I think your plan to put the profit into a trust for the grandchildren will disarm David to some extent. At least, it's not like you are giving it all to Samantha and Adam. I'm touched by your affection for the boy. You haven't seen enough of our two to have quite the same bond, although they do care about you. David is ringing me tonight, or at least he's promised that he will, circumstances sometimes overtake him. Let me give him a potted version. He's usually so full of what he's doing to take in too much from this end. I'll tell him not to go off the deep end, but to think about it and then call you at the weekend when he's back. Would that be OK?'

'Louise, that would be wonderful. Thank you so much.'

Jack realised that there was more depth to Louise than an outsider might imagine.

DAVID RANG JACK on the following Sunday evening, full of excitement from his first visit to New York. Jack waited patiently for the conversation to come round to his topic.

'Er, Dad, Lou has told me about your plan to move north. That's quite a shock, although I do like the idea of setting up a trust for the grandchildren. Is the move really something you want to do?'

'Yes, David, it is,' replied Jack mildly, 'my life is fairly empty and aimless here, I feel like I am wasting whatever time I have left. I can see a chance to be useful to people who need help in a way that would give me satisfaction. Kenton isn't what it used to be. You don't need me down here. And, as you say, I can put a decent sum of money aside to help my grandchildren without them having to wait for me to pass on.'

'Dad, I know we don't always see eye to eye, and I now know better than to try to make you change your mind. Louise and I have talked it through, and I can see the positive aspects. We'll miss you and we mustn't lose touch, you'll always be welcome to come to stay with us. I don't really know Derbyshire, once I was caught by the snow and had to spend a night in Buxton, that wasn't very comfortable. And you'll go out to Christchurch again soon to see Elizabeth, won't you?'

'Have you talked to Elizabeth about it?'

'No, I haven't.'

'Well, I'll be honest, she wasn't at all happy. Sounded quite sentimental about the old family home. She said she'd talk it over with Howard and I haven't heard from her since. As she'd met Samantha and Adam, and seemed to get on so well, I thought she would be more agreeable.'

'I haven't spoken to her since Christmas, I must admit,' said David, 'Gosh, that's over three months. I must give her a call and see what she says. You've got a solicitor on the case, I take it?'

'Yes, I have. I went there first to make sure that I was very clear on what was involved and what the costs were.'

'Well done, Dad. All right, keep us posted, talk again soon.'

Jack couldn't believe that it had been that easy, with David, at least.

THERE WAS ONE more person left that Jack felt that he should tell, his sister Brenda, up in Lancashire. I hope she doesn't think I'm doing it to be closer to her, thought Jack, that's the last thing on my mind. He called her twice but there was no answer, which was unusual for her, she always seemed to be at home.

A FEW DAYS later a neighbour of Brenda's, who Jack

didn't know, rang him, having found his number in her address book. She said that their postman had seen Brenda lying on the hall floor and called an ambulance, but she had died a few days earlier of a heart attack. Jack felt guilty that it was more than a year since he had last spoken to her. What a lonely way to end up, he thought, that's not the way I would want to go.

CHAPTER 48

Ripley, October 1991

IT WAS NOW six weeks since Jack had moved into Crossley Street, only a short walk across the High Street from Samantha's house, which was near the hospital, where all the roads were named after trees. It was not much further for him to go to Adam's school. His house was in need of some maintenance and decoration, so he had been busy putting emulsion on the walls and cleaning up the outside paintwork. The previous occupants had left plenty of rubbish which he'd had to dispose of. He'd said 'Hello' to his immediate neighbours, but no more than that. There was an area behind the house which was more of a yard than a garden. Work on that could wait until the spring but he had bought a shed to set up as his new workshop.

As a regular shopper he was pleasantly surprised by the prices of groceries, much cheaper than Kenton. There was a Sainsbury's on the edge of town, also within walking distance. He had found a friendly coffee shop where he could treat himself to a bacon sandwich. Ripley didn't have a train station, but Jack could see that there were plentiful bus options to take him to Derby, Nottingham, Belper and Matlock, destinations which he planned to explore. He was starting to find his way around the town, perhaps a little rougher around the edges than Kenton. He was starting to catch on to the local lingo. One of the main shopping streets, Grosvenor Road, was rendered as "Gross Veenor Road."

He had mowed Samantha's lawns for her and had plans for a vegetable garden there next year. It would need some digging over first. She was more than happy to give him a free hand with the gardens, front and back. The hydrangea that he had planted in the front garden on Boxing Day was surviving but would need pruning in the Spring.

It was still an exaggeration to say that Elizabeth was happy with the move but, perhaps through Howard's influence, there was a sort of acceptance.

WHEN THE SCHOOLS went back in September, Samantha had, as she had suggested, extended her working hours to go full-time. Taking Adam to school each morning had now become Jack's routine responsibility, as was collecting him in the afternoon, giving him a fixed daily timetable. He knew this wasn't for ever, because Adam would go to the secondary school in a couple of years' time and would be old enough then to find his own way home.

There was the usual crowd of parents and grandparents waiting by the gates on this particular afternoon when Jack arrived. He felt the buzz of conversation drop as he approached, confirming that he was still seen as a stranger. He was pleased to see Linda, the mother of Adam's friend Lee, in the crowd. She was standing by a man of Jack's age, and she beckoned him over. He felt a lot of eyes focused on him.

'Hello, Jack, are you alright?' she asked.

'Yes thanks,' he mumbled in reply.

'Can I do introduce you to my favourite uncle,

Jim?'

The man stepped forward, hand outstretched. 'Ey up, I'm Jim Spray.' He was taller than Jack, lean and gaunt and wore a cloth cap, even though it was quite a warm autumnal day.

'Pleased to meet you,' said Jack feeling a very firm handshake.

Linda explained to Jim that Jack was a 'sort of grandpa to Adam"' and that he had just moved up from London. Jim grinned.

'I expect you'll find us very down to earth here, not like London folk,' he said.

'I was born in Lancashire, actually, so I'm not a true Londoner,' replied Jack, keen to make that distinction clear. 'I've never been one for the West End or the bright lights, so it's not a lot different really. I've settled in pretty well so far.'

'Where are you living?'

'I've bought a house on Crossley Street, that suits me very well.'

'Oh, that's handy for everywhere, isn't it? Shops and buses, like?'

JUST THEN ADAM and Lee emerged, kicking a battered football across the playground. Adam had quickly accepted that Jack would be meeting him now. After they had parted ways with Lee, Linda and Jim, Jack asked him about his day.

'Mr. Keen has been telling us about the Sahara desert, weren't you in the desert in the war, Jack?'

'I was in the desert, but not the Sahara. We were further north, mainly in Egypt.'

'What was it like?'

'Horrible.'

'Really? Why?'

'Too hot in the day, too cold at night. Flies, snakes and scorpions. And the sand gets everywhere, and I mean everywhere. And, of course, there was a war on as well.'

'It's not like a beach, then? Kirsty Bettinson said that she thought they would have deckchairs and sun shades like when they went on holiday to Morocco.'

'I hope Mr. Keen put her right on that.'

'He said that deserts were very dangerous, and that people died there because there wasn't any water.'

'He was right about that.'

WHEN THEY WERE back at Samantha's house, Jack let them in with his key. He made himself a cup of tea, a glass of squash for Adam and a slice of madeira cake for both of them. They sat in a comfortable silence while Adam read the *Eagle* comic, which Jack had brought for him, while he read his newspaper. Later, Jack prepared the vegetables for their evening meal. Samantha arrived home at five-thirty. She'd had a busy day and flopped into an armchair while Jack made a cup of tea for her. After their meal she roused herself to prepare the spare bedroom. Charlotte, her half-sister from Hull, was coming to spend the weekend with her and Adam.

CHAPTER 49

Ripley, September 1992

IN THE YEAR since Jack had moved North, he and David had had regular phone conversations. These had tended to be rather stilted affairs as David did not often have much to say of interest to Jack. In turn, he found it difficult to talk about his life with Samantha and Adam, or even the chaps he met on Friday nights in the pub, when David hadn't ever met any of them.

However, when David called one late summer evening, the occasion was different. After very brief pleasantries, David went straight to the point.

'Dad, Lou and I have been talking, and I've also chatted to Elizabeth about this. I've a week's holiday coming up soon. How would you feel about coming down here on the train to stay with us for a few days, just on a single ticket, and then I would drive us both back up to Derbyshire. Perhaps stay with you a night or two, or in a hotel, if you'd prefer. I'd really like to meet Samantha and Adam and see where you are, get a feel for the place. What do you think?'

Jack didn't know what to say at first. He had thought that an invitation would eventually arrive to go down to Surrey to see them all again, but he hadn't dared to hope for more than that.

'David that is a surprise.' He paused for a few moments while he digested what had been proposed. He appreciated that it was a make or break moment, a chance to rebuild some bridges. It would be too easy to find an excuse to decline the offer.

'That would be great. I definitely want to catch up with you all again, don't go to any trouble, will you?' He took a few more moments more to contemplate the full implications of David's suggestion.

'Well, I really would love you to come up here and meet Samantha and Adam, that would give me a lot of pleasure. You'll stay with me, of course. It's not palatial, but I try to keep it tidy. I reckon we'll cope all right. When are you thinking it would be?'

AND SO IT was arranged. Soon afterwards, as his train crossed the M25 and travelled at speed through Edgware, he felt a momentary pang of nostalgia for the suburban sprawl where he had lived for so long. He was close to his old home, but he recognised that he didn't feel any urge to return there.

His days with David and Louise passed comfortably. Simon and Lucy were friendly and relaxed in updating him on their lives. They talked of their ambitions, indeed expectations, that they would go to university; he to study Economics, she to pursue Modern Languages. Louise expertly interrogated Jack on Derbyshire, to better understand his new life. David had sensibly not planned any great excursions to stately homes, although on a trip to Wisley, Jack was able to buy plants that he thought would decorate Samantha's front garden.

At the start of their journey back north, David offered to make a detour to take Jack back to see his old home.

'Thank you David, but no. That's all behind me now.'

Once they turned off the M1 at Junction 26, Jack

was able to point out a few local landmarks as they neared Ripley; Eastwood where D.H. Lawrence had lived, and the sites of some of the old coalmines, now closed. It was late afternoon, so they went directly to Samantha's house, where, in Jack's absence, Adam's friend Lee and his mother Linda had taken responsibility to deliver him home.

'It's not unlike Kenton round here, is it Dad?' commented David generously.

'No, not too much difference,'

There was a brief exchange with Linda and Lee before they headed off for home. Adam was tongue-tied at first, but David surprised Jack by sitting down with him, asking about Notts Forest, as Jack had briefed him. He heard about Adam's concern that while they had beaten Liverpool in their first match in the new Premier League, they hadn't won since.

'Do you like your school?' asked David.

'Most of the time, I do,' the boy replied, more at ease now.

'And what do you like best?'

'I like Maths, I'm good at that. And English, I like writing essays.'

'Oh yes, what about?'

'Making up stories, I enjoy that.'

WHEN SAMANTHA ARRIVED home, Jack, as he normally would, made them cups of tea. Again David surprised Jack by taking the initiative to ask Samantha about her job, while he went on to explain something about his own. He also asked for more detail of the Charcot-Marie-Tooth disease which Adam was suspected of having, which Samantha gave in some detail, emphasising the long-term prognosis. Adam listened in silence.

Jack had decided that he would take David for a

meal that evening at a local pub, so they left David's car parked outside Samantha's house and took their bags to walk from there round to the nearby narrow street and Jack's new home.

'It's nothing much I know,' said Jack, but I'm really comfortable here.'

David looked round appreciatively. 'You've made it really nice and homely, Dad.'

Jack showed David to the spare bedroom. Adam had stayed over with him a few times and they discovered that he'd left a book under the pillow. Jack went to prepare more cups of tea and left his son to make himself at home.

The next morning, after they had both taken Adam to school, they went for a drive around the more scenic parts of Derbyshire, with David being very impressed by the cable cars at Matlock Bath, as well as Chatsworth House, the home of the Dukes of Devonshire.

They were back in time to collect Adam from school. As soon as they were home, he proudly showed David his books of football stickers, but it was clear that his knowledge of modern players was much more extensive than David's. He also showed off a chess set that he'd had for his birthday, explaining that one of their teachers, Mr. Keen, ran a chess club after school, which he was enjoying. Jack wasn't even aware that David knew how to play the game ('Simon and I play sometimes of an evening, Dad') but he and Adam were soon engaged in a game. Jack felt quite excluded and jealous, as he had never played. Samantha prepared them a simple meal of salmon. After that another game of chess was proposed.

'You're pretty good at this aren't you?' said David after he had conceded defeat again.

Jack was annoyed with himself that he hadn't trusted David's social skills more.

When Adam had gone to bed and red wine had been poured, David said, addressing Samantha, 'I don't know how you'll feel about this, but I have a proposal to make here.'

Jack didn't know what was coming and gripped the arms of his chair. Samantha said nothing but raised an eyebrow and glanced at Jack, who shrugged his shoulders in return. David cleared his throat and continued.

'We, that's me, Louise, Simon and Lucy, we're going to Walt Disney World in Florida for the week at October half-term. How would you feel if Adam came with us? All expenses paid of course, he'd be our guest. Simon's quite keen on chess as well. And football, come to that.'

Samantha was astonished.

'Blimey, are you sure you want to do that?'

'Yes, we're all very happy with the idea. I can see that he's a smart boy, I think he'd get plenty from it. Could you cope if we take him away from you for a week?' The last part was said with a pleasant smile.

'Phew, well, thank you. I hadn't expected anything like this.' She laughed. 'No problem at all, I think I could survive on my own for a week. I'm certain that he'd love that, he's never been on a plane. He might be a bit quiet at first, until he gets to know you all better.'

There was a silence as Jack and David could see that she was still absorbing the offer.

'It might give me an opportunity to go to visit some friends that I haven't seen for a long time. Or stay with Jenny in Watford again, if she'll have me. I've not had a real holiday in a long time. That's really generous of you, David, I do appreciate it. I can see that you were getting along fine together there tonight. What do you think, Jack?'

'I'm speechless.'

BEFORE DAVID HEADED for home the next morning, they walked Adam to school. Jack hung back while David repeated the holiday offer to Adam. The boy turned to Jack, his eyes shining with excitement and amazement.

AFTER DAVID HAD left, Jack, home alone, settled in his rocking chair with a cup of coffee and a chocolate biscuit. He had never thought of it in such terms, but now he realised that since Samantha had arrived on his doorstep, they had both been on personal searches for something that had been missing in their lives. He thought they weren't yet over, but just entering new phases. He felt he had a real purpose in his life now, and it gave him contentment to be helping others in his final years.

He did wonder why David hadn't discussed with him first the offer to take Adam to Walt Disney World. Was he afraid that Jack would try to talk him out of it? Having seen Samantha and Adam's reactions, he thought now that it was a great idea, but he needed to watch that David didn't become too controlling of this new life. He'd seen again at firsthand how skilful his son was at achieving his own objectives.

'Ah well,' he thought, 'the day might not be too far away when he has to take more responsibility for me.'

CHAPTER 50

Nottingham, May 1993

AS HIS SEVENTIETH birthday drew near, Jack found himself thinking more and more about his past. For him an important part of that was in Nottingham, easily accessible from Ripley. While he had been to the city for the football and cricket with Adam since his move north, he had not really visited the city as such. Now, thirty-eight years after his original stay there, something told him that it was time for him to go back.

One morning, after Adam had left for his new school, he caught the bus to Nottingham from Ripley. The routes had all changed since 1955, but eventually he found one to take him out from the city centre to Sneinton, dropping him where he used to catch the bus every morning to go out to Colwick. Soon he was standing across the road from Pamela's old house. He had, of course visited it less than two years before, with Elizabeth and family, when Samantha and Adam were waiting to greet them. This time was different because he was on his own. Also the house had been sold, to new occupants who had installed bright orange curtains in the front room window.

It felt appropriate to Jack to be there now, for what he told himself would be a last visit. Almost like a pilgrimage, he thought. He reflected on how so many unrelated decisions change lives.

If Brian Gladwin hadn't had delusions of building

the small local business he had inherited into a national chain, anticipating B&Q and the others by twenty years or more...

If Jack hadn't accepted the job to set up the first branch of this imaginary new chain...

If Elaine, Brian's secretary, hadn't found such congenial digs (as they were called in those days) for him...

The long list of 'Ifs' goes on for ever, he thought. Just occasionally, over the years, he had allowed his mind to wonder what life would have been like if he made a different decision on that January afternoon in 1956 and had moved to Nottingham and become Samantha's stepfather.

He walked up to the top of Pamela's road and turned right, as she and he had done on that summer's evening. In his mind he could hear her heels tapping on the pavement, as he was oblivious to the many changes around him in that area. The pub was still there at the top of the hill, farther to walk than Jack had remembered. It was a mid-week lunch-time, but the pub was open. Most of the garden where he and Pamela had sat had been tarmacked over to create a car park. The taciturn youth behind the bar served him with a pint of bitter but could only offer crisps for his lunch.

He sat in the bar and sipped his pint. No, the taste of Nottingham beers hadn't improved since 1955. Two elderly men, with thick Eastern European accents, both smoking, sat at a corner table, talking loudly, sometimes in a language that was strange to Jack, discussing the war in the Balkans on which they clearly had differing views.

Jack finished his beer and his crisps, took his empty glass back to the bar, which was ignored by the barman, and then left. He stood outside for a moment, by the few tables that had been left in what remained of the garden. They looked as if they were the same ones at which they had sat all those years ago. He walked back down the hill, past Pamela's house, and carried on into the city centre. He located the Ripley bus and headed straight back to the place he now called home, feeling satisfied that he had done his duty to Pamela, honouring her memory. He wouldn't go again.

He understood now that their search had resulted, for both him and Samantha, in them finding something that they didn't know they were looking for.

ACKNOWLEDGEMENTS

This book would not have been written if I hadn't signed up for an MA in Creative Writing with the Open University just before lockdown hit us. I had no intention of writing a novel but, having created a character to whom my tutors and fellow students responded enthusiastically, I ploughed on. Thanks to my tutors, Nicky Harlow, Louise Tondeur and Ed Hogan and my ever supportive new friends, especially Sarah Le Marchand, Jenna Lyons and Christine Colliar.

I am grateful also for the professional guidance that I have received from Becky Hunter, Holly Seddon and Stuart Walton at Jericho Writers, whose summer school at York was also extremely beneficial. I was fortunate to meet the author Nicola May at the London Book Fair who gave me good advice on self-publishing and signposted me to Scott Pack, who gave me a thorough manuscript assessment, urging me to improve it, to Ifan Bates, who came up with the wonderful cover and BB eBooks who did the formatting.

Thank you to Simon Prideaux for his generous medical advice and to Tony Ounsworth for his knowledge of Hull. Also to the Charcot-Marie-Tooth Society and James Elder at the BT Archives for their assistance and information.

I must mention the aficionados of the King and Queen and at Real Magic Books for their literary and musical inspirations. And also those family and friends who, by requesting frequent updates on progress, gave me impetus to press on.

Above all, my thanks to my partner, Viv Suttie, without whose firm direction I could well have pursued a less stimulating degree in History and this book would never have been written.

Made in the USA
Middletown, DE
23 October 2023

41133699R00179